THE NIGHT THEY STOLE MY BABY

A totally addictive psychological thriller with a shocking twist

DARREN O'SULLIVAN

Joffe Books, London
www.joffebooks.com

First published in Great Britain in 2024

Cover art by Nick Castle

ISBN: 978-1-83526-570-3

To the two Lisas in my life.
Who picked me up and made me to get back to work.

PROLOGUE

Then — 25 December

She ran.

She ran deep into the wildlands, as fast as her legs would carry her, stumbling over the uneven ground, frosty and hard from the harsh winter night. At first her bare feet hurt, almost as much as the gash that trickled crimson down her thigh, then they burned, then she felt nothing at all. The numbness crept up from her toes, through her ankles until her knees ached. But she didn't stop running, not until she reached the tree, their tree, where they once dug and played, where they once laughed and sang, the tree where they once hid.

Once there, she sank into the depression in the earth beside the gnarled roots, her body partially sheltered from the rain that jabbed at her exposed skin like needles. She needn't have bothered sheltering. She was soaked through, and the icy cold had seeped all the way to and frozen her heart. She hid anyway — hiding was what she knew — and once her small body was cocooned in the wet earth, once she knew Mother wouldn't find her, she allowed herself to cry.

Emily had never seen a dead person before, she had no comprehension of how she could tell if someone was alive and asleep, or gone. Still, as soon as she saw her lying there, she knew. She wanted to shake the image, but as she closed her eyes, the image sprang back, lit in festive reds and greens, and then was gone again, as the Christmas tree lights she'd hung in the room flickered on and off. Part of her wanted to try to help, but she knew it would be pointless. It was in the way her body lay, her limbs twisted, not abnormally so, not broken or snapped into new positions, but still twisted. And the way her mouth hung open, her jaw drooping towards the floor as her facial muscles had failed and gravity had taken over. It was still Freya, still her sister, and yet her face had somehow melted like a wax figure in the sun, making her face seem longer and thinner.

As the rain began to intensify, and the cold set in, making her whole body hurt, she couldn't stop herself seeing her dead little sister. The image played on a loop.

The lights flick on, her dead sister stares back.

Off, total darkness.

From the town a mile away, Emily heard the church bells toll carried on the harsh winter wind. The distant chime punctuated the sound of rain, wind, and the roar of the nearby angry sea. One, two, three, she counted. It briefly masked the peal of Mother's question looping in her head. Four, five, six, seven. It masked her own questions of what she should have done differently. Eight, nine, ten.

As she counted the final two tolls, the gravity of what that meant hit her so hard she struggled to take a breath. Eleven. Twelve.

It was a new day, the first new day without her sister, and it was 25 December. Christmas Day.

Looking up to the night sky, Emily willed a light to streak across it, Santa coming to her house to save Freya. Instead, dark clouds pressed down, willing to crush her, the wind howled, the rain fell, and the wildlands that once gave comfort held her in their tight and unforgiving grasp.

It was Christmas Day, Freya was gone, and Mother's question rang over and over in her mind.

What did you do?
What did you do?
What did you do?

The question wouldn't go away, not until Emily found the answer, and then the question stopped. And the answer looped instead.

I killed her.

I killed my sister.

I have just killed my sister.

PART ONE

CHAPTER ONE

Sixteen years later

'This is entirely pointless,' I said, unable to look at myself in the wardrobe mirror anymore. Each outfit I had put on seemed either inappropriate somehow, or simply didn't fit. The blue one I wore, the one that had once made me feel good, now made me feel fat, and I struggled to pull it back over my head. Maybe one day I would wear it again, but then lots of new mothers never bounce back to their former glory. Dropping the dress on the bed, I sighed, feeling too hot and bothered to try another outfit on. From her sitting place on the edge of the bed, Michelle spoke.

'Why not that one? You looked nice.'

'I looked like a beached whale.'

'You're literally a couple of weeks away from having a baby. You're not a whale, you're pregnant.'

I looked at her in the wardrobe mirror and smiled. With anyone else, I wouldn't dream of standing in front of them in just my underwear, not anymore, but Michelle was different. She was my best friend, my family. As close as it gets to, at least. She knew all of my secrets. Almost.

'I may be pregnant, but I'm also fat.'

'Don't be daft Emily, you look great. You're glowing.' Michelle casually sipped her rosé, *my* rosé that I wasn't allowed to drink anymore. Behind her, Taylor Swift played from her phone, and, despite feeling hideous, the combination of my friend and my favourite artist eased my glum mood.

'I look anything but great,' I replied. At this stage in my pregnancy, I wanted to be in a pair of maternity shorts and a T-shirt, I wanted to be sitting in the living room, watching crap TV with a fan blowing into my face, keeping me cool.

With the blue dress on top of the other outfits that I would likely never wear again, I rummaged the rail once more. As I swiped through the clothes, I could see Michelle in the mirror staring at my bump, unblinking. She didn't know I was looking at her, and I could see a longing in the way she stared. I could almost hear her questions. *When will it be my time? What does it feel like? Does Emily know how lucky she is?* I didn't comment, nor did I show that I had seen her looking. It wouldn't be fair. 'I swear to God, I will never find anything that fits me anymore,' I said, and I saw her look away, ready to make eye contact when I turned to face her. 'I'm destined to be a whale. A sweaty, beached whale, dying in the heat.'

'Oh, come on Emily, it's not that bad,' she said, sending a smile my way, but one that still spoke of sadness.

'It's too hot.'

'It's lovely. Christ, after the shitty spring we've just had, we're finally getting some nice weather.'

'It's not nice when you're this pregnant,' I said, removing a light-green dress from the rail that I desperately hoped would fit, or at the very least camouflage me against the grass at the barbecue, making me invisible. 'Tell me why I agreed to this again?'

'I need a designated driver; I'm going to get on it today,' Michelle said, and I scoffed. 'I'm kidding! Soon you're going to have your baby, and then none of us are going to see you again, are we?'

'Of course you will.'

'It will be different,' she said. She tried to sound neutral, but I could tell she felt something — abandoned, forgotten, or perhaps it was just the shitty hand she had been dealt in not being able to have children of her own.

I nodded, unsure how to reply. She was right, of course, it would be different, because instead of me arriving as care-free, good-for-a-laugh, good-for-a-drink Emily, lucky and uncomplicated Emily — at least on the outside — I was going to be the non-drinking, overtired mother Emily. I knew how much that title, mother, could change a person's world, change who they are. And as I thought it, a pang of dread filled me, wondering if I would end up like mine. I had seen what she changed into; I knew that some women weren't good mothers. I knew that some mothers were unkind. And for the thousandth time since discovering I was preg-nant, I wondered how much I was still like my mother. How much of her was lingering somewhere inside? How much of her nature still existed in my bones? My mother was bad, but once I was worse. I wondered if that version of me would find its way out when my baby came. I pushed the questions down. All the way down.

'Em?' Michelle said, seeing my momentary dread. 'Are you OK?'

'I'm fine. Just uncomfortable,' I said, my thoughts shift-ing back. Our group of friends had no kids. I was going to be the odd one out. I once told Michelle my fear of being left out, and she tried to pacify that fear, but still it lingered, waiting in the shadows to occasionally whisper that I would be all on my own again.

In the early days of the pregnancy, that scared me into trying to find new friends quickly, so I'd not be by myself. But since I started feeling my baby, my daughter, kicking and rolling inside me, since I heard her heartbeat for the first time, its gallop rendering me helpless to do anything but cry tears of joy, I liked that I was going to be the odd one out, for now. They would catch up — some of them, at least. I had hoped Michelle would more than anyone else.

'Whose idea was this barbecue?' I asked, trying not to dwell on my thoughts.

'Mine — well, mine and Jack's.'

'Well, as much as I wish it wasn't so bloody hot, it's a nice idea.'

'I thought so too,' she said, getting up and walking towards the door. 'Back in a sec, need a wee.'

In her absence, I took some measured breaths and settled myself. I focused on the here and now and appraised myself in the mirror. Being pregnant hadn't just meant gaining weight where my baby was growing; my ankles were wider, my face was rounder and I had more weight on my hips and upper thighs. But as much as I liked to complain, I didn't really care. I only said as much to distract myself from the thing I was truly worried about. Would I ever hurt my daughter? Would I ever hurt her, like I have hurt before? And what kind of mother would I be? Would I be kind, loving, as I thought I would, or would I become like my own mother? Would I struggle? Would I be cruel and unkind and resentful? It frightened me enough that I looked more and more like I remember her looking. But would I be like her too?

I rubbed my stomach, my baby, and the love I felt told me that despite my worries, despite my fear, despite my past — despite my crime — I'd not be like Mother. I knew I'd love this baby with all of my heart. I would protect her, cherish her, and I would right my terrible wrongs through caring for her. It was me and her, against it all, for ever. Even with this resolve, for a moment, I could hear my sister's voice telling me I was going to fail again. Telling me I would kill again. But she was dead, and I'd not projected her image into my world since the day I found out I was having a daughter. That part of me was gone.

'You OK?' Michelle asked when she came back into the room and saw me.

'Stop asking me that, I'm fine.'

'Well, I'm twitchy. What if you went into labour right now?'

9

'I've still got two weeks, and they say most first-time mothers go beyond their due date anyway.'

'But what if you did? I'd freak out.'

'It's going to be fine, Michelle. Mothers rarely go into labour and pop out a baby in minutes. If I went into labour right now, we would mosey to the hospital with plenty of time.'

'I don't know how you're so calm about it all.'

'I just am,' I said. Sensing her unease, I continued, 'Michelle, don't ditch me when my baby comes and I insist on showing you a thousand pictures of her sleeping.'

'I won't,' she replied, already back on the bed, sipping the wine.

'You're kinda the only family I have.'

'Em, I'm not going anywhere, I want her to call me Aunty Michelle.'

'Me too,' I said as I pulled the green dress over my head. 'Freya will love you.'

'Freya?' Michelle asked, taking another big sip of the rosé. She wasn't kidding when she said she was getting on it tonight.

'Yeah. Freya. What do you think?' I asked, the dress now on, stretching over my belly.

'Freya . . .' she said again, contemplating the name.

I took a deep breath, almost said my daughter would be named after my sister. But Michelle didn't know I had a sister. She didn't know where I came from, didn't know who I really was.

'Do you not like it?' I asked.

'I do, it's beautiful,' Michelle said. 'Where did the idea come from?'

'I saw it on a TV programme,' I lied. 'I thought it was nice.'

'It's perfect. Freya Claywater. She sounds like an author or an award-winning journalist or something.'

I laughed, feeling relieved she didn't push me further on why I had chosen the name.

'And don't worry, you can show me all the pictures of Freya you want.'

'Good.' I smiled, pushing down the final wave of guilt I felt for my sister. My daughter would take her name, so I could make amends for my crime. And honour her as I should have. I could speak my sister's name, out loud, for the first time since that Christmas, and maybe, *maybe* I could find peace, replace that trauma with something pure, something wonderful.

'As calm as I might seem, I can't bring a baby into this world without you.'

'And you won't, of course,' Michelle said, putting down her wine glass and getting up to help me sort the twisted hem of the dress. 'But, you know, things change with a baby.'

'Yeah, they do,' I said, reappraising myself in the wardrobe mirror. The dress was a little tight, a little shorter as it had to drape over my baby, but it was comfortable enough. I looked at my legs. If I wore a pair of shorts underneath, the dress was just long enough to cover the scar that sat at the top of my thigh.

'No one will see,' Michelle said, noticing me checking.

'Are you sure?'

'Yes,' she replied.

My scar was ugly, but for anyone who saw it the story was I fell off my bike into a bush when I was eleven. That I did it here, in London, not in Scotland, and not that Christmas.

But I knew, I always knew, and every time I saw it it reminded me of what I had done. Of the crime I had committed. Only my grandparents knew some of the truth, some of what happened that night, of how I didn't cope in the aftermath. The nightmares, the visions of my sister that haunted me. Only they knew some of what really happened, and they had both passed away, taking my secrets with them.

If I never said it aloud, if I didn't speak of it, then it never happened.

'You look amazing,' Michelle said behind me, snapping me away from staring at my scar.

'It will do.' I smiled, pushing it all down.

'And your boobs. Augh, I'm so jealous.'

'There is nothing sexy about pregnant boobs.'

'I disagree, make the most of those,' Michelle said, laughing as she walked to pick up her wine glass again.

'You all right to drive?' I asked, watching enviously as she finished her wine.

'I've only had one, this small one. I'm fine.'

'Right, shall we get this over with?' I said, grabbing a pair of tan flip-flops from the base of the wardrobe. I knew they didn't compliment the dress. I didn't care. Heels were now a distant dream and my feet got too hot in shoes or trainers.

Leaving the room, I walked across the landing of my house and towards the stairs. I passed Freya's room, the room next to mine, and looked in. It always made me feel calmer, safer, and I was satisfied that it was ready for her, filled with toys and nightlights and mobiles above the cot, which I had built and decorated by myself. I knew she wouldn't sleep in it for the first six months of her life, as she would be in with me, but I wanted it ready for when she did. Michelle paused beside me, looking in. I could see her longing once more, and I felt bad for her. Here was me, single, surprised at Freya's coming, and, until I found out I was pregnant, being a mother wasn't something I ever wanted. I didn't feel the biological clock ticking, I didn't feel time was running out. If anything, I had made peace with the idea that someone like me, someone who had done so much wrong, shouldn't ever be a parent. My understanding of such things was tainted; I was convinced I would be like my own mother, and no child needs that. Michelle had been trying for years, but had never once fallen pregnant. It was cruel. But then, that was life, wasn't it? Cruel. I would ask Michelle to be godmother to my baby, to take care of her, in case anything happened to me. In case I felt I was becoming like my own mother. I hoped it would be enough.

'This room is perfect,' Michelle said. And I knew she meant it genuinely, but I sensed a sadness there too.

'The cot nearly killed me, and why are there never enough screws?' I said, trying to raise a smile, to lift her from her thoughts. She never said anything, but she was my best friend. I knew. 'And I'm not just talking about the ones for the furniture either,' I added, the sort of filthy gag that usually came from her.

She laughed. 'I guess being up the duff might make it tricky to get laid,' she said, smiling, her attention back on me and not her own what-ifs.

'Nature's cock-block,' I said, and Michelle laughed again, the questions and longing gone from her eyes.

'Right,' she said decisively. 'Let's go.'

Taking the stairs slowly, I made my way down. When I was young and had first moved here, I'd loved how steep the old staircase was. I dared myself to jump from higher and higher up, until I broke my ankle attempting to run from the bathroom at the top of the stairs and launch myself from the top to the bottom. I'll never forget the moment I took flight, soaring down in what felt like slow motion. I was convinced I could do it, I could land on my feet at the bottom, like the Six Million Dollar Woman. I was so sure I would land on my feet and continue running like the stairs were just one small step. I was so sure, right up until the last moment when I knew I was going to hit the bottom step. My ankle turned, snapped, and, as I crashed into the wall, I knew I had hurt it badly from the sound alone. My poor nana nearly fainted when she saw, and, two operations later, I now had a metal pin holding it together. Even after, the stairs still presented adventure, risk, fun. Now, the steep stairs made me nervous. A lot about the house did. It was beautiful, but too big for just me and my baby, and it being a Grade II listed house from the 1850s, baby-proofing had been a nightmare. When I first moved here with my grandparents, the local kids teased me about it. They said it was haunted, that murders had happened inside. They were probably right, people died in houses much younger. I brushed it off back then; it didn't scare me, not when I had come from the wildlands. Not when I was already haunted. Even though the house was too big for me, I couldn't sell it; it was all I had left of my family. The old house, surrounded by newer, smaller homes, was handed down to me, and I would one day hand it down to my daughter. I needed to modernise it for that to work. The first thing: the staircase. I knew I would have a heart attack with her around them as they are now.

Walking along the hall to the kitchen, I checked the back door was locked and grabbed my bag. Michelle was waiting by the front door and, as she opened it, brilliant hot light flooded into the entranceway, forcing me to squint. The heat from outside flooded in moments later. It was hot today, hotter than I thought. The old bricks in the walls kept the place cool.

'Come on, we don't want to be late.'

'Late? I thought this was a relaxed, turn-up-when-you-want-to kinda thing?'

'Well, it is, but I want to work on my tan.'

Michelle stepped out into the day, the light absorbing her, and I followed. As I closed my front door, for a split second I thought I could see a little girl in the hallway, my sister. It shocked me. I thought she was gone — I'd not seen her in months, not since I'd found out about my baby — and now she was back. What did that mean? Deep down, I knew she wasn't a ghost, but she was there, staring at me. Looking at me in the same questioning way. Asking, when are you going to tell the truth? I blinked, and she was gone. But she was never really gone, not as I had hoped. I knew then, she was always watching, always waiting.

I silently answered her, *never*. Never would the truth come out. Especially not now, not with my daughter so close to being born.

Locking up the house, I forced a smile and waddled down the path to the open passenger door of Michelle's car.

CHAPTER TWO

The traffic was so bad, it took a little over twenty minutes to get from my house to Jack's. It would have been quicker to walk, even in my condition. However, the gentle drive — music playing, windows down — made me glad we didn't.

We parked outside Jack's house and I heaved myself out of the car. We made our way to the side gate that led into Jack's back garden, as we had done a hundred times before.

Jack had been a mutual friend of ours for four years now. What had started as a drunken encounter on a night out ended in a deep, lasting friendship. Michelle had hit on him, and he'd told her he was gay and set to be married. I remember Jack being awkward when he halted her not-so-subtle advances, and I think he'd expected Michelle to be embarrassed and leave, but she didn't. She congratulated him, asked about his fiancé — Adam, as we learned — and when he apologised, telling her he was flattered by her interest, she replied that she didn't mind as she liked the idea of having a hot gay friend. He laughed, as did I, and that night the two of them became thick as thieves. Jack was my friend too, but he and Michelle were like peas in a pod. Adam was quieter than Jack, and he let Jack take the lead in most things. I guess a healthy relationship needs some of that, and opposites can attract. Adam was a little more like me, and as such we were polite and kind, but both kept our distance.

As we walked down the side of Jack and Adam's new-build home, I expected to hear the sound of music, people chatting, laughter. However, it was quiet.

'Are we the first ones here?' I asked.

'Dunno, must be,' Michelle said, shrugging her shoulders.

Rounding the corner into their back garden, I saw a marquee, open on three sides and pinned to the floor with guy ropes. Three chairs under, shaded from the sun. A barbecue was out, lid closed, and a paddling pool was full to the brim towards the rear of the garden. I looked towards the house; the back patio doors were open, leading to the kitchen, and I headed towards them.

'Jack?' I called out, looking through the door. The kitchen was empty. 'Adam?'

'Are they not there?' Michelle said from behind me.

'No.'

'Oh, maybe they're in the living room?'

Stepping in, I gingerly walked through the kitchen. I had been in Jack's house many times, but without an invitation I felt weird, like I was trespassing. 'Jack?' I called out again, moving towards the door that led to the living room. Inside, the blackout curtains were drawn, making the whole room dark. I didn't much like the dark, but it was short-lived.

'Surprise!'

I leaped back in shock as the lights were thrown on, and for a split second I felt myself wanting to run and hide. Fear shot through me like lightning but passed just as quick. It took a moment for my eyes to adjust, and, when they did, I saw a dozen people, with Jack and Adam in the centre of them, laughing and clapping.

'What's going on?' I asked, trying to control my pounding heart.

'It's your baby shower,' Michelle said behind me, wrapping her arms around me, giving me a hug.

'Did you not guess?' Jack said, approaching to also hug me.

'No!'

'You mean, Michelle was able to keep it a secret?'

'Y-Yes,' I stammered.

'I told you I was good with secrets,' Michelle said, playfully slapping Jack's arm.

'Oh, how wonderful,' Jack said.

'Jack, have you forgotten that I'm eight and a half months pregnant? I nearly wet my pants!'

Everyone laughed, and with the moment a roaring success for Michelle and Jack, the masterminds behind the surprise, everyone came to greet me. There was Adam, Hayley, Penny, all the girls from work, and Jack's two nephews, who insisted on being there because there was food and a paddling pool. And to my surprise, at the back of the group was Lucas. He smiled, raised his glass, and I smiled back. I was glad he was there. It made me feel like I mattered, that his daughter mattered. Once everyone else had said their hellos, Lucas came over. Michelle watched, keeping an eye on me.

'You look amazing,' he said.

'I look huge. I didn't think you'd be here.'

'Jack rang me a few weeks back. I know things didn't work out with us, but I still care.'

'I'm glad you made it.'

Giving Lucas a gentle kiss on the cheek, I turned to see Jack had joined Michelle in watching over me. I gave them a smile, letting them know I was OK.

'Michelle, Jack, you really shouldn't have done all this.'

'Are you kidding?' Jack said. 'You'd deny us the joy of buying baby clothes and toys?' He gave my hand a squeeze.

Adam led us all to the garden and took drinks orders and, while he and Jack made the drinks, we all gathered under the marquee, my chair in the centre of the gaggle, Michelle beside me. Lucas kept to the outside of the circle, watching on. Michelle saw me looking and glanced over at

Lucas. Giving him a smile, I sank into my chair. When I first told Michelle and Jack that Lucas and I weren't going to raise Freya together, they were angry. Michelle was so angry she didn't speak. But after I explained that it truly was a mutual decision, that we both knew it would be wrong to force a relationship for her, that we could both love her, in a different way, they seemed less angry. He hadn't run out on me. It was for the best.

Lucas wandered off towards the barbecue, and I turned to Michelle.

'Michelle, you are so naughty.'

'Yeah, but you love it.'

'You hid it so well.'

'What can I say? I'm good with secrets,' she replied, and in that moment I wanted to tell her everything, but knew I never could. No one was that good with secrets. No one but me.

'Thank you,' I said. 'And getting Lucas to come, it means a lot.'

'It's nice to see him here, isn't it?'

'Yeah. It is.'

As Jack's nephews began to play and the music started, Jack and Lucas fired up the barbecue and Adam arrived from inside with bottles of prosecco for those who could drink — everyone besides me and the kids — and a rather lavish something for me in a cocktail glass that he said was alcohol free. And as he filled everyone's glasses, Michelle stood. Once the drinks were filled, she raised hers.

'I'd like to toast our wonderful friend Emily, who is about to be the first of us to dive into the world of parenthood. God help her.'

Everyone laughed, including me.

'But, seriously, as much as they say motherhood is terrifying, difficult, hard—'

'Easy, Michelle,' I joked. I looked over to Lucas, who wasn't smiling anymore but fiddling with the label of his beer bottle. It wasn't just me who looked though, everyone did.

It seemed, despite everyone saying they were cool with Lucas and me not being together, people still held on to the idea he had done something wrong in this.

'And let's not forget the fact she will be squeezing something the size of a melon out of something the size of a lemon,' Jack added, making everyone laugh, including Adam, who then told him off for being so crude.

'That too,' Michelle continued. 'Despite all that, I couldn't think of a single person who is more capable, more ready, and who will be better at parenting than her.' She made a point of looking at me for the last part.

'Hear, hear!' Jack said.

'Em, you're the bravest person I know, and you're going to be the fiercest, most loving mother in the world. To Em.'

'To Em,' everyone said in unison, raising their glasses, and I looked at Lucas once more. He took a tiny step back, removing himself slightly. Michelle saw it too.

I wished I could believe what Michelle said. I wished I knew for sure that my past, my genetics, my crime, wouldn't ruin motherhood for me. I fought not to let a little tear escape. Fought and failed, but thankfully, before anyone could notice, Jack announced it was time for gifts and, one by one, wrapped boxes and gift bags came from behind the closed side of the marquee. There were babygrows, rattles, toys, teddy bears, beautiful baby dresses and shoes, as well as more sensible gifts like nappies and wet wipes from Adam.

'Wet wipes?' Jack said. 'I married a man who buys wet wipes for a baby shower?'

'Hey, someone has to be practical.'

With each gift unwrapped, I felt the love in my heart grow. I had spent the last eight and a half months trying to ready myself to have my baby, to have my little girl, my Freya. Eight and a half months preparing to bring her into this world without a constant father figure or grandparents, without any biological family besides me. And now, knowing those who were closest to me, those who I called family, were all here, celebrating it, I knew I was ready for her to meet them.

19

Once all of the gifts were unwrapped, Jack said he was going to start on the food, and everyone drifted into smaller conversations. Lucas approached, and, clinking his beer glass against my drink, he sat.

'You OK?' he asked.

'Yeah, I'm OK.'

'I think I should go.'

'You don't have to.'

He nodded. 'I get that people will think—'

'I don't care what they think, we know this is right, right?'

He looked at me for a long time, and then leaned in and kissed me on the cheek. 'Do you need anything?'

'No, we're all good,' I said, enjoying that I was now a 'we'. 'Will you be there still?'

'I wouldn't miss it for the world.'

I smiled. 'Well then, see you in a couple of weeks?'

'See you in a couple of weeks.'

Lucas stood, squeezed my hand and walked away, giving Michelle an awkward smile as he headed back to the barbecue. Michelle sat beside me, and we both watched as Lucas said his thank-yous before slipping out of the garden.

Once he was gone, Michelle turned to me.

'You OK?'

'Yeah. Yeah, I am,' I said truthfully.

Michelle nodded and, a little drunk, moved on quickly by leaping up to help Jack, giving me a moment to look around, rubbing my tummy as I did. Freya was kicking. Even though seeing Lucas did bring up some feelings, I knew what we were doing was right for all of us, and I felt peace for knowing that one thing. My friends were all chatting, happy, and I watched Jack's nephews splashing in the paddling pool. I let myself imagine the day I had this in my garden, with my own daughter doing the splashing. Jack's nephews were playing a game, and I watched them. One was maybe ten or eleven, the other a couple of years younger. It made my heart ache a little. They were discussing an idea and I strained to listen to them.

'Don't start counting until I'm under,' the oldest one said.

'I won't.'

'OK.'

'Ready, steady, go! One, two, three . . .'

The smaller of the boys started to count aloud as the bigger dunked his head underwater. They were trying to see who could hold their breath the longest.

'Five, six, seven . . .'

The bigger of the boys lay flat on his front, arms out, legs too, like a starfish, unmoving, and as much as I tried not to, as much as I knew it wouldn't do me good, as much as I knew it wasn't the time, I couldn't help but think back to a time when I too played games, before that night, before that Christmas.

'Eight, nine, ten . . .'

CHAPTER THREE

Then — 17 December

'Eight, nine, ten. Ready or not, here I come!'

She turned. The room was empty, almost as if no one had ever been there, and for the briefest moment she remembered when it was just her, before Freya was born. She smiled. Freya was getting good at hide and seek, and, even though it was only the first day of the Christmas break from school, Emily already knew it would be easier than last year. Freya was older, she understood more, she was able to care for herself more, and she was beginning to learn how to be around Mother, to have an easier life. But still, even with her younger sister able to stand on her own two feet a little more each holiday from school, it was still going to be tough. If the Christmases before showed anything, it was that Mother was at her worst over the festive period. She was sadder, angrier. More dangerous. But she wasn't always. Once Christmas was full of joy, laughter, movies and hot chocolate and sleepovers in the living room. Before Freya was born. Emily missed those times.

Pushing those Christmases down — remembering didn't help anyone — Emily quietly sang, 'I'm going to find you' and waited to hear her little sister giggle. Nothing. Smiling, she began to move silently, tiptoeing, and as she did she couldn't help but work out how many days it was until she and her sister could go back to school.

Nineteen. Nineteen days.

Hide and seek would only get them so far.

The winter break was always harder than the summer. In the summer, both girls would go outside from dawn till dusk, playing in the wildlands behind their house. They would catch butterflies, walk to the stream to see the minnows swimming. They would lie in the shade of a tree if the sun was too warm or the heavens opened. They chased crickets and grasshoppers and paused to examine ant nests in the soil. They would watch razorbills, terns and gulls fly overhead, their mouths full of small fish from the sea. The six weeks of summer holidays were calm, easy, free. In summertime, Emily didn't hate her life so much or resent her sister, who through no fault of her own had ruined what she and Mother used to have. Summer gave the feeling of hope.

Winter kept them cooped up in the house, prisoners to the unforgiving Scottish weather. When school was open, they escaped for those six hours and pretended to be like all the other children, but in the breaks nothing spared them and, although the winter break was half the length of the summer, it felt ten times longer. The short days, the wild weather that beat them inside. It was almost too much, but Emily knew she had to accept that, keep her spirits up, keep Freya entertained and safe, make her feel loved. Life before her sister was born was easier, kinder. Mother showed tenderness and warmth. She missed it. But again, it wasn't Freya's fault. She didn't ask to be born, she didn't insist Mother became sad, and angry for it.

Emily began to move quietly through the living room, checking behind the curtains, even though she knew Freya wouldn't be there. Last year, Freya hid in that place every time they played, her body exposed from the knees down under the bottom of the curtain. Last year, Emily could have found her blindfolded, as Freya always giggled anyway. Now, Freya had learned to move like a ghost, quietly wafting through the house. She was old enough to realise that, living with Mother, being quiet and unseen was better than the alternative. Emily had learned that for herself in the months after her sister had been born. Invisible was best. Silence was best.

'I know you're here somewhere,' Emily whispered, waiting to hear something, but the room was quiet, still. Leaving the living room, she walked along the short, narrow, unlit corridor towards the kitchen, and quietly opened the door. Outside, night had drawn in, and, catching her reflection in the glass of the back door, she jumped, thinking she had seen a ghost. She shivered, maybe at seeing her own image, thin and pale, or maybe because of the cold. It was likely both.

'I know you're in here,' she said, her voice singsong and small, trying to push down the unease she was beginning to feel. 'I'm going to find you.'

Checking the cupboards, most of which were bare besides crumbs and the odd dusty piece of pasta, she left, closing the door behind her. Back in the corridor she moved quietly through the dark. It had been a few months since the bulb in the hallway had blown, and still it hadn't been replaced. But she didn't mind. Over the past few months, her eyes had coped in the darkness of the house well enough.

Reaching the bottom of the stairs, she knew, with the living room and kitchen checked, the only place Freya could have gone was up. Going up was risky, going up could end in trouble. And she didn't know if her sister was brave or stupid. Mother's door was shut, and they both knew what that meant. They both knew what would happen if you opened it before Mother was ready to have it opened.

Emily wanted to call out, barely a whisper, telling her sister the game was over. She dared not even do that.

On her hands and knees, she began to crawl up, hoping the stairs didn't creak. Once she was at the top, she looked down the hallway. The door at the end was untouched.

Mother's door was still closed, and she thanked God Freya hadn't done something so foolish. Emily turned and went into their bedroom. Inside, she quietly closed the door. Only when the door was closed did she dare to whisper.

'Freya? Fry? Are you in here?'

She waited for a sound, a shuffling, a voice, but nothing.

'Where are you? Freya? The game is over. We shouldn't play up here. You know better than that. Come out, we can play again, downstairs.'

She checked under both beds, inside the wardrobe, panicking as the wardrobe door squeaked when she opened it. She hoped her sister was there, but all she saw were piles of clothes, some clean, some dirty. Some not fitting anymore.

'Come on, I'm not playing,' she said, panic starting to lace her words. She knew what would happen if the closed door at the end of the corridor opened, and the longer she stayed upstairs the more likely that would be. Sometimes Freya was a godsend, sometimes Emily wanted to kill her.

'Fry? You're going to get us in trouble.'

Leaving her bedroom, she looked into the bathroom. A tap dripped, the shower curtain hung from the rail like a drunk clinging onto a doorframe. Freya wasn't there either.

'Please, please, we can't play anymore. Where are you?' she whispered, getting increasingly annoyed with her sister as she looked back into the hallway. She had checked all the rooms, all but one.

All but Mother's.

Emily reasoned that her sister wouldn't go in there, she knew better. However, there was nowhere else she could be.

'You haven't, have you?' she whispered to herself.

Gently, she began to move towards the closed door, and only when she was close enough was she able to see that the door wasn't fully shut as it should have been, but slightly ajar. She gently pushed it open, just enough to look inside. On the bed, in the darkness, she could make out a mound, an arm hanging out over the edge, a burned-down hand-rolled cigarette in her fingers. She wanted to call for her sister, tell her to come out quietly, but fear robbed her of her ability to speak. What if Mother woke? What would happen to her? Then, beside the bed, beside the mound, under the blankets, she saw a little face. She felt panic rise in her chest, quickly replaced with anger at her sister for being so stupid. But she had to push it down. Slowly raising a finger to her lips, she mouthed to her sister to keep quiet.

Freya nodded, and they both held their breath as the mound on the bed twitched. It moaned something that Emily couldn't understand, but whatever it said, it sounded angry, like sleep itself was pained somehow. Then, just as Emily feared it would rise up and look at her, its eyes boring into her soul as only Mother could, it rolled over, and settled once more.

'The game is over,' Emily mouthed.

Freya shook her head. 'No it's not, you have to touch me to win,' she whispered back.

Emily placed a finger to her lips, shushing her little sister once more. Freya didn't know how bad it would be if Mother woke. She knew Mother had a temper, but Emily ensured most of that temper was directed her way. She would take the blows so Freya never had to, even if most of the time Freya was the reason for Mother's rage.

It meant Freya feared Mother less. And Emily, although proud she had kept her word to protect her sister, was frustrated, because the older Freya got the bigger the risk was for them both. And even though she never said it, all of it was Freya's fault. Before her, life was kinder. Before, there was only Mummy. Now, Mother had many forms. There was Angry Mother, Sleepy Mother, Quiet Mother, Sad Mother, Dancing Mother, Fake Mother, Fun Mother — who had been missing for a long time — and the worst, Monster Mother. When Monster Mother was around, Freya was hidden from it all. Hidden under her bed or in the wardrobe. Always a game, like now. Freya didn't know just how quickly the game could turn ugly.

She beckoned Freya over, telling her to creep, and she shook her head again. 'You have to tag me for the game to be

26

over,' she said. Emily knew Freya wouldn't budge, rules were rules, so reluctantly she pushed the door open a little wider and, keeping her eye on the mound on the bed, stepped into the room. She knew she shouldn't be there, that neither of them should. This room wasn't like the other rooms in the house, this room was darker than the others, colder. She felt like the walls watched her. Watched her in the same way Mother watched her when she had a bottle in her hand, her special water, the clear liquid making her face screw up each time she drank from it. A few years back, when she was around eight or nine, Emily tried Mother's special water. She wanted to know what made it so special, and why Mother hid it in her bedroom. It tasted like something you would clean a toilet with and after drinking it the world wobbled until she was sick. But it didn't make Mummy sick, it made her laugh, dance, sometimes cry, but mostly it made her sleep. And then, the next day, it made her angry. Always angry, until she drank some more.

Drawing level with the bed, inches from the sleeping mound, Emily stepped on something sharp with her bare foot, and fought not to scream. Screaming would only lead to more screaming. The pain in her foot was brilliant and white, like a snowstorm, but it was nothing compared to the pain she would experience if Mother woke. With tears threatening to cloud her vision, she sat on the bare floor and smiled at Freya, who looked worried. She winked, showing her younger sister all was OK, and then, taking a deep breath, she pulled out a small shard of glass from the ball of her foot. She fought to hold in a cry and succeeded but for the smallest yelp. The mound on the bed moved, and she froze, wide-eyed. Mother rolled over, her face inches from her, her breath foul, like a dying animal. She dared not move, not until she was sure Mother wouldn't stir. As she held her foot in her hand, blood ran down, over her heel and onto the floor. She wanted to cry, but crying didn't help. It never helped. Not anymore.

Once Mother was settled again, she crawled past her to her sister at the head of the bed and touched her shoulder.

'There, I got you, we need to leave before Mother wakes.'

Her sister nodded, her face grey from seeing the blood, and they began to crawl away. Emily paused in front of Mother, helped her sister past, and, as Freya reached the door, she stood and opened it to leave. The hinge squeaked angrily, and the mound stirred.

'Go into our room, get under your bed now,' Emily whispered and Freya nodded, looking not at Emily but at something behind her. As Freya scurried away, Emily turned and came eye to eye with Mother — not Fun Mother, not Dancing Mother, or Sad Mother or Happy Mother. It was in the eyes, a hatred only one Mother ever showed. Emily was standing in front of Monster Mother.

CHAPTER FOUR

As the afternoon went on, my friends got steadily more intox-icated, and by late afternoon exposure to the heat and too much prosecco meant people began to get sleepy and drift home. By six thirty, it was only Jack, Adam, Michelle and myself.

Michelle and Jack were sitting in chairs, their feet in the paddling pool, both radiating from sunburnt shoulders and noses. They were chatting about whether they would have kids one day, and I listened as Jack said he and Adam had spoken about it, and they would, when the time was right. I couldn't help but smile. *When the time was right!* If everyone waited for when the time was right, no one would have kids anymore. The time certainly wasn't right for me. Nor was the man. Lucas and I were not right for each other, we both knew that going in. He was too much of a free spirit, too open with his thoughts and feelings and, well, I was grounded here, tied to the home I grew up in, my grandparents' home, tied by my past, to secrets I would never speak of. I wasn't going anywhere. Lucas, however, had the world to see. We agreed it wasn't right that we try to make it work for the sake of our baby. And I knew we would be all right, and find a way to make it work. Even though it had been awkward for him, he'd come to my baby shower, he'd been there when it mattered. I didn't doubt he would be present at her birth, at those special moments. He was a kind man, if unable to settle. He would love his daughter, there was no doubt of that, I just knew he would have to love from afar. And that would have to be enough. My daughter would at least know her father in some way, more than I had as a child.

I hoped, after Freya was born, he would realise what I already knew, that timing didn't matter for shit. That love was love, and it magnetically drew us all in. And what felt important before felt like nothing in comparison. Lucas would get there, one day, I knew it. But we would never be a thing. I would raise my daughter alone, me and her, us against the world.

I didn't say any of this, of course. Instead I quietly listened as Michelle, drunk and relaxed, spoke a little about not being able to conceive.

'Babe, have you ever considered it was him?' Jack said. The 'him' in question was her ex. They had tried a few times, and when it didn't happen their relationship had failed.

'No, we both tested, it's me,' she said, smiling, but it didn't fool anyone. 'They said it might happen, it would be difficult, but it might. Besides, I gotta have a partner first, right?'

'Are you not seeing anyone?'

'I was,' she said. 'But I had to call it off.'

'Shame.'

'Yeah, it is, I liked him a lot,' she said, and then, noticing that both Adam and I were listening, she looked away. Then she got up, excused herself and went inside the house.

'I'll go,' Jack said, getting up to follow her, to make sure she was OK.

Adam noticed my worry. 'She'll be fine. She's drunk. Have you got your birth plan sorted?'

I appreciated his attempt to move the conversation along. 'Just about. I've still got time, but I know what will go into my bag.'

'Will your mum be there for the birth?' he asked innocently.

'I'm not close with my mother. Not seen her for a very long time.'

'Families are tricky,' he said, and I nodded. If only he knew. 'Will she visit perhaps? Meet her granddaughter?'

'She's probably long dead.'

'I'm sorry.'

'No, it's OK, honestly. I was brought up by my grandparents.'

'I see.'

'I'm glad for it. My mother . . . she wasn't a good woman.'

'Not all are,' he said. 'It was good that Lucas came today.'

'Yeah, it was.'

'He seemed a little off though.'

'I guess today was about me and my friends. Some still think he's running away from his responsibilities.'

'Do you?' Adam asked.

'No, no, this is right. Lucas and I, we've argued a lot about Freya.'

'What about her?'

'At first' — I paused to look around, making sure Michelle couldn't hear — 'we argued about keeping her. He didn't want me to go through with it when we first found out, but I just couldn't . . . I guess we were doomed from that moment really.'

'And now?'

'Less now, but we occasionally bicker about how she should be raised.'

'Does he have the authority to say how she'll be raised?'

'Some, yes, he is her father. And although we're cataclysmically wrong for one another, he is a good man. I just didn't like his idea for her future. Lucas said he wanted her to see the world, to be a global citizen, like him.'

'A global citizen?'

'Yeah, wanky, I know. But he wanted her to be wanderlusty, like him.'

31

'With a newborn?'

'Yep, but I told him that, although I would go fifty–fifty if he wanted, I wasn't going to let him take her to bum around the world with him, and I didn't want that life for me either.'

'How'd he take that?'

'As well as he could. I won't stop him travelling with her, but she won't be going here, there and everywhere with him. I think, over time, he'll see her less and less for it.'

'I'm sorry.'

'It's OK. I'm OK with it now. I don't mind it being me and her, for the most part.'

'Aren't you angry with him? I would be.'

'I was, of course, but not now. He'll be in her life, he'll show up, like he did today, and I know he'll not miss those big occasions.'

'Oh, shit, I forgot: just before he left, he gave me a gift to pass on.'

'Did he?'

'Yeah, I said he should just hand it over. He said you were with Michelle and he didn't want to interrupt. I'll go grab it now.'

Adam was back within a minute, and in his hand was a small box, wrapped in silver paper. Lucas's gift. I thanked him as he handed it over. I tore open the packaging to find a jewellery box. Opening it, I looked inside. It was a pin with a small angel on it, holding a sword.

'What is it?' Adam asked.

'A brooch.'

Adam looked at it. 'It's nice. What does it mean?'

'I have no idea,' I said. But it rang a bell, I just couldn't place where I had seen it before.

'So,' Adam continued, 'have you got someone with you on the day?'

'Michelle is going to come with me when I go into labour. Lucas too. I was going to ask if you and Jack would visit after.'

'Oh God, yes. We'd be honoured,' he said, taking my hand in his. 'Jack sees you and Michelle as family.'

'I do too,' I said, and Adam smiled.

Behind us, Michelle and Jack re-emerged, laughing raucously at something Jack had said.

'See, told you she's fine. They've both had too much to drink though. They're going to be a handful tonight.'

'Rather you than me,' I said, yawning. 'Sorry, the heat's knackered me out.'

'Don't say sorry, you're carrying a whole new life inside you. If I were you, I'd be a heap in the corner.'

'I'm gonna go home, if that's OK?'

'Of course. Do you want a lift?'

'No, it's OK, I could do with walking. Sitting down too long makes me uncomfortable.'

'Are you sure?'

'Yes, thanks Adam.'

Adam helped me out of my chair, and I ambled over to Michelle and Jack. 'I'm done, heading home.'

They didn't want me to go but, as they were wasted, they didn't put up a fight. Kissing Michelle, I thanked her for the surprise.

'I fucking love you, Em.'

'I love you too.'

'No, no, I fucking mean it. I fucking, *fucking* love you.'

Adam, laughing, peeled Michelle off me. 'OK, OK, put her down. She needs to go home.'

Michelle landed one final wet kiss on my cheek and then I was free. Jack, who was so drunk he couldn't get up again, waved and called out he loved me as I headed towards the stack of gifts I had received.

'Leave this, I can drop them around tomorrow,' Adam said.

'Really?'

'Of course. Are you sure you don't want a lift?'

'No, thank you,' I said as Freya started kicking. 'The walk will do me good.'

'OK, message one of us when you're home?'

'I will. Thanks Adam.'

Adam walked me to the side gate and hugged me good-bye. I had one final look back at my friends, who were chatting shit at one another.

'Good luck with these two.'

'Thanks, I think I'm gonna need it.'

Smiling, I turned and left, and began my slow walk home, enjoying the cool summer evening.

CHAPTER FIVE

There's something special about a summer evening in London. The sound of birdsong, children playing in their gardens, the smell of barbecues everywhere. It felt so simple, like life wasn't this challenging thing we made it out to be when it was wet and cold. It was light, bright, easy-going. And it wasn't just me who thought this; as I walked, everyone I saw was smiling, talking, laughing. A group of teenagers bopped past, listening to music from a phone. Seeing me approach, they stepped onto the road to save me having to do so. I thanked one young man, and he said it was his pleasure. Older folks passed too. One woman caught my eye and her face told me she missed a part of herself for seeing me, but in a fond, nostalgic way. The walk was doing me good. I could feel the tightness in my hips loosen a little, and the ache in my feet subsided as my blood flow returned to them. It was hard work, walking with so much extra weight sitting low in my pelvis. But I loved it. A walk in the cooling breeze was the perfect antidote to an afternoon in the sun feeling hot and uncomfortable.

A quarter of a mile from my front door, I approached the underpass that went below the main road, a short, well-lit passage that would only take me a moment to dip through.

As the shade of the concrete cooled the air, I sighed. It was the first time all day my skin didn't itch because of being so hot. Walking down the underpass was easy enough, but I kept my hand on the rail doing so. I didn't want to lose my footing and take a tumble. I had to laugh; this underpass was the same one that had caused me to need several stitches in my knee fifteen years ago. I was with Christine, an old school friend, on our rollerblades, and she dared me to go down as fast as I possibly could, and doing so was fine, something I had done maybe fifty times before, until, unbeknown to me, a bike had similar ideas from the other side. We collided at the bottom. The rider got a few bumps and bruises, I took a chunk out of my left knee. I hobbled home that day, bloodied and limping, and once again Nana almost fainted. Another trip to the hospital, another sleepless night for her. Now, fifteen years later, I'm shuffling down the same underpass, heavily pregnant, clinging on to the safety rail. It's funny how life can change. Thinking about it, I never considered how hard it was for Nana, taking me on with all of my baggage, all of my complications. I wish I could have understood that when she was alive.

Reaching the bottom of the ramp, I paused before walking up the other side of the underpass. It was tough going and midway I had to stop, steady myself and suck in a few lungfuls of cool unmoving air, before I stepped back into the warm, cloying city atmosphere. From behind me, a man approached, fast, his hands stuffed in his pockets, and although I knew he was there I jumped when he spoke to me.

'Can I help?'

He saw me physically recoil.

'Shit, sorry, I didn't mean to scare you,' he said.

'No, you're fine,' I said.

'Are you OK?'

'Yes, thank you, just enjoying the cool air.'

'OK, just wanted to check. Have a nice evening.' He smiled, but it didn't quite reach his eyes.

'And you.'

The man walked on, and at the top of the ramp he didn't look back as he turned left and walked away. I felt silly for jumping, it wasn't like me. Being pregnant had made me over-cautious, I guessed. Each day closer to my Freya being born, the past, that Christmas, felt closer too.

I continued up the ramp and back into the light and heat of the day compared to the cool tunnel. Turning the opposite way to the man, I walked down my street. I wanted to get in, run a cool shower and melt into it before eating my body-weight in crisps and binge-watching something in bed. Perfect.

Drawing closer, I went into my bag and pulled out my keys, and, as I sorted through them to ready the one for my front door, I heard rapid movement behind me, some-one running in my direction. Before I could react, a brilliant white light flashed before my eyes and a percussive sound exploded in my head, then I began to fall. My arms went to my stomach, to protect my baby as my face bounced off the hot tarmac. In a dazed heap, I felt a sharp pinch in my shoulder, and, as the world began to fade, I saw the feet of someone running; I thought they were coming to help, but they weren't, they were running away.

Then, the world went black.

PART TWO

CHAPTER SIX

Then — 18 December

Emily woke and instinctively looked over to her sister, but her bed was empty. Panicking, she shot up, forgetting that she had stood on glass, and when she placed her weight down she almost cried out in pain. She bit her lip; Mother would be in a bad mood already.

Hobbling downstairs, she walked into the kitchen. There was no sign of Freya, just Mother, who was sitting by the back door, blowing smoke into the air.

'Where have you taken her?' asked Emily, daring to hold her eye. 'Where is she?' Usually, she didn't dare speak to her mother when she was a monster, it never ended well, but she knew Freya was being punished for the game of hide and seek.

Mother didn't respond; she seldom did. She grunted, moaned, scoffed, but rarely did she speak, not unless she had drunk her special juice. And even then, her words were slurred, they didn't make sense, they were angry, sad. Rarely did she look at her own daughters.

'Where is she?' Emily asked again, her fear temporarily masked by her courage to help her sister.

Mother took a long drag, her bony features illumined by the intensifying glow of the cigarette tip, and exhaled. She didn't blink.

'Why do you care?' she said, barely a whisper. It unnerved Emily. When Mother whispered it was more difficult to work out if she was Sad Mother, Angry Mother or Monster Mother.

'She's only little,' Emily said. 'Where is she?'

'She's big enough now to know. You knew when you were her age,' Mother said, and Emily nodded. When she was Freya's age, Freya was a baby; when she was Freya's age, Mother had finished her evolution into what she was now.

'Mother, please.'

'Ever dutiful towards your sister. You know full well where she is,' she said quietly, without menace, without venom. She could have been saying it as if Freya was somewhere nice, somewhere fun. But it was anything but those things. Emily looked past Mother to the back door; it was closed, but beside it sat Mother's wellies, fresh mud on them.

'You both know the rules. And she broke them last night, didn't she?' she said, turning away and dropping her cigarette into a glass, before walking towards Emily. She wanted to be strong, to be brave for her little sister, but as Mother passed she couldn't help but cower, waiting for something — a slap, or a punch. But that wasn't Mother's way anymore. She rarely hit, not now Emily was bigger and stronger and no longer cried. She found newer, crueller ways to make sure they both feared her. Emily was at least grateful that Freya hadn't yet felt Mother's hands on her. She hoped it would stay that way.

Mother brushed past her, and once Emily heard her haul herself slowly up the stairs she dared to breathe again. Midway, Mother stopped. 'It was better before, wasn't it?' She was mumbling and Emily struggled to hear her. 'When it was just the two of us. Do you remember back then? We were happy, weren't we?'

Mother continued upstairs, into her room, slamming the door behind her. Knowing Mother wouldn't come out again for a while, probably hours, Emily dared to move towards the

41

back door and look outside. Daylight was breaking, and she wondered if the sun would find a way through the thick and heavy clouds. Rain would come, rain always came. Listening once more for the sound of Mother, and hearing nothing, she quietly put on her coat and wellies and opened the back door.

The garden was small, two of the three sides of fencing having blown down, exposing a vast sweeping nothingness behind, miles and miles of untouched Scottish wildlands, thick brambles and bushes that were unpassable apart from the narrow walkways carved into them by deer, foxes and wildcats. In the summer, Emily loved the wilds. She loved the space, the distance she and Freya could create from home and Mother, the freedom the wilderness granted. They could play and laugh without worry. They could scream — joyfully for the most part, and the other kind if needed. She felt free. In the winter, it was different. The winter wilds acted like a prison, so much inescapable nothing. But she wasn't there to look at the wildlands. She was there for the brick shed that sat at the end of the garden.

The brick shed was only eight feet square, built decades ago out of solid granite to withstand the winter winds. When Emily was at school, she learned about the war and the bomb shelters; the shed reminded her of that.

Walking towards it, the wind whipped the side of her head so fiercely she could barely hear, and it was so cold she had an earache that spread into her jaw within seconds. Walking was tough too; the bog-like garden tried to pull her wellies off. She kept moving, blinking through the wind to see if she could spot Freya at the door of the shed, poking her fingers or toes out under the gap, like Emily did when she was younger, in the months after Freya was born and had to 'learn from her mistakes'. She couldn't see them, and, reaching the door, she knocked quietly on it.

'Freya?'

From inside, she heard movement.

'Fry?'

'Emily, is that you?'

'Yes, are you OK?'

'Mother said I was naughty.'

'Yes,' Emily said, unsure what else she could say. She hadn't been naughty, but she had been stupid.

'I'm cold.'

'I know,' Emily said, weighing up the options. Freya should stay in there, just like Emily had countless times, until Mother was ready. She deserved to; it was her fault she was there. But she was too young, it was too cold and, even though it would likely put Emily in the shed, she had to help her little sister. It was her duty. 'I'm going to get you out. As soon as I'm sure she's asleep, I'll get the key and I'll let you out.'

'No, don't,' her sister pleaded. 'She'll punish you.'

'I'm your big sister, it's my job,' Emily said, hoping her anger towards Freya couldn't be heard over the wind.

'No! Please, Em. Please. I'm OK. I can wait.'

Emily rested her head on the cold metal door. Freya was right, she would be punished, but, as much as she was afraid of that, she didn't have a choice. It was her job. Freya would be inside, warm and safe, and that was all that mattered.

'I'll be back soon, OK?'

Marching back to the house, Emily could hear her sister begging her not to, but she had made up her mind. Mother could punish her as much as she wanted, but not Freya.

Inside, she kicked off her wellies and climbed the stairs to Mother's room. The door was shut, and she quietly drew level. Pressing her ear to it, she could hear her snores, Mother's heavy, special juice snores, and, knowing she wouldn't wake, she opened the door. The key was on the dresser, an old beaten-up brown unit with a mirror attached that was so dirty Emily couldn't see her own reflection. Grabbing the key, she slipped out of the room and retraced her steps back down to the shed and unlocked the door.

Freya was in her pyjamas, shivering, her skin pale, her lips blue, and it took everything for Emily not to cry.

Taking off her coat, she covered her sister and cradled her as they walked back to the house. Once inside, Emily carried her on her back up the stairs and into their bedroom, then helped her strip and change into dryer clothes, before putting her in her bed.

'Em, I'm so sorry for going into Mother's room last night, I was only playing.'

'I know, but you have to learn, OK? You can't keep making these mistakes,' she said.

'But why not? Mia from school says she and her mummy have sleepovers and everything. Why can't we with Mother?'

'Because.'

'Because what?'

'We just can't, OK?' Emily said, biting her tongue so she didn't add any more. She wanted to say that once she'd had that with Mother, and now it was gone for ever. 'Just . . . no more mistakes, all right, Fry?'

'All right. Sorry.'

'It's OK,' she said, giving her sister a hug.

Freya smiled, and her stomach growled.

'Stay here, warm up. I'll go see if I can find you something to eat,' she said, knowing that she wouldn't find anything.

As Emily walked towards the bedroom door, Freya whispered, 'Are you going to get into trouble for letting me out?'

'No, I reckon I can convince Mother she did it. You know she forgets things.'

'And what if she doesn't believe you?'

'Don't you worry your head with that, OK?'

'OK.' Freya closed her eyes and snuggled down.

Despite Emily saying not to worry, she couldn't help it. Mother was not going to be happy, and as she crept downstairs she heard her parting words: *It was better before, wasn't it? When it was just the two of us. Do you remember back then? We were happy, weren't we?*

CHAPTER SEVEN

I heard a giggle, one I once knew, one from long ago, one that haunted my dreams, and I tried to open my eyes. But I couldn't see anything. I thought I was blind, but it wasn't darkness, it was the opposite. It was light, bright light, and it blinded me. Like the flash from a camera bulb. However, this flash was permanent and unmoving. It made my eyes burn.

I tried to move, to turn my head, but I couldn't. I wasn't pinned down, I just couldn't move, like I was paralysed. But I couldn't be, because I could feel pain in every single muscle. My body hurt all over — fire crackled under my skin and razor blades slashed my throat. My muscles felt like they had been pressed through a mangle. In the brilliant white light, I thought I could see her, my sister — that question written on her face. Then, the memory of what happened materialised slowly, floating out of the black, and as it rushed towards me she faded into the white.

The flash, the explosion in my head, the pinch in my shoulder, someone running, someone screaming.

I closed my eyes, opened them again; the light was less intense for it, and shapes began to come forward. I expected to see my road, my house in the distance, the summer day still warming the tarmac underneath me. I expected to see people around me, helping me get up. I reasoned I must have passed out, the heat of the day all too much, and maybe I had landed on something sharp. God knows there are enough broken bottles on the road where I live. But as my eyes focused, I saw a heart monitor, and then I heard it beeping — rhythmic but climbing. I looked to my left and saw a window, and I couldn't understand why I was inside. Perhaps I had fainted and then somehow dragged myself into my house. It couldn't be, there was a heart monitor, besides, it didn't look like my house. It was familiar though, somehow.

I tried again to move, to understand what was happening, but it was impossible. It hurt, everything hurt. I lifted my arm and felt a sharp pinch. I looked, and there were tubes hanging from it. Beyond, a bed. In it, an old lady, who was sound asleep, propped up by several pillows. My right hand tried to move to my stomach, to my baby, and even though I was confused, even though I could barely move, I was angry that reaching for my baby wasn't the first thing I did. I had only been there, in the brilliant white, for a few seconds, but I should have looked for her before I tried to work out anything else.

Would that be the type of mother I was? Her child coming second?

Despite my arm feeling weak, hollowed out, like the bark of a tree that had fallen and rotted away, I managed to reach down to my bump. I felt it, my swollen stomach where my baby was growing, but it felt different, wrong somehow. I still had a bump, but it didn't feel like the same bump I had stroked a thousand times. It felt less solid. I thought it must be that my arms were heavy, numb, like the rest of my body, and my mind was confused. But, as I pressed, trying to feel an elbow or a knee, I couldn't feel anything. I still had a bump, but it was softer, definitely softer. I moved over my stomach, down to where I knew my daughter's head to be, waiting to come into the world, needing to feel my baby's tiny head inside me. As I did, I winced as white-hot pain exploded from my lower stomach. My hand had touched something that didn't belong to me, something that was not *of* me. It felt like thread — thick, tough cotton thread — and as I traced my hand on it, ignoring the pain, I felt a line of it. Pulling myself up, I looked. There was a wound across my lower abdomen, stitches holding me together. At first, I didn't understand, and then the realisation hit, and the world spun out from under me, and a noise came out of my mouth, something that didn't sound human. It was primal: rage and fear. I was feeling a wound, a caesarean wound.

She was gone. My baby had been taken out of me.

'Oh God, someone help! Where is my baby, where is my baby?' I screamed, my words slurring and weak.

The beeping from within the room increased, started galloping; my heart was about to explode. I tried to get up, tearing the wires from my left arm, and, as I did, the pain was incredible, blinding me once more. But I needed to move, I needed to find my baby.

I felt dizzy, unable to focus, and three people ran in. I couldn't read their faces, their details washed out, but two held me down so I couldn't get up, and then I felt a sharp pinch in my arm, and the world began to fade away once more.

As the world disappeared, I heard my own voice crying out, trying to fight the effects of the drug, and over my cries a voice spoke, trying to calm me. 'It's going to be OK. Emily, listen, you need to stop fighting, everything is going to be all right.'

As I slipped into unconsciousness, the last thing I heard was my own voice, small and completely powerless. 'Where is she? Where have you taken my daughter?'

CHAPTER EIGHT

Then — 18 December

She searched high and low, but returned to their room empty-handed. It didn't matter; Emily was used to hunger pains, and Freya was shaken up from the morning's events. So, tired from the cold, she slept.

Emily watched over her little sister. She knew, deep down, none of it was her fault. She didn't choose to come into this world and change everything. It wasn't her fault, but Emily blamed her for the life they lived. The love they lacked. She loved Freya and she hated her too. And before she said or did anything, she left her asleep and went downstairs to sit alone, in the silence, waiting for her sister or Mother to wake. Freya woke first and, sleepy-eyed, joined her sister in the living room.

'Is there any food now?' she asked as she hit the bottom step.

'No, Freya, there isn't.'

Freya nodded, and, finding her doll — her only toy, one that Emily had stolen from school the year before — she began to quietly play. Emily watched on in silence.

Mother woke mid-afternoon, her footsteps heavy, and both Freya and Emily held their breath. When she came down the stairs into the living room and saw Freya sitting there, the doll in her hand, she gave Emily a look that burned through her skull. She wanted Mother to shout, to scream and hit, to drag her out of the room and punish her for letting her younger sister free. But she didn't, she just looked at her, gently nodding, telling Emily that she knew what she had done, and she would be punished when Mother was good and ready. Even at eleven years old, Emily truly understood what hatred was.

Hours passed, and still Mother did nothing, said nothing, and, as the day morphed into night, Emily needed to break the hanging silence.

'Freya, go play in our room,' she said.

'No, I don't want to.'

'Just go to your room,' she hissed, before stopping herself. Both she and Freya heard Mother's voice in the way Emily had spoken. It scared Emily. It scared them both.

'Please, Fry? Just for a while?' She spoke more softly, helping Freya to her feet. 'I need to talk with Mother, and she might get angry.'

Freya didn't need to be asked again, and she went up the stairs as quickly as she could. From the top step she looked back down, and Emily could see worry in her eyes.

'It'll be OK. Close the door,' Emily said, before turning and walking towards the kitchen.

Mother sat at the table, looking out into the garden, into the nothingness. Blue-grey smoke curled from her burning cigarette. She glanced over to Emily when she walked in the room, looked her up and down, smiled with pure malevolence, and then returned her gaze to outside. Emily didn't move, didn't speak, but waited. She knew better than to speak first with Mother.

Minutes passed, Mother smoked and Emily waited. Eventually Mother stubbed out her cigarette.

'Well?'

'We need food.'

'Then get some.'

'There . . .'

'There what? Spit it out.'

'There's nothing in.'

'Oh, for fuck's sake,' Mother said, getting up and moving to the cupboards. Throwing the doors open, she looked in, and, although Emily couldn't see Mother's face, she knew that when Mother found nothing either she was angry.

'You do realise food isn't free?'

'Yes, Mother, I know, I—'

'If you and your sister weren't such fucking pigs you would make it last longer.'

Emily bit her tongue. She wanted to tell her that they weren't pigs, that she was careful with food, she had always been. She had no choice. But with two of them needing to eat, and only enough food for one person, it would quickly disappear.

'I'm sorry, Mother.'

Mother searched the rest of the cupboards, but Emily knew there was nothing, not even a stale cracker. If there were, she would have found it already. Mother looked at Emily, the anger hot and venomous. The anger faded, replaced with a smile that didn't reach her eyes. Another face to her — not a monster, this one was Vengeful Mother. Emily knew what her mother was thinking, and it wasn't good.

Mother then turned and went to the only cupboard she didn't look in, the only cupboard with a lock. Her cupboard. Removing a key from around her neck, she unlocked it. Emily didn't get to see inside Mother's cupboard, she usually had to leave the room, but today Mother swung the door wide open. She did it on purpose, Emily knew this, and she wanted to look away to spite her, but she couldn't take her eyes off the food. Stacked and organised were tinned beans, crisps, crackers, chocolate bars, bread. And bottles of her special juice. Emily's mouth began to water and her stomach rolled angrily.

Without speaking, Mother pulled out some food and arranged it on a plate. A few crackers, a packet of crisps, one small chocolate bar. And as she did, she smiled knowingly at Emily, no doubt thinking she looked like she was being nice, but Emily was wise to Mother. She was playing nice, pretending to be caring. Really, this was Emily's punishment for letting Freya out of the shed. Mother was getting out just enough food to feed one person, and Emily would have to choose. Would she share with her sister, and they both feel hungry shortly after, or would one eat and feel full, and the other go without?

Mother knew Emily had a duty to Freya.

She missed the days when Freya was a baby and her mother would simply shout and hit. Simpler times.

Once Mother had laid out the food, she locked her cupboard, and without speaking she returned to her chair and lit another cigarette. Tentatively, Emily picked up the plate.

'Thank you, Mother.'

'Oh, you're more than welcome,' she replied with a smile that made Emily feel sick.

Taking the plate upstairs, she went into her bedroom and closed the door behind her. Freya was sitting on the floor, playing with a doll. She gasped when she saw the food.

'Where did you get that?'

'From Mother,' Emily said, handing the plate over to her sister.

'Chocolate?'

'Yes, Freya, chocolate.'

Freya began to cry happy, fat tears, and Emily fought to hold it together at seeing her sister's joy. Only that morning she had been shivering and afraid, locked in a shed. Now, seeing the chocolate, all of that melted away, as did Emily's resentment for her. Emily understood why Freya cried; it was for something as close to joy as they could feel, and Emily felt that joy transfer into her. They hadn't had chocolate for the longest time. It was a gift, a moment of light, a taste of hope. Once Freya had calmed down, she noticed there was only one plate, one chocolate bar.

Downstairs, Emily heard movement. Mother was up to something, and they paused. It wouldn't be unlike her to

51

take the food back, to taunt them with it. So, they sat quietly, hoping she didn't. Emily heard her mother pick up her keys, then the front door slammed. She had gone out instead.

Another gift.

Another taste of hope.

Emily got up and went to the window and saw Mother plodding away from the house, her hands stuffed in her pockets. She'd be back late, slurring and unsteady. Until then, the girls could make noise, wash, play downstairs, even watch some TV.

'Where is yours?' Freya asked when Emily joined her again on the bedroom floor.

Emily swallowed, fighting hard to stop her tears. The happiness she'd felt at seeing her sister's joy had morphed to sadness. 'I ate mine downstairs with Mother.'

'All this food is mine?' she said, her eyes lighting up once more.

'Yes, all of it is yours, now eat.'

'Can I start with the chocolate?'

'Yes,' Emily said, smiling. 'Just make sure you eat it all,' she added, trying to sound like a mother should. Telling herself it wasn't Freya's fault.

Freya tore open the wrapper to the chocolate bar quickly, and, taking a big bite, she chewed slowly, moaning in appreciation as she did. She smiled at Emily and chocolate dribbled down her chin.

She giggled. 'It's so yummy.'

'I know,' Emily said, watching on, trying hard to push down the pains in her stomach. 'Mine was too.'

CHAPTER NINE

Night had fully set in, and my hand went straight to my stomach. I hoped it was a dream, a nightmare, a horrid and vivid projection of my guilt in knowing, after what I did all those years ago, I shouldn't be allowed to be a parent. But as I felt the stitches, I knew what had happened was real. My baby was gone, and I didn't know why. I fought to lift myself up, to swing my legs onto the floor so I could look for her, but the effort almost made me pass out. I began to call for help. My head was swimming like I was drunk, and my words didn't sound like my own. I tried to say I needed help, but the sound that came out of my mouth was missing all of the consonants. A hand reached out and touched my left arm, and I turned my head, blinking hard to try to keep my focus.

'Hey, it's OK, Emily. You're OK. You're all right.'

Michelle smiled at me, but the smile was confined to her mouth. Her eyes told me I was anything but all right.

'Where is she?' I managed to say, my voice scratchy and parched. 'Where is my baby?'

Michelle squeezed my forearm. 'She's safe, so are you.'

'Is she hurt? Why isn't she with me?'

'I know you're confused, a lot has happened, but she's fine, you are too, and your baby will be with you soon. Emily, look at me.'

I did as she asked.

'She's all right. Just try and stay calm and I'll explain it all.'

'Michelle, what's happened?' I said, bursting into tears. 'Where is my daughter? Who's looking after her? Who has my baby now? Please.'

'Lucas. Lucas has her. He's coming soon. You need to rest.'

'I don't want to rest, I want my baby. Why is she not here? Why was she born without me knowing?' I was desperate, my breathing jagged and sharp.

'Emily. Emily, look at me,' Michelle said forcefully, and again I did as I was told.

'Take some deep breaths with me, OK? In and out. That's it, in and out.'

I followed her lead, and my breathing settled.

'You've been asleep. Freya was discharged, and, as she was well, Lucas agreed to take her home until you woke. It was agreed she would do better at home than here with you not being able to care for her.'

'She's with Lucas?'

'Yes, she is. I know this is so confusing, but I promise everything is OK.'

'What happened to me, Michelle?'

'Em, you have to rest. I promise, Freya will be here soon.'

'Please tell me why I'm here. Why isn't my daughter still inside me? Why was she born without me?' I tried to sit up.

'Hey, hey. Stop, you'll hurt yourself,' Michelle said, before calling for help. A nurse came in.

'She's trying to get up.'

'Miss Claywater,' the nurse said calmly, 'you can't get up just yet.'

I ignored her and continued to try to force myself upright, and, as I did, her firm hands went to my shoulders, pushing me back down on the bed, and before I could protest further something was added to the IV pole that went into a cannula in the back of my hand, and I drifted off once more.

* * *

When I opened my eyes again, I was sure I could hear someone at the end of my bed, quietly talking to themselves — a small voice, a child's voice — but when I looked, no one was there. But I knew: my sister had followed me to this place. She was always watching, pleading with me to undo what I had done, to give her her life back. As my mind swam up from the dark place it had drifted into, I knew even before I touched my stomach the awful truth. I knew, and still I cried when I couldn't feel my baby. I looked around the room. Adam was dozing in the chair. Outside, pink and orange hues lined the sky. Dawn.

'Are you OK, love?' a voice asked. I turned, startled, and then remembered the old lady in the bed next to me. 'Did you have a bad dream?'

I didn't know what to say. Yes, yes, I was having a bad dream, this was all just a bad dream. I had lived in it for sixteen years.

'I've heard what they were saying, about your accident. I'm so sorry for what happened. You'll have your baby again soon. It seems you have lots of people around you who love you.'

'Thank you,' I whispered, and as I turned away, unable to say more, Adam stirred, smiled and reached for my hand.

'Hey,' he said, 'how are you feeling?'

'Where is she?'

'Freya's coming. It's still really early.'

'What time is it?'

He looked at his watch. 'Just after four.'

'What happened, Adam? Why did they cut her out of me?'

'I think it's best we wait for a doctor.'

55

'Adam. Just tell me. My baby isn't here, and no one is telling me why. She was born, she was born without me. I have to know why.'

I watched him take a deep breath. One I understood from past experience meant bad news was coming. Someone took a deep breath that Christmas in my childhood. Several people did in the months after, and again two years ago when my grandparents died. The deep breath wasn't good.

'Just tell me. What happened, what accident? Please, I don't know what's going on and I have the right to, so—'

'All right,' he said, cutting me off. 'All right.' He took a deep breath again, and then he just said it. He didn't try to soften his words. He was direct, shockingly so. 'It wasn't an accident. You were attacked.'

'What?' I said, and then I recalled the flash, the noise and the footsteps.

'Do you remember?'

'I remember passing out.'

'You didn't pass out. Someone attacked you.'

'What? Ummm, I mean, do you . . . do you know who? Did my baby get hurt?'

'No, she's fine, she wasn't hurt at all, and they don't know who did it.'

'They?'

'The police. It was serious, really serious. They'll want to talk to you.'

I began to panic. The police. I didn't want to talk to the police, not now, not ever. 'Why did they take my baby out?' I said, forcing myself to focus.

'After you were knocked to the ground, you were injected. They didn't know this at first, not until you were here, but they discovered you were injected with insulin, a big dose.'

I recalled the sharp pinch I'd felt. Was that the feeling of a needle going into my skin? Had someone tried to kill me? A blow to the head was one thing, a mugging, but to be injected? In that moment, someone wanted me dead, and I didn't know why.

'The blow knocked you out, the insulin put you into a coma. You nearly died. Fuck, I'm so sorry. I should have insisted that I take you home.'

I couldn't process what Adam was saying. *Attacked, injected, coma.* It didn't make sense. All I could understand was, my baby wasn't with me.

'How long have I been here?' I asked.

'I've been told not to say.'

'Adam. Just fucking tell me.'

'Ten days,' he said quietly, reluctantly.

'What?'

'It happened ten days ago.'

'My baby is ten days old?'

He nodded.

'And I've not even met her,' I added as tears began to fall. But then a question flashed into my mind. I didn't know how it would be possible, but had this happened because of that Christmas in the wildlands?

'You were really poorly, Emily,' he continued. 'Once they knew you were in a hypoglycaemic coma, they had to perform an emergency caesarean to make sure Freya was OK. But she's fine. She's perfect.'

'Is she?'

'Yes, they acted quickly, got her out. She was observed for two days and then discharged to Lucas. He was here the whole time, Em, he didn't leave, not even when visiting hours were over. She's fine. Freya is fine. The doctors did a great job, with both of you.'

'I want to see her.'

'I know. She's coming.'

'I don't even know what she looks like,' I said, a fat tear rolling down my cheek. Adam didn't try to wipe it, and I was glad that he let me be.

He stood up and pulled his phone from his pocket. Unlocking it, he tapped the screen a few times and then put his phone in front of me. It took a moment for my eyes to adjust but when they did, I was looking at a picture of my baby. My girl. My Freya.

She was wrapped in a green hospital blanket up to her waist, her little arms out and up by her head. Sound asleep. Under her right eye, she had a white plaster.

'You said she wasn't hurt?'

'The surgeon had to get her out quickly. He nicked her cheek, but her eye is fine. She might just have a little scar, that's all.'

I nodded. She was beautiful, so much more beautiful than I could have imagined. I couldn't take my eyes off her tiny face, her tiny nose, her tiny hands. My baby, my baby. I didn't blink until my tears filled my eyes, making it impossible to see.

'She's perfect,' I said. 'Can you send me that picture?'

'Yes, of course.'

'I need her with me now.'

'I know. She's coming.'

Adam's screen went black and locked itself and, without me needing to ask, he unlocked it again so I could look at my little girl.

'Emily. The police need to talk to you.'

I nodded without taking my eyes from the picture. I wanted to know what her cry sounded like, what it felt like for her to hold my finger. I wanted to feel her soft skin and her warmth. Fresh tears fell. I had missed that first moment when a mother and baby bond. And I'd never get it back.

I took a deep breath as a doctor came into the room.

'Ms Claywater,' he said, smiling sympathetically at me. He appeared calm, and it calmed me a little too, although I couldn't shake the fact that I had been attacked. I wondered, was that why my sister was back? Did she know what was going to happen to me? Was this her way of telling me I was finally going to pay my penance?

'Ms Claywater?' the doctor said, snapping me from my thoughts.

'Sorry, please, call me Emily.'

'Emily. I'm Doctor Bhari. It's good to see you back with us again. You gave us all quite the scare.'

'So I hear.'

'You're a lucky woman — you and your daughter. It could have ended quite differently for you.'

I nodded, having absolutely no idea what to say in response.

'Ms Clay . . . Emily,' he continued, 'we were asked to inform the police once you were conscious. They want to talk to you, about the incident, would that be OK? I can tell them to go away if you want more time.'

'No, it's fine,' I said, swallowing. I tried to remind myself, they didn't know, no one knew. My secret stayed in the wildlands all those years ago. In the eyes of the law, it was settled, it was done. The blame lay elsewhere. I was just a little girl. A little girl with a different name. They didn't even look at me then as a suspect, so they wouldn't now. That Christmas, I was seen as the victim, a poor young girl, despite the truth. Now I was the victim again, the crimes couldn't be connected. Even reassuring myself, I still didn't want to speak to the police. But I had to, or else it would look like I was hiding something.

Adam stood and excused himself, and as he and the doctor left a man walked in, mid-forties, kind eyes.

'Hi, Ms Claywater, I'm Detective Myers.'

'Hello, Detective.'

'How are you feeling?'

'Like shit,' I said truthfully, and he nodded, taking a seat beside the bed.

'Are you OK to answer a few questions?'

'Yes,' I said, noting to myself to take a deep breath.

For thirty minutes, he and I talked about that day, what I did, who I was with. He didn't ask anything about my past, and I felt relieved for it.

'When you walked home, did you see anyone, speak with anyone?' he asked.

I said no, I was on my own, but then I remembered the teens who stepped into the road for me, the older lady who smiled longingly, and the man who asked if I was all right in the tunnel.

'Can you describe him to me?'

'No, sorry.'

'Had you seen him before?'

'No, never.'

He nodded, told me to rest up, and that he would be in touch soon. I was expecting more questions, but they didn't come. Not yet, but they might still. As he left, Adam came back into the room.

'You all right?'

'Yeah, tired. I'm fine. Where's Michelle?'

'She's gone to Lucas's, she'll be back soon.'

'With Freya?'

'Yes, with Freya.'

I smiled and looked up to the ceiling, my heart light, so light I felt I could float away. I was nervous too at seeing my girl, nervous and excited. The pain in my body melted away, replaced with the warmth of knowing that imminently I would hold my daughter in my arms, that she would look at me, her eyes and mine locking together for the first time.

'Will she know?' I asked.

'Know?'

'Will she know I'm her mummy?'

'Of course, you grew that little girl. She'll know.'

From somewhere outside my hospital room, I heard Michelle's voice asking someone to move, and I felt butter-flies come alive inside my stomach. She was about to walk in with my little girl. I was going to hold my baby for the first time. She was here, my baby was here.

Michelle came in, and I expected to see my daughter in her arms, or in Lucas's behind her. But she was alone, her face grey.

'Why didn't you answer the phone?' she said to Adam, her voice high and tight.

'I haven't got reception. Why?'

'Where is she?' I said.

She didn't respond.

'Michelle, where is Freya?'

'I've tried calling everyone,' she said.

'Why isn't she with you? Where is Lucas?'

Michelle hesitated, and then she took a deep breath, just like Adam had.

'Where is he, Michelle? Where is my baby?'

'Michelle?' Adam added.

'I went. His house is empty. Car is gone. I spoke with a neighbour — they said they've not seen his car on the drive for two, maybe three days.'

'What are you saying? Where is my daughter?'

'I don't know,' she said.

'What do you mean, you don't know?' I said, my voice cracking. 'You told me she was safe, you said he was coming. Two or three days? Why haven't you seen him in two or three days?'

'I've spoken with him every day. I thought he was, I . . .' She trailed off. 'Adam, have you heard anything?'

'No, nothing! But I'm sure there's a logical explanation.'

'Where is my daughter!' I shouted. I tried to get up, to force my legs into action, but they felt hollow and weak. My scream must have alerted the medical staff, as before I could try to take a step I was grabbed and pushed back down onto the bed. I fought, but it was no use. And once again, I watched helplessly as a doctor administered some medication and the world faded away, and as it did I could hear Michelle saying something to me, trying to comfort me, her voice becoming ever more distant.

CHAPTER TEN

Then — 18 December

Emily was watching the birds battle futilely against the wind of the wildlands when she heard Mother's voice carrying over it. A laugh that felt false, forced. A laugh that hid so much pain. It was distant but drawing closer. It lifted her from her daydream of flying away, somewhere new, somewhere where the sun was shining, where warmth was constant, where she could be safe. A nest all of her own, high in a tree, away from people, away from harm. Shaken back into reality, she ran into the living room to get her sister.

'We need to move.'

Freya moaned in protest. It wasn't often they were able to sit in front of the television, cartoons playing. She was watching a film with songs about a mermaid with red hair; she'd not seen it before.

'Emily, please, just five more minutes.'

'No, Freya, move. Mother's coming.'

Whereas only moments before, Freya had been sleepy from her banquet of chocolate, crisps and dry crackers, content at her belly feeling full for the first time in weeks, now she seemed gripped with fear.

'Come on, move,' Emily said, pulling one final time, lifting her younger sister to her feet. 'Go upstairs, now!'

Freya began to run, followed by her sister, and as they reached the bottom of the stairs the front door unlocked, and swung open, almost hitting Freya.

Mother was home, and on her arm was a man.

'Ahhhhhhh, you're up. These are my babies, aren't they beautiful?'

Fake Mother.

The man nodded, polite, but he wasn't interested in the girls.

'Girls, this is Uncle Paul,' she said, and Emily wondered if she genuinely thought they believed it.

'Say hello, then,' she said, cuffing Emily around the head, laughing as she did. The man laughed too, but Emily didn't. The force of the blow made her head swim.

'Hello, Uncle Paul,' the girls chorused.

'Hello, girls, are you excited for Christmas?'

'Christmas? Is it soon?' Freya asked innocently, but Emily knew it wouldn't be seen that way.

'There, see, see?' Mother said, but to whom and what about, she didn't know. 'Now, girls, go to your room. Uncle Paul and I need to talk about grown-up things.'

Emily could tell Freya was intrigued as to what they might discuss, but Emily knew better, and, before Freya could speak, she gently pushed her sister up the stairs, mumbling goodnight on her way up.

Going into their room, Emily closed the door behind them and took a deep breath before turning back to Freya, painting on a smile.

'Uncle Paul?'

'Yes, it's Mother's brother,' Emily lied.

'Why haven't we met him before?'

'We did. You were too little,' she lied again. Freya was too young to know what their 'uncles' actually were. She would eventually get wise, as Emily had a few years back, but although she knew Freya wouldn't be shocked by it, even though she knew Freya was wiser than her six years suggested, she wanted to try to preserve something in her. She waited for Freya to question when Uncle Paul was last around, but she simply nodded, yawned and stretched.

'Now, it's time for you to go to sleep, it's late,' she said when she noticed Freya staring at her, a question right on the tip of her tongue.

'No, I want to stay up with you.'

'No, Freya, little ones need their rest.'

'You're little too.'

'Yes, but not as little, I'll go to bed soon.'

'But—'

'Come on Fry, please?' She almost added that if she did, there might be more nice food in the morning, but she didn't want to get Freya's hopes up.

'Now, come on.'

As Freya began to protest again, footsteps came up the stairs, and both girls froze, listening. The steps passed their door, and less than a minute later the toilet flushed. In the crack under the door, Emily could see a shadow pause as it made its way back to the stairs. Two feet blocking the dim light underneath. Mother's feet. Emily put her finger to her lips.

'Shhhhhh.'

Freya nodded. After a moment, Mother moved and descended into the house. She was saying something, but Emily couldn't make out what.

Freya climbed into bed without the need for Emily to ask again, and Emily tucked her in, pulling the covers up high, knowing it was going to be a wintry night ahead. Watching her sister, she could see Freya was sleepy from the sugar crash following her rare feast, as each blink was long and heavy. Sitting on the floor beside her, Emily reached over and stroked Freya's hair, quietly humming a song that had been with her since for ever, that reminded her of a different time. Mother used to hum it to her when she was around Freya's age. When she didn't understand what fear or hunger or cold was. She pushed it down, remembering that life hurt, and it made her hate Freya all over again.

'Em, is it really Christmas soon?' Freya said, snapping her out of that dark place, a place that had become increasingly familiar, that was more and more like a friend every day.

'Yes, it is.'

'Will Santa visit this year?'

'He will. Now go to sleep.'

'How do you know he will come this time?'

'I just know, OK? No more questions.'

Once Freya was asleep, Emily stood and walked to the window to look out onto the street. The rain was falling, signs of sleet in some of the fat drops, and she wondered if they would have a white Christmas this year. She knew they wouldn't get gifts, but snow would make it all right. Snow would make Freya forget that Santa hadn't been again. Turning to look at her sister, she knew hoping for snow wasn't enough. She needed Freya to be happy, so she would behave, make no more mistakes. Then maybe Mother wouldn't have a reason to be angry, and they could have a Christmas like the ones she remembered. When all the magic was real.

Looking at her sister, she wondered how long Freya would have before she lost her magic, and the part of her that felt duty bound knew she needed to do something to ensure it stayed for as long as it could. An idea struck her. In the loft were some decorations — tinsel and lights from before Freya came. She had to get them. Santa had to visit now, just in case.

From downstairs she could hear laughter, but it wasn't kind laughter, it was something else. She tried not to listen and instead focused on the row of houses opposite that looked identical to one another, some with lights on, some dark. She wondered what it must be like living in one of them. What were the adults like? Was there kindness, food, warmth? Did they know how she and Freya lived? She wondered if everyone lived as they did. Probably not.

Outside, a small car pulled up and a man got out with bags of food from the supermarket. He locked his car and hurried up the path of one of the houses opposite and disappeared inside. Even though she couldn't see much inside the bags, even though she couldn't smell any food, her stomach growled angrily.

Downstairs, the laughter had turned to the sound of moaning, and, moving from the window, she knelt down by her little sister and gently covered her ears. Just in case. Duty bound.

She must have fallen asleep, because when she opened her eyes the rain had stopped, the moaning had stopped too, and, daring to open her door, she looked into the hallway. Mother's door was ajar, meaning she was asleep downstairs. As quietly as she could, Emily opened the airing cupboard and pulled out an old stepladder. Mother borrowed it once from another uncle, she couldn't remember his name. She needed it to take down a beeping fire alarm. He told her she needed to replace it, and yet Mother never had. Nor did she give the ladder back.

Unfolding it, she climbed up and pushed the hatch open to the attic, then, using the shelf on the airing cupboard, she pulled herself up. It was dark, pitch black, and, without any light, Emily stumbled along the thin planks of wood laid between the support beams. Finding some boxes at the back of the loft, she opened them one at a time and fumbled through them, trying to identify the contents by touch. In the fourth box, she found the Christmas decorations. Dragging the box to the open hatch, she climbed down onto the stepladder and listened. The house was still silent, and she pulled the box down, struggling to hold it as she descended. Once she had safely placed both feet on the landing floor, she quietly put the ladder away and went back into her room. And even though she was tired, hungry and cold, Emily smiled. Tomorrow, Freya would wake up and Santa's helper would have been, because, as if by magic, their room would be ready for Christmas. It would make sure Freya was good, and that would make Mother happy. It was a risk but, she reasoned, as long as they didn't have the lights on often, Mother would never know. As Emily began to decorate the room, silently so as not to wake Freya, she wondered if she was doing so because of the love she had for her sister, but it wasn't that at all. Emily wasn't sure she knew what love was anymore. She once knew, but had learned that love was cruel, punishing. No, it wasn't love that wanted to shield Freya from it all, but duty. A duty she wished she didn't have to face day after day. A duty she would do anything to rid herself of, so that maybe she could love her sister, and Mother would love her.

CHAPTER ELEVEN

I woke, the world fading in once more, and, although I could see Jack and Michelle and Adam in the room, I couldn't quite read their faces and I couldn't quite understand their words. Their voices were muffled, like they were speaking through a thick wall. They were standing by the window, the bright daylight behind them, a conspiring circle. Michelle had her back to me, and as they spoke they did so in whispers. I sensed they felt tense, but I couldn't quite place why. As I turned my head, it swam, and I rested my unfocused eyes on the bed beside me. The woman who had been there, the older lady, wasn't there anymore, and her bed had been stripped down. I hoped it was because she got to go home. On the other side of the bed, I thought I could make out the shape of a girl, my sister, standing in the shadows, watching. Her eyes bored into me. 'Another Freya gone, another Freya failed,' she said without the need to open her mouth.

Her unspoken words forced me to blink, to recoil from the truth, and when I looked again she was no longer there.

The world began to settle, the muffled voices sharpening into focus.

'This is so fucked up,' Jack said, his tone hushed.

'Yeah,' Adam said. 'Michelle, you know him pretty well, right?'

'I mean, maybe. More than you two, for sure.'

'Is this the sort of thing Lucas would do?'

'No, not at all. Their relationship was complicated, but he's a good man. I know he wanted Freya to have a life like his, but taking her? I didn't think he'd be the type.'

'No, me neither,' Jack said. 'But for him to just take off without telling anyone, it doesn't look good.'

'Can I speak openly?' Adam asked. 'Truth be told, I didn't really like the man.'

'Why?'

'I don't know, he just made me feel a little uncomfortable. And when he came to the barbecue he was really off. Thinking about it, he looked like he was up to something.'

'What do you mean "up to something"?' Michelle said.

'I don't know, he was shifty. Wouldn't hold my eye. I get he's intense, but I found him too intense. Too mysterious. I know that was why Em liked him, but now I'm wondering if he was hiding something.'

'What kind of thing?'

'Well, that he was going to kidnap a baby, for one.'

'And you're only saying this now?' Michelle said, her voice clipped and angry. She sounded hurt.

'I dismissed it, thinking it was just his way, the artistic, free-spirit type. But . . .'

'But what?' Michelle asked.

'Now I think, that day at the barbecue, he was planning to attack Emily.'

'No, no, he couldn't have,' Michelle said.

'I don't know, maybe Lucas is the type. Maybe his "mystery" is in fact something darker? Maybe he isn't as good and kind as Emily thinks.'

'So what has he done with Freya? Where would he take her?' Jack said.

'Emily told me he wanted Freya to be wanderlusty, like he is. She said they argued about it,' Adam said.

'Are you saying he intended to take her away?' Jack asked.

'I'm not saying anything, but Emily wanted Freya to stay here, in London. Lucas wanted her to go and see the world. What if he did this to ensure he got what he wanted?'

'By nearly killing her?' Michelle said.

I moved, trying to prop myself up, but the effort hurt my stomach and I winced. My friends turned to me, and I watched them paint a smile on their faces. The effort looked almost as painful as my torn stitches.

'Heeeey,' Michelle said, coming over to me, sitting on the edge of the bed and taking my hand. 'How are you feeling?'

'Where is she?' I asked, ignoring her question, and I watched as her smile dropped.

'We don't know.'

'What do you mean, you don't know?' I said, my anger and fear bubbling up.

'The police are looking for her, they're doing everything they can. They will track Lucas down.'

'Why wasn't someone looking out for my daughter?'

'We were,' Michelle said. 'But Lucas, he is the father, and—'

'Have they been to his house?'

'Yes, they went in, and most of his stuff is gone along with all the baby things, which means he packed it all. They wonder if he has family that he's gone to.'

'Why would he do that?'

'Maybe he's freaking out — a newborn, you being attacked, maybe he needs support,' Adam said, taking over when Michelle couldn't speak. 'The police are looking into it. I'm sure they'll have answers for you. I'm sure it's just a big misunderstanding.'

'*Misunderstanding?*'

'Maybe he's scared. Christ we were all scared, Em, you were in a bad way for a while,' Jack said, taking my hand.

'So, what do I do now?'

'Rest, recover, get out of this hospital,' Michelle said, mirroring Jack by taking my other hand in hers. 'So that when they find Lucas and Freya, they can bring her straight to you, in your home. Your family home. Em, I probably know the answer to this, but given what's happened, I wanted to ask if you wanted me or Jack or someone to reach out and try and find your mother?'

'No.'

'Are you sure? I know you and her haven't—'

'I said no. I don't want her here. I doubt she's even alive now, but even if she is, I don't want her here.'

She nodded. 'I assumed as much.'

'When? When will they let me go home?'

'I asked this morning, a few days.'

'A few—?'

I was interrupted by the sound of Michelle's phone vibrating on the trolley table. She turned quickly to grab it and looked at the caller ID. 'I don't know the number.'

'Answer it, put it on loudspeaker, it might be Lucas,' I said.

Michelle nodded and answered, holding the phone so we could all hear. 'Hello?'

'It's Detective Myers. Is Emily there?'

'Yes, yes, I'm here.'

'How are you feeling?' he asked.

'Where is she?'

'We're working on it, trust me, OK?'

'I want her here.'

'Emily, I need to ask you a question. Can you tell me what connection Lucas might have to Middlesbrough or Newcastle?'

'What, why?'

'Has he got friends there, family that you know of?'

'I don't know, I can't remember. Why?'

'Any friends or family in the North East?'

'I don't know, why are you asking?'

'ANPR's picked up his car on the A19, heading north. I hoped there was a different reason than what we assume as to why.'

'A different reason?' I asked, struggling to keep up due to the drugs.

'Newcastle is a port city,' Jack said.

'Oh, shit,' Michelle said quietly.

'We're ahead of you,' Myers continued over the phone. 'If he tries to board a ferry to leave the UK, we'll find him. Port control is aware of the situation.'

'What if he's already gone?' I asked.

'We'll find him, and Freya,' he said.

'OK,' I said, trying to sound reassured.

'Emily, there is one more thing I want to ask you. We've done a background check, but I want to confirm — do you know if Lucas is diabetic?'

At first, I didn't understand his question, but then it hit me, and what that meant.

'Yes, type one,' I said.

'Oh shit!' Michelle said, understanding also.

'OK, thank you. I'd better go. Rest up, you'll need your strength when your baby comes home,' Myers said, urgency in his voice.

I pleaded for him to stay, to tell me more, but he hung up.

Suddenly the gift Lucas left for me at the barbecue came to mind, the small angel brooch. I knew I had seen it before somewhere. It was the crest of the town I grew up in, the crest of Dumfries, of the wildlands. Lucas knew who I was. Lucas knew where I was from. Somehow, he knew what I did that Christmas, the brooch was his way of telling me he knew, and he was going to take my daughter away.

'Emily? Emily?' Jack said, drawing my attention. 'Why would he ask if Lucas is diabetic?'

'Because it tells us something,' Michelle said.

'What?' he asked. 'I don't get it?'

'Jack,' Adam hissed, 'Lucas carries insulin.'

'And insulin was what put me in a coma. Insulin was what nearly killed me,' I said.

PART THREE

CHAPTER TWELVE

Thirteen days missing

Seventy-two hours, three whole days, and nothing.

I couldn't bear it, I just couldn't.

Three days of being awake and not having my baby, three days of waiting for the police to tell me they had found her, that they were bringing her home. Three days of my stomach lurching each time the phone rang, only for it to drop when it wasn't what I needed to hear.

I replayed over and over the conversation Lucas and I had had after it was clear I wasn't going to give up on having my baby. The way he'd pressed to give my daughter the life he had, travelling far and wide, seeing the world. I could hear him pleading for it, and how he and I would never work if we didn't agree. I had said, when she was older, he could take her. Now I knew he wasn't willing to wait that long.

I thought I knew Lucas, but to inject me with insulin, to almost kill me — it seems I didn't know him at all.

Then, the same could be said about me by anyone. No one knew me either. My past, my true identity, no one but Lucas. It was why he took her, and, as everyone else struggled to find his motivation, I knew, and I couldn't tell anyone.

I understood torture, I understood waiting, I understood grief; those three words were the foundation of my early childhood, but not like this. And my only comfort was a photo of my little girl that I didn't take, a photo that would be dated now as she would surely look bigger. It was the first time I knew that the torture would surely kill me. But then, I once took a life. Maybe I had to pay with my own. Maybe Lucas knew it would kill me, not having her, maybe that was his point. Protect his Freya, knowing I would die and pay for my crimes.

I just didn't understand how he knew.

Michelle could see I was struggling, that I was dying inside not having my daughter, and once I was discharged she insisted that either she, Jack or Adam would be with me at my house at all times. And as Michelle slept in one of the guest rooms for the third consecutive night, I paced. My bright, happy home, which had offered such solace before, now felt lifeless without my daughter there. In the day, I could cope; there was noise, light, movement. There were regular conversations with the police, and Jack or Adam would tell me stories.

They helped, but the lack of rest was beginning to take its toll on my already battered body and, after another sleepless night, Michelle found me in the conservatory at the back of the house, sitting on a rattan sofa, the morning light streaming through an open door, the sound of birdsong filtering in, mocking me.

'Did you sleep?' she asked as she took a seat opposite me.

'Not really,' I said.

'Em, you need to rest, you need to recover.'

'What for?' I asked, turning to look her in the eye.

'Because, when they find her, she's going to need a fit and healthy mum.'

'Michelle, what if they don't?' I said. I waited for her to argue that they of course would, that she was probably on her way to me now, as she had been before, but there was a pause before she spoke.

'They will, they'll bring her home.'

'It's been three days. Lucas could be anywhere.'

'I still can't believe he would do this,' she said, and I didn't comment. I could. The brooch said he knew who I was and what I had done. I just couldn't work out how he had discovered the truth.

'I hate that I'm sat in this conservatory right now,' I said, moving my thoughts along.

'Why?'

'I'm sat here, comfortable, warm, the morning sun on my face, and she's . . . she's God knows where. She could be somewhere dark, cold, she could be de—'

Michelle cut me off before I could finish. 'Hey! Hey! No.'

'Michelle, we have to—'

'No! You aren't going there.'

'Too late,' I said quietly. 'I know you want me to stay hopeful, but children aren't spared from trauma, they aren't spared from tragedy.'

'Fuck off, Emily.'

'What?'

'I said fuck off. I'm not having it. You're just going to let yourself go there?'

'I'm trying not to, I am.'

'Try harder!' she said, almost shouting at me.

'Michelle, please, don't.'

'Don't what? Don't stop my best friend going to a dark place? Don't stop her from giving up?' She paused, waiting for me to tell her I wasn't giving up. I felt so powerless, so hopeless that I couldn't. 'Right, fuck this. When was the last time you washed?'

I hadn't since coming home.

'Get showered.'

'What? Why?' I said.

'We're not doing this.'

'What?'

'This. Sitting and waiting and doing nothing. Get off your ass. We've got a busy day ahead.'

Before I could ask her what our 'busy day' involved, she was gone, and as I sat, stunned by her telling-off, I heard her talking on the phone in the kitchen.

'Hey, Julia. It's me. Yes, yes, she's OK. Listen, that thing we spoke about yesterday? We're going for it . . . Yes, I agree, time is important. That's wonderful. Message everyone. We'll see you in an hour.'

Heaving myself off the sofa, I walked towards the hall-way, and as Michelle hung up she looked at me.

'Do you need help getting upstairs?' she asked, her anger gone, replaced with a purpose I didn't understand.

'No, I can manage. Michelle, what's going on?'

'Just get showered and dressed, OK? People will be here in an hour.'

'People are coming here? Michelle?'

'Just do it. I'm not fucking having this wallowing bullshit. It isn't gonna help find her.'

'Why are you so angry?'

'Because you're giving up. Because Lucas has your daughter. Because . . . because I failed you, we all failed you. I'll not fail you again.'

'Michelle?' I said, softening as my friend began to cry.

'The police are looking, they're doing their bit. You need to step up and do yours, Emily. I do too.'

'I don't know what it is I'm supposed to do,' I said quietly, ashamed that I should be so clueless as to what to do to help my baby.

'You know what helps find missing people?' Michelle continued, wiping her eyes. 'People. You need to get out there, put your face on the TV and in the papers. Speak to the world, and they'll help you.'

I stumbled back. I had spent a long time, over half of my life, hiding away from the world, hiding who I was, and now Michelle was trying to make me step into the spotlight. And I knew I was screwed. If I did, someone might recognise me from that Christmas in the wildlands, and if I didn't, I was condemning my daughter to an unknown fate. I had no choice.

'OK,' I said. 'OK.'

I turned to continue up the stairs and Michelle stopped me.

'Emily. I should have never let you walk home alone. I should have looked after you, after her.'

'It's not your fault,' I said, trying to believe it. If she'd been pregnant, I knew I would have walked her home.

'I'm a bad friend, but I promise to make this right.'

Michelle never spoke to me like this. She was kind, funny, flaky. I'd never heard her so fired up. So sad. I moved towards her to give her a hug, but before I could get close she wiped her tears, lifted her chin and stepped away. Burying her pride and pain, she picked up the phone and began talking to God knows who.

'Hey, it's me. We're going for it. Great, see you soon.'

'Who was that?'

'Adam. Now, get moving.'

Heaving myself up the stairs, I tried to force down the nausea growing in my belly, a new sick feeling to sit upon the constant sick feeling I felt. Michelle had made it clear I was going to go public, and so I stepped into the bathroom and turned on the shower. Leaving it to warm up, I went into my bedroom and opened the wardrobe to pull out some clothes. My eye was drawn to the furthest corner; tucked away under a stack of jumpers was a box. *The* box. The one I shouldn't have kept. Its contents were the only link between the me I am now and the me who lived on the wildlands. Part of me wanted to lift it down, open it up, but I didn't need to. I knew exactly what was inside. There was a cardigan, my sister's cardigan, a teddy and a knife. I realised, if Lucas had found it, that might be how he knew who I was and where I was from. That might be why he took her away from me. Lucas had always wanted to know about my early years, but I never told him. I shouldn't have let my guard down with him, I shouldn't have let him get close enough to be able to find out the truth.

'Em?' Michelle said from the doorway, making me jump, and I quickly closed the wardrobe door. 'Are you OK?'

'I'll be down in a sec.'

Michelle smiled sympathetically at me. 'Listen, I'm sorry I got angry.'

'It's OK.'

'I just—'

'It's OK, honestly.'

She smiled again, and went back downstairs. I went back to the bathroom, and as I began to undress I caught my reflection in the full-length mirror. My stomach was still swollen; I almost looked pregnant. My breasts were achingly swollen too, despite how much I expressed. But my eye was drawn to below my belly button, to the thin smile-like scar that ran across me. My daughter was pulled out of that scar; through that small incision she was born into a world that was proving to be cruel. I ran my fingers over my stitches, trying to imagine that moment when she was dragged into the world. Away from me. I imagined her crying before being lifted onto my chest, her skin on mine. I tried to hold on to that image, that fake memory, but it faded, like my reflection as steam fogged the room. It was replaced with another image, one of Lucas finding the things I should have destroyed sixteen years ago. I saw him holding the knife, piecing together who I once was. Making his plan to take her away from me.

CHAPTER THIRTEEN

I was out of the shower and dressed just as people began to arrive at my front door, and as I descended the stairs I saw an older woman standing beside Michelle.

'Julia, this is Emily,' Michelle said.

'Hello Emily,' she said, taking my hand in hers, and then wrapping it with her other one. She looked at me with such kindness, such pity, I didn't know how to respond.

'Julia is one of Mum's friends, she runs the local church community centre. She's helped me organise volunteers and let us borrow some things we'll need.'

'Thank you,' I said.

'Anything to help.'

'But volunteer for what?'

'We're turning your kitchen into our base of operations,' Michelle said, matter-of-fact, like I was supposed to understand what she was talking about.

'Follow me, Julia,' Michelle said, leading her into my kitchen. I followed obediently behind. I had no idea what Michelle had planned.

'OK, so I'm thinking we put the whiteboards up in the conservatory; we can run a phone from there. The kitchen table we'll clear and use for maps, information. We can keep the kettle boiled, snacks stocked. There's even a bathroom on this floor, so no one needs to go upstairs — if that's OK?'

'Of course, this is her home,' Julia said.

'Do you need help unloading the van?' Michelle offered.

'No, it's fine, I've got people coming.' Julia smiled politely and went back towards the front door.

'How many?' I asked, still completely lost as to what was happening in my home.

'A dozen or so,' Julia said, before continuing outside. Once she was gone, the front door closed behind her, I turned to my best friend. 'Michelle, what the bloody hell is going on?'

'I've been worried about you spiralling. So, I spoke with the boys, and we agreed that you sitting there wallowing isn't going to find her, and me just trying to keep your spirits up won't either. So, we're taking action.'

'Action?'

'This is now our centre of operations to find Freya. We'll use social media to our advantage, we'll write out everything we know and we'll connect the dots.'

'But the police said not to talk to anyone.'

'And that's their prerogative. Media makes things messy for them, but it can help us. People are smart, people are driven, and with a missing baby people will want to help.'

'Missing baby? Michelle, this is my daughter you're talking about.'

'Yes. Yes, sorry, I'm getting carried away,' she said, her hands up in defence. 'With Freya missing, people will want to help.'

'But the police said—'

'Are you happy to sit and wait? Are you happy to do nothing?'

'No, I want my daughter with me.'

'So, let's find her, then.'

With that, Michelle went into the conservatory and started moving the furniture around, leaving me standing in the middle of my kitchen, stunned. I turned back to see the front door open again, and Julia carrying a large whiteboard in her arms. Once she had cleared the lip of the front door, she put it down and wheeled it towards Michelle. Through the open front door I saw cars stopping on the street. Several of them. And once they'd parked, people, strangers, got out and made their way into my home. I watched as Michelle moved in a blur, hugging, talking, thanking. Within half an hour there were fifteen people, including me, spread throughout the kitchen and conservatory.

Michelle stood on a chair to speak to everyone.

'Right, welcome everyone. And on behalf of Emily, thank you for coming.'

'Yes, thank you,' I echoed quietly.

'Right, so, we all know why we're here?'

There was murmuring of assent.

'Good. That little girl needs her mother, and we are not going to stop until we find her.'

A cacophony of affirmation.

'We all have social media, today we flood it. We post about her, we tell her story — Freya's story. We post a picture of her and a picture of her father, who has taken her. Someone somewhere has seen something that felt odd, out of place, and dismissed it. Someone somewhere has seen a man struggling with a newborn. There are over 68 million people in this country, someone has to have seen them, and the more we share, the more we beg others to share, the more people will see and know what is happening. We'll use a hashtag,' Michelle said, getting swept up in her own energy. 'For every post, for everything we say, we'll use this.'

She grabbed a green pen and wrote it in big letters on one of the whiteboards that was positioned near the back door. Nine letters that brought a tear to my eye.

#FindFreya

'Facebook is our biggest platform,' she continued. 'I'm assuming everyone here has an account?'

People nodded — everyone, I think.

'We'll create a page, one we can all follow and share. OK?'

Another murmur of affirmation.

'But I want us to hit every social media platform out there where people can find and share. Lucas has to be somewhere. Is anyone proficient with these platforms?'

Two younger people in the room raised their hands. I didn't know their names.

'Great. Tom, Frankie, you two are in charge of that. Can you create profiles, using *Find Freya* as the username?'

'On it.'

'Once this is done, we'll have an email and all of the socials. Until then, let's go old-school. I'll get some pictures printed. Let's hit the streets, start telling Freya's story.'

There were several nods of agreement. People were charged, ready for a fight. And I wondered, if Lucas were here right now, what would they do to him? I knew what I would do.

'And we will find him.'

More nods spread through the room, one person clapped, and Julia shed a tear. She smiled and wiped it away when she saw me looking.

'Any questions?' Michelle asked, and after a beat of silence she continued. 'Good. I know I don't need to say this, but time is important. We need to move.'

As people began to scurry into action, I took a breath, amazed by the woman Michelle was showing herself to be. I knew she cared, I knew she loved me, but I never knew she was capable of this. She flashed me a smile, and I smiled back, before retreating to the living room, needing a moment to collect myself. Looking out of the window, I wondered where my daughter was. I wondered if she was OK. As I did, I was stunned to see media vans pulling up outside.

'Michelle?' I said.

She came running into the room. 'Are you all right?'

'Look.' I pointed to the vans.

She smiled. 'They're right on time.'

83

CHAPTER FOURTEEN

Then — 19 December

Emily didn't know what time it was, but it was dark when she looked out of her bedroom window and watched the new uncle leave the house. He didn't look back when he slammed the front door. He simply stuffed his hands into his pockets and walked out into the pre-dawn light as if he wanted nothing more than to disappear. Emily watched him walk, wondering if he would ever visit again. Sometimes her uncles did, sometimes she never saw them again, and nor did Mother, as far as she could tell. If Mother needed to have an uncle visit in the future, she hoped this one would come back. He didn't look at her in that way she didn't fully understand but knew was bad. This latest one barely looked at her at all. Again, invisible was best.

After putting up the decorations in their room, Emily struggled to sleep. Excitement and worry coursed through her blood, robbing her of rest. Instead, she returned to her sister's side and stroked her hair as she slept.

Duty.

If she stayed awake, there would be no nightmares. If she stayed awake, she could make sure Freya kept warm and safe. She watched her sister smile in her dreams. She wondered what she was thinking of that brought her such joy. Part of her was jealous of it. Whatever she was dreaming of, it was a moment of fantasy that Emily wouldn't ever see. Yes, she was jealous, resentful too, but another part of her hoped that, whatever it was that made her sister smile, it lingered long after Freya woke, and kept her smiling throughout what Emily knew was going to be a tough day. She hoped it lingered and kept her sister quiet, for whenever an uncle visited it usually went one of two ways. Mother either slept all day, or she was more of a monster than usual. A sad rage would consume her. Last time, Mother said she wished both she and Freya had never been born, that they'd ruined her life. But Emily knew that it wasn't true. Life before Freya was better, softer, and she saw Mother knew it too. She also called Emily her imprisoner. Emily didn't understand how Mother could think that way. Emily had never locked her in the house, had never dragged her to the shed and dumped her on the cold, hard floor for sometimes days without food, forcing her to drink rainwater that came through the roof of the shed. Emily had never stopped Mother leaving, stopped her from eating. Only Mother herself did these things. And yet, when she told Emily she and Freya had imprisoned her, Emily could see she completely believed it.

After the uncle had disappeared into the early morning mist, Emily waited to hear something from Mother. The house was quiet, eerie, and after a few minutes Emily couldn't bear to wait any longer. Ensuring Freya didn't hear her and wake, she quietly opened the bedroom door and stepped into the hallway. Mother's door was shut, and Emily feared that at any moment Mother would hear her, fling the door open and release the monster. But as she drew closer, all she could hear was her mother's gentle sobs. Drawing closer still, Emily placed her ear on the door and listened. She was prepared for Sleeping Mother, even Monster Mother. This, however, was the one who rarely came out.

Teary Mother.

Emily stayed at the door, listening to Mother crying, tears rolling down her own cheeks, and, in that moment, she wanted a hug from her more than ever.

Then it went quiet, and, panicking, Emily tried to move back to her room. As she slowly stepped away, the door was flung open, making her jump. Mother stood holding the door handle, staring at her.

'Sorry, Mother,' Emily said. And she was, she was sorry Mother was sad, but more, she was sorry she'd been caught.

'It doesn't matter, Bebe, nothing matters,' Mother replied, using a nickname Emily hadn't heard in a long time. Emily wanted more than ever to give her mother a hug, like she once could so readily, but she didn't dare, and after a moment Mother smiled sadly and closed the bedroom door once more.

Mother had smiled. The Mother who Emily once knew was still there, somewhere, if she could only find a way to pull her out. If only she could work out what she needed to do to get her mummy back.

CHAPTER FIFTEEN

Michelle's actions ignited something in me, and as the morning wore on I found myself gaining strength, determination. Adam had joined the search too, taking a day off work to help. His presence made me feel safer. Jack would join when he could. But with Michelle so charged and having Adam there to be so caring, I felt brave enough to speak to the local papers, telling them my story, my focus solely on finding my daughter. They asked questions, thankfully nothing to do with my past, scribbled notes and offered their sympathy. And after, I made a point of speaking to everyone who was in my home, helping raise the profile, telling them mine and Lucas's story. Julia had brought several people from the church, and the young couple who were taking charge of social media were Michelle's neighbours. There was even an elderly man who'd seen the posts, learned what was happening and offered to help. It gave me hope. And the whiteboards that were erected in my conservatory were getting filled with everything we knew about that day of the baby shower that I could remember, and the ten days after that I couldn't. I scanned them, learning things I didn't know from when I was in the coma, but there was a statement on the board nearest the back door that caught my eye. It was in red pen, in capital letters.

IN MOST CASES OF A CHILD GOING MISSING, THOSE INVOLVED ARE THOSE CLOSEST.

I didn't know why someone had bothered to write it, as it was obviously Lucas who had done this. Beside it was a mind map, and in the middle it asked the question: *Why would Lucas take her?* Branching out were several theories — his desire to raise her differently to me, panic about being alone with a newborn, getting stuck somewhere. But I knew the reason: Lucas knew of my past, knew who I was. He knew I'd killed a little girl who was also called Freya, back when I was young. Not being able to say as much made me feel sick, and Michelle saw.

'Hey? You OK?'

'I just need some air.'

As soon as I stepped outside, the few reporters who were there sprang to life, wanting to talk and get my picture, so I walked around to the side of my home, away from their watching eyes. I could hear them still, calling for me to come back around, but I ignored them. Standing in the shade of my home, sandwiched between mine and the neighbours in a narrow passage, I leaned on the cool brick wall and took some measured breaths. Everything was moving so fast, and I was struggling, both physically and mentally, to keep up. I felt my chest tighten, like a hand inside me was pulling on my diaphragm, and before I could stop myself I began to cry. Everything I expected the world to be, everything I had daydreamed about, didn't exist. My baby was nearly two weeks old. She would be cooing, crying, feeding, sleeping. And she should be with me doing all these things. She should be in my home, sleeping in her Moses basket, crying for me, my milk, my smell, my calming voice. Not his, not fucking his.

'Em?' a voice said, startling me, and even though I knew they had seen me crying I tried to hide it. 'Are you OK?'

I looked up to see Adam standing in the passage, having approached from the back of the house, concern in his eyes.

'Yeah, well, no, but I'm trying to keep it together.'

'I can't imagine how hard this all must be for you,' he said, taking a step closer, joining me in the shade. I didn't reply. There was nothing to add.

'You're doing better than I possibly could.'

'I don't feel like I am.'

'Trust me, we all see it, you're being so brave, so strong.'

'Thanks,' I said, offering a half-smile.

'We will find her, you know that, right?' he said, and I nodded. I didn't want to doubt him, I wanted to know she was coming to me, like I thought on that first day when I woke up. But it was there, my doubt, a distorted little golem, quietly waiting. For what, I didn't know. But it was the same one that had always been with me. The one that was there, present and taunting when I was a child.

'Em?' Adam said when I didn't answer his question. 'You know that, right? That we will find her?'

'Yeah.'

'Good. You've just got to keep your chin up.'

'Easier said than done.'

'I know. You sure you're all right?'

I nodded and smiled weakly towards him, and it seemed to be enough.

'Want me to stay with you?'

'Can I have a minute?'

'Of course, I'll leave you to it,' he said, smiling and taking my hand in his, giving it a squeeze before stepping back around towards my garden and the hubbub of the conservatory.

I stayed in the shade and listened to the hustle and bustle from inside, until, feeling calmer, I moved to walk back inside. I could have followed Adam into the back, but I didn't want to walk through the room where Michelle was doing whatever she was doing. I didn't want to get in the way, so I opted to go through the front door again. I knew I needed to continue to talk, to share, to help. To step back into the noise and notes and conversations and do my part. Standing upright, I took a step into the sun, its warmth making my skin goosebump, and as I turned to walk back towards the door I saw a man standing among the press. He was staring back towards me, unmoving, and I squinted in the sun to try to make out his face. I couldn't make out his features — he was about a hundred feet from me, and I was blinded by the sun — but he was about the right height, the right build.

'Lucas?' I called out, and the man turned away.

'Lucas!' I shouted, and, even though I couldn't make out his face, it had to be him, or else why would he walk away from me? I started to half walk, half run towards him. 'Lucas, wait!' I called as he began to walk quicker. I upped my pace, racing through the front gate, and ended up surrounded by journalists trying to get their scoop.

'Get out of my way, please. Please. Lucas!' I shouted, and one of the journalists understood what was happening. I'd seen the man who'd taken my baby. He helped me through, and once I was clear I tried to break into a run, but my stomach muscles were still too weak, and each step pulled on my stitches. 'Wait, please, Lucas, please. Where is she? Where is my daughter?'

'I'll get help,' the journalist said, running back towards the house.

'Lucas!' I called out as he broke into a full run. I tried to match him, but it was hopeless. With each stagger, he bounded further away. I wanted to push on, to run like I once could, but I was unable to, I was failing, I was failing again.

'Please, Lucas, just give her back to me!' I shouted.

I reached the end of the street and turned onto the main road, where I followed for about two hundred yards before I had to stop. Propping myself up against a garden wall, I watched him moving further away, but not entirely disappearing. I wanted to pursue him, but I couldn't. Pain rippled through me, and my legs felt like they would give out at any moment. And I fucking hated myself for being so weak. So feeble. As I began to cry, I heard movement from behind me, and saw Adam running towards me with the journalist.

'Em? What is it?'

'It's Lucas, I think I can see Lucas.'

'What? Where?'

I pointed in front of me, and the man saw me do so. Adam ran off, and I watched as they caught up and grabbed him. Within seconds, Adam raised his hands, offered an apology and stepped away. It wasn't him. Adam began to walk towards me, panting from the effort of running. But I didn't look at him, I looked through him to the man beyond. He turned back to me, and with the sun now behind me, in front of him, lighting his face, I could see his features clearly. It wasn't Lucas. He was older, weather-beaten, and he looked at me like I was out of my mind. I glanced at the journalist who had helped me, and his expression said exactly the same thing. And I knew that couldn't be good.

CHAPTER SIXTEEN

Adam led me home, through the fired-up journalists and into my living room.

'I feel so stupid,' I said.

'No, don't. You're under a lot of pressure, and he looked like Lucas. You were right to go after him.'

'You think?'

'I know. Let me get you a tea. Are you OK for a minute?'

'To be honest, I need a minute.'

'I thought as much.'

'Adam?' I called as he opened the door to go towards the kitchen.

'Yes,' he said.

'Have you ever made a mistake?' I asked, the words blurting out before I had a chance to pull them in.

'A mistake?'

'Something you regret.'

'Oh, Emily, I have literally hundreds of things I regret.'

'Have you ever hurt someone?'

'Ashamedly, yes. Plenty.'

'Did you ever feel like you should be punished for it?'

'No. Mistakes are what make us human. We can only try to get it right, but trying doesn't mean we will. As long as we try and learn from them, and don't repeat them, then there's nothing to punish. Someone once said to me, if you don't have regrets or make mistakes, then you aren't growing and learning to be a better person.'

'I like that,' I said.

'It helped me when I was in a bad place. Em, why are you asking?'

'I did something a long time ago, when I was a kid, and I'm wondering if I'm being punished for it now.'

'Who would do that?'

'I don't know, God?'

Adam walked towards me and sat opposite, taking me by my hands.

'Whatever you did, whatever mistake you made, this has nothing to do with it. You are not being punished by some higher being, if there is such a thing. Whatever happened when you were young, you're not the same person. You're a good woman.'

'You sound so sure.'

'I am, we all make mistakes, we all regret things, it's just how it is. How old were you when you made this mistake?'

'Eleven.'

'Em, lovely, you were a kid, you can't be held accountable.'

'You don't know that.'

'I do, children can't be held to account for things going wrong in life. If you did something wrong, I would put paper money on it being an adult's fault. Not yours.'

'Thanks, Adam.'

Adam left me to my thoughts. My mind drifted back to a memory of me and Lucas in the living room. It was early in our relationship, if you could call it that. We were on the sofa, under a blanket, watching a movie. I was staring at the screen, and became aware that he was looking at me.

I turned and looked back at him.

'What?'

'Nothing,' he said.

'Lucas, what?' I asked again, smiling towards him.

93

'It's just, you're so fucking beautiful.'

He kissed me, long and hard, and in that moment I wanted him, needed him inside me. We'd not had sex yet, I was wary of jumping in too fast, but in that moment I didn't care. We made love on the sofa, there and then, and after, we giggled like teenagers, relief and release working in equal measure.

Another memory came back to me of a time, a few months later. The day I found out I was pregnant. I had prepared a little box, the positive test, and a card in it for him, to soften the blow. I remember trying to push down the sick feeling I had in my stomach, not knowing how he would take the news, not even knowing how I truly felt about it.

I had planned a dinner, his favourite takeaway. We would eat, and then, relaxed and full, I would share the news. I had ordered the takeaway and, as it was on its way, he texted me to say that he was going out to see a film with a friend. He didn't ask if I wanted to come, he didn't ask if it was OK. He had just decided.

I remembered eating alone, wondering if this was the future for me.

I stopped myself remembering any more. It hurt too much.

Shaking off the memory, I looked out of the window into the street. There was a van parking up. On the side of it, three letters. BBC.

No sooner had the van come to a stop than a woman jumped out. A camera rig quickly went onto her shoulder and she began to advance, the camera pointing into my living room. I didn't want to be on TV, I didn't want anyone to see who I was. So before she could get too close, I ran into the kitchen.

'Michelle!' I shouted. 'Michelle?'

'What's wrong?' she asked, looking concerned.

'The BBC are outside.'

'The BBC?' she said, pulling out her phone. She went to the BBC app, and scrolled the headlines. She gasped and showed me the screen. I read the headline:

SEARCH FOR MAN WHO KIDNAPPED DAUGHTER WHILE MOTHER WAS IN COMA

'I knew the media would get involved, but this is the BBC, this is national,' she said. The volunteers all clapped and cheered.

'Oh shit.'

'This is good, Em. More people knowing and looking for her.'

'What do we do?'

'You talk to them.'

'What? No, Michelle, I can't,' I said. Speaking with the local paper was hard enough, and that journalist who saw my outburst at a total stranger was still there. This was the national news. If it got airtime, someone somewhere would know who I really was.

'You can.'

'What do I say?'

'Tell them who you are.'

'Who I am?' I asked, terrified. No one could know who I was.

'Yes, you're a mother to a beautiful little girl who you haven't met. Because Lucas took her from you.'

I nodded. I didn't want to talk to the BBC, but then, if it got airtime, it would surely help me find my daughter. It was a risk, as my secrets might spill, but it was a risk I needed to take.

CHAPTER SEVENTEEN

Then — 20 December

Emily knew it would be a huge risk, but she also knew she had no choice. She and her sister needed to eat. She wanted to not think about food, but instead focus on the small smile Mother had shown her. She wanted to wrap herself in it, hold onto it for as long as she could, but every time she tried her thoughts came back to the more urgent thing: how would she and Freya find their next meal? When she found a solution, it both excited and scared her in equal measure. Excited, because if she pulled it off she and Freya would eat well for days, maybe all the way into the new school term. But she was scared too; if she was caught, she didn't know what Mother would do to her. When Mother's sobs eventually turning into gentle snores, Emily and Freya made their way from their bedroom into the living room. There would be no TV like the day before but, as long as Freya stayed quiet, they would have a few hours of space. With her sister playing with her doll on the sofa, wrapped in her blanket, as the weather outside had worsened as the day wore on, an icy winter wind straight off the sea battering their home, Emily set out to see if she could answer at least one of the questions on her mind. In the kitchen, she once again searched for food, hoping that she had somehow missed a larder that never existed. The cupboards remained empty. She tried the fridge, knowing it would be just as bare. Sure enough, after her eyes adjusted to the bright light, she saw there was a tub of margarine, some onions with shoots growing from them, and a translucent container of something tinged with black that she dared not open.

'Anything?' Freya whispered from the doorway. She had sneaked in to watch Emily without her realising.

'Nothing.'

Emily watched her sister's shoulders sag, and her heart ached for it. That morning, Freya had woken to see the decorated room and was filled with joy and hope when Emily told her Santa had sent a helper. Now, that hope was gone. It had lasted only an hour. She knew she needed to try to do more somehow. Emily needed Freya to be good, to show Mother it could work with the three of them.

'Em, I'm hungry.'

'I know.'

'What are we going to do? Should I wake Mother?'

'No, don't,' Emily said, looking out of the window to see the snow falling, pushed horizontally by the driving wind. It was cold out there, too cold.

'But I'm hungry.'

'I know, but we can't wake Mother, OK?' Emily snapped. Freya didn't know about Mother crying in the night, about that smile, the tiny, fragile moment of something from the life before. Emily knew Mother would have to come out of her room on her terms, and hopefully with that small smile still in the corner of her mouth. If she was interrupted, it wouldn't be good for either of them. The idea of a day in the shed, in the cold, wasn't welcoming. Better to be hungry than that. Better to be anything than that.

There was one more cupboard to try, Mother's top cupboard, but the lock was snapped shut and the key was around Mother's neck. Waking Mother was bad enough, waking

Mother by removing her food key would no doubt have ramifications beyond Emily's wildest nightmares. Emily climbed onto the sideboard and tried it anyway out of desperation. The lock held firm. She knew she could probably rip it off the hinges, but what then? Mother would wake, she would be put in the shed, she would remain unloved and both she and Freya would stay hungry.

'Em, I feel sick,' Freya said. Emily turned to her little sister. She looked so small.

'We don't have any food, Fry. Drink some water, it will help.'

'No, I want something to eat,' she said, her voice getting louder, too loud.

'Fry. Stop.'

'No, why can't we have food, why can't we—'

Emily placed her hand over her sister's mouth, trapping in her voice, and she pressed hard, too hard.

'Stop, you're going to get us into trouble!'

Freya mumbled something and, feeling her fight leave her, Emily released her hand. There was a small patch of blood on her palm where she had pressed so hard, Freya's lip bled.

'Get dressed, we're going out,' Emily said. It was now or never.

'Where?' Freya asked.

'Don't ask questions, Fry, just get dressed. Wrap up as warm as you can.'

'But—'

'Do you want food or not?'

'Yes.'

'Then go, and do it quietly. Don't wake Mother.'

'We can't go out without telling her.'

'Are you hungry or not?' Emily snapped.

'Yes, but—'

'Well, come on, then. Go, get dressed.'

'Em, please don't shout at me,' Freya said. Her eyes began to brim and, seeing that, Emily took a breath.

'I'm sorry, Fry. I'm hungry too. Now, let's get sorted, so we can both eat.'

'OK.'

'But remember, don't wake Mother.'

'I won't,' Freya said.

Freya did as she was told and made her way upstairs to get changed. As she did, Emily gathered their coats and looked for hats and scarves. She only found one of each, and, even though her coat didn't zip up anymore, she put both the hat and the scarf on her sister when she came downstairs.

'Right, wellies on,' Emily said once she was happy Freya wouldn't freeze to death.

Freya headed for the front door, but Emily stopped her. 'No, we have to go through the back, just in case.'

She took Freya by the hand and they went to the back door, gingerly opened it and stepped out into the bitter wintry morning. Closing the door behind her, Emily led Freya around the side of the house, to a hole in the wire fence of their garden. Pulling the fence to one side, Freya slipped through and Emily followed behind. As they stepped into the front garden, Emily held her sister back.

'We're going to check the bins.'

'The bins?'

'For food.'

Freya nodded, and began to move towards the black bins by their own front door.

'Fry. Not ours, there won't be anything in it. We need to look in someone else's.'

'Someone else's bin?'

'People throw food away all the time. Keep up, OK?'

'Where are we going? Whose bin are we going to look in?' Freya asked, her voice small against the wind.

'Just keep up.'

The girls stepped out into the driving wind. Snow quickly stuck to the front of their coats and, despite trying to keep hers closed, Emily's billowed in the wind, and the effort to hold it closed meant her exposed hands burned as the chill set in. Beside her, Freya had her head low, battling forward, and Emily stepped in front of her, to act as a shield. She felt her little sister hold the back of her jacket, and, even though she was cold, Emily couldn't help but feel warmer for it. But again, mostly out of duty.

Five minutes after they set out, with the cold taking its firm grip on them both, they arrived at a small shop. Ducking down the side, sheltered in the building's shadow beside a large commercial bin, Emily told Freya to keep watch.

'Shops sometimes throw food away, maybe there's something in here,' she said, heaving the lid open and climbing inside.

'Emily? *Emily?*'

Emily lifted her head out of the bin, and dropped a loaf of bread on the floor beside her sister's feet. 'Check it's OK to eat,' she said, before disappearing again.

Freya opened the packet and pulled out a slice. Thick green mould covered the entire surface.

'No, it's gone bad.'

Emily lifted her head out of the bin. 'Yeah, all of it in here has gone bad.'

'What do we do?' Freya said.

'We keep looking,' Emily said, climbing out of the bin. 'Fry, stay here, stay small. We're going to eat today.'

'Where are you going?'

'Just stay here. Get behind the bin. Don't speak to anyone.'

'Where are you going, Emily?'

'Just . . .' Emily said, almost snapping. 'Stop worrying, OK? I'm going to get us some food from the shop.'

'How? You don't have any money,' Freya said. Emily heard her, but she didn't respond. Instead, she turned back into the force of the wind, before stepping inside the shop. The shopkeeper, an elderly man, smiled her way and looked behind, waiting to see the small child's parent. When he realised she was alone, he frowned, before turning his attention to a customer who approached with a loaf of bread and a pint of milk.

Emily looked around. There was the man at the till, another looking at the magazines. She'd hoped for more people to be inside, but it would have to do. She refused to go home empty-handed, or empty-bellied. Grabbing a basket, she wandered up the narrow aisles that dwarfed her, picking things up and putting them back down again. Looking up at a curved mirror, high in the corner of the shop, she could see that, as the shopkeeper served the man, he looked up to see where she was. Her heart raced. She'd never stolen before, and she almost lost her nerve. She would have too, if it wasn't for the six-year-old outside, shivering and hungry, who she needed to feed when no one else would.

As Emily passed the chocolate, a memory flashed into her mind of a winter before Freya was born. Her and Mother sitting on the sofa, watching *Tom and Jerry*. Emily had chocolate on her face, and Mother wiped it tenderly. The memory wanted to linger on, but she knew better than to let it. Wishing she could put some of the chocolate in the basket, she turned away; chocolate wouldn't alleviate the hunger they both felt. She picked up some bread, some fruit and crisps. Then, turning around the corner, the furthest away from the till, she picked up two tins of beans. She knew there was a can opener somewhere in the kitchen, and they could eat them cold, so Mother wouldn't know. She could also rinse the cans out and find some string and make some walkie-talkies for Freya for Christmas, and Mother would play. Mother would be happy.

With her basket as full as she could carry, Emily looked back down the first aisle she had walked along. Above her the curved mirror sat, and she knew where she was she couldn't be seen. In front of her was the exit. She had one shot. Emily would wait until a customer left, and then, as the door was open, she would make a run for it.

CHAPTER EIGHTEEN

I stood on my doorstep and spoke to the BBC, telling them the same things I had told the local paper, and, despite the fear I felt about my secrets finding their way out into the world, I didn't care. My daughter was bigger than my problems, she was bigger than my past. As I spoke with them, Jack arrived and waited in the crowd for me to finish. I was glad he was there. I could direct my questions towards him. I knew he was on my side.

The journalist who'd helped when I thought I'd seen Lucas asked if I was struggling to cope. I knew what he was doing, he was trying to spin a story about me being unhinged. Maybe I was, maybe I was losing my mind, but that wasn't for him to say. So I ignored him, and focused on talking about my daughter, who I hadn't yet met.

When I'd finished, I stepped back into the house with Jack beside me, and the energy of the conservatory felt different somehow. Charged, ready for a fight.

'Has something happened?' I asked quietly, and Adam approached.

'So, remember the police officer said they saw Lucas's car heading up the A19, and we thought he was maybe going to the port in Newcastle.'

'Yes,' I said, bracing myself to be told that they had discovered he had left the UK. If he had, I knew I'd never see my daughter.

'Well, we might have found a link between Lucas and Middlesbrough, which is the city you hit before reaching Newcastle.'

'You did? What did you find?'

'A man has messaged, someone called Matthew Baker. Does that name ring a bell?'

I wracked my brain, but the name didn't stick. I shook my head.

'He told us he knew Lucas from way back, I thought it might have been before you two met. So, anyway, Matthew and Lucas worked together for a freight company, packing lorries at a warehouse.'

'I remember him saying he did that for a while.'

'The company was based near Middlesbrough. Matthew lives there.'

'Does he know where Lucas is?' I asked, my stomach lurching. 'Does that mean Lucas hasn't left the UK?'

'We don't know, but he said Lucas had more friends in the area, an ex-girlfriend too. He gave us a few names, we're trying to find them on Facebook. If he was heading that way, maybe someone knows where he is. Maybe he's gone to meet someone from his past?'

I was hopeful for something more, something that would make me feel I was closer to my baby, but if he had gone to Middlesbrough he was still in the country. I lowered my head, and a fresh tear fell. Adam took my hand.

'Hey, I know it's really tough, but we will find her.'

'OK,' I said quietly. I could feel people watching me, pity in their eyes. The whole room reeked of it. I forced myself to look up. My head felt almost too heavy for the task, but somehow I did it. I then heaved myself onto my feet. 'OK,' I said again, lifting my head high. 'What now?'

Adam guided me to a whiteboard where a list of things to do, proactive things, had been written in capital letters.

One idea was to make a new video to post on social media, there were a few radio stations lined up for a live telephone call, and, as the day wore on, those who had volunteered drifted, vowing to come back and help after some rest and a shower. I thanked them for giving up their time, and, as they left, I kept going. I told our story maybe a dozen times to a dozen different people, completely exhausting myself.

'Emily, you need to stop. Go to bed, it's been a long day,' Jack said quietly.

'No, I want to keep going for as long as I can.'

'You do need some rest.'

'So do you, and Adam, and Michelle.'

He nodded. 'We do, but you need it more.'

With the evening fully set in and the kitchen now quieter, I went to make a drink and took it all in. Every surface and table was covered with notes, every whiteboard full of information. In big capital letters the hashtag *FindFreya* screamed at me. I almost screamed back that I didn't know how.

There were maps blu-tacked to walls, and dozens of empty coffee cups strewn around the room. The effort, for me, for Freya, was almost too much.

Michelle and I began to tidy the cups. She tried to insist I sit down, but I needed to do something, so I ignored her and washed up every single one. And knowing I wouldn't budge, Adam suggested he nipped and got a takeaway, which everyone agreed was a good idea. But I didn't think I could eat. As I began to dry the crockery from the day, I heard a knock on the door. I didn't think much of it, so continued with my task. Then I heard a voice. One I wasn't expecting. Hearing it made me almost drop the cup I was drying.

'Hey, Em. Detective Myers is here. He wants to talk to you — in private?'

'OK?'

Leaving the kitchen, I went into the living room and saw Myers, who was sitting down. He didn't smile, and I closed the door behind me nervously.

'Emily, how are you doing?'

'I'm OK,' I said plainly.

He nodded. 'Wanna sit?'

I did as he asked and waited for him to talk. Had something happened to my baby? Did he have bad news? I tried to prepare myself as best I could for the blow, but when he spoke I was caught off guard.

'It seems you haven't been completely truthful with us. So, you and I are going to have a chat, and you're going to tell me everything,' he said.

'I don't know what you mean,' I said, my voice sounding tight.

'Oh, I think you do, Ms Claywater, or should I say, Ms Jones?'

CHAPTER NINETEEN

I was stunned. I had expected someone to find out — with my life held under a microscope to find my daughter, it was a matter of when, not if. But even knowing it, I wasn't sure what to say.

'Emily?'

'Yes, sorry, yes, I've not heard that name in a long time,' I said quietly.

'Why didn't you tell us?'

'That I changed my name?'

'That you are Emily Jones, *the* Emily Jones from the news that Christmas in 2008,' he said.

'I didn't think it would matter.'

'I don't follow.'

'It was a lifetime ago, I was a different person, this has nothing to do with—'

'Who knows that you're her?' he said, interrupting. 'Your friend, Michelle?'

'No.'

'Jack, Adam?'

'No one,' I replied. 'No one knows.'

'Not Lucas?'

'No one,' I said again, looking him in the eye. 'I think,' I added.

'You should have told us. This opens up a whole new avenue of investigation.'

'Now you know,' I said, quietly hoping that what he did know wasn't the whole truth. My mother had taken the blame for my sister's death. The world assumed, because of who she was, the type of woman she was, that it was her fault, despite how much she denied it.

'Emily, I need you to be honest. Do you think what happened has anything to do with that Christmas?'

'No, I mean, how can it? The only person who is maybe alive from that night is my mother, and I don't know where she is. Do you?'

'No,' he said.

'But you know something about her?'

'After she did her time for your sister's . . .'

I looked away.

'Sorry,' he continued. 'After she finished her sentence, she spent several years in and out of psychiatric hospitals.'

'Hospitals?'

'Your mum was a very poorly woman.'

'I see,' I said. For my entire adult life, I had reasoned Mother must have been unwell, possibly bipolar, possibly suffering postnatal depression, bordering on psychosis. She must have been very unwell to do what she did. And I didn't know how I felt, learning the truth. 'And now?' I asked quietly.

'We don't know. She's not been seen in years. No bank account access, no name on the electoral register. Nothing.'

'So she's dead.'

'That's what we think.'

'Can people die and it not be known these days?'

'You'd be surprised. Lots of people go missing every year, over a hundred thousand, and those are only the people who have someone around to know they're missing. If your mother was alone and something happened, no one would know.'

'I see.'

'How does that make you feel?'

107

'Nothing,' I said, but really, I did feel something, a loss perhaps, relief too. But both were small. I expected more.

'If she's dead, there's no one else connected with Emily Jones left alive. Not her, or my grandparents, or my sister.'

'Even still, this is something we should have heard from you.'

'Why? What has it got to do with my daughter? What difference does it make?'

He ignored my question and continued, 'Have you kept anything that links you to your past?'

'No,' I lied, thinking of the knife in my wardrobe, directly above our heads. 'Nothing. As you know, I was taken into emergency foster care, and then brought down here to be placed with my grandparents. I didn't have anything other than the clothes on my back, which were binned as soon as I arrived in London.'

'We have a theory, now we know the truth, that maybe Lucas found out about your history. Who you are, what happened to you that Christmas, is a big secret to keep. Maybe he was spooked.'

'Spooked enough to attack me?'

'Maybe. Again, we're trying to explore all options.'

I nodded.

'And where you grew up,' he continued, 'is there any link at all?'

'No, nothing. I haven't been back, haven't thought about that place since,' I added, which we both knew couldn't possibly be true.

'We might have questions about that Christmas.'

'What? Why?'

'Because you're Emily Jones, from Christmas 2008. You're the girl the whole country was talking about. And now your daughter, who is also called Freya, is missing.'

'You don't think . . .' I started to say, terrified that my daughter shared the same fate as my sister.

'No, no, nothing of the sort. From what we understand about Lucas, and what we know now, we think he feels he's protecting her.'

'But why?'

'We don't know. Why do you think he would want to protect her from you?'

'I don't know,' I lied again.

Myers nodded, and stood up. 'OK, as soon as we get anything, you'll know.'

'Detective Myers, can you keep quiet about who I was?'

He nodded. 'I don't see any reason why it should be made public.'

'Thank you.'

'But you've been on the BBC news, I can't promise the world won't soon know. Stay near your phone; we might have more questions.'

'Of course,' I said, looking away from him.

'Emily, is there anything else I should know?'

'No, not that I can think of.'

'All right,' he said, holding my eye.

Myers said his goodbyes and left. I slumped back into the kitchen and nodded to my friends, who all looked at me with concern.

'Nothing. No news,' I said quietly.

I prayed that he would find my daughter before he could dig any further into my past. Either way, I knew I needed to tell Michelle. If she found out who I was, and it wasn't from me, it would make me look guilty — the secret to my childhood I'd hoped to keep buried along with my sister, my grandparents and now my mother. But I had to exhume it, at least some of it.

'Michelle, there's something I want to tell you. Something about who I am, or who I once was,' I said. And I meant it, I would tell her who I once was. But I wouldn't tell her everything. What happened that Christmas was to die with me, just like it died with everyone else. My worst mistakes, my worst crimes, would go with me to the grave.

CHAPTER TWENTY

Then — 20 December

Emily didn't have to wait long to make her escape, as the man with the bread and milk said his farewells and walked towards the door. He opened it, stepped out into the snow, swearing as he did. As he walked away, the door began to close. Running as fast as she could, Emily grabbed a handful of chocolate bars and headed for the door, and as she pushed past into the forming blizzard she heard the shopkeeper shouting behind her.

'Oi, stop!'

Emily rounded the corner, panic in her eyes, and as she drew closer to Freya she started shouting instructions.

'Take this, run home, get in the house and hide it upstairs.'

'What?'

'Just do it.'

Emily gave Freya most of the food, keeping the chocolate bars, hoping the shopkeeper assumed that was all she had taken. Freya cradled the rest in her small arms and ran, as she had been told. As she disappeared into the snow, the shopkeeper rounded the corner, panting and angry. He hadn't seen Freya, and Emily thanked God for it.

'You little shit!'

'I'm sorry,' Emily said. She meant it too. She hated that she had to rob.

The shopkeeper grabbed her by the arm and held it so firmly it hurt.

'Where do you live?'

'Lothian Road.'

'What number?'

'Fourteen.'

'Ahhh, you're Carol's kid. That explains a lot. Right, I'm taking you to your mother.'

'No, please, I'm sorry. Please, I didn't mean to. She's sleeping. I'm sorry.'

'It's too late for sorry.'

Dragging her back into the shop, the shopkeeper snatched the chocolate bars from her hands, put on his coat and shouted an instruction to his wife. 'Janet, look after the shop. I've got a thief to deal with.'

He grabbed her by the hood of her coat and frogmarched her back through the snow towards her home. Emily thought she could see Freya ahead, and, knowing they would catch her up, she pretended to slip on the ice and fall.

'Shit,' the shopkeeper said, trying to help her to her feet.

Emily took her time getting up from the frozen ground, and when she looked again Freya was nowhere to be seen.

Arriving at the front door, the shopkeeper banged on it. It took several attempts to rouse Mother.

'Hold on,' her voice bellowed from inside, and, as Emily waited with the shopkeeper, her heart galloped once more. Eventually, the door swung open. 'What?'

'Is this your child?' the shopkeeper said, and Mother's eyes went from him down to Emily.

'Aye?'

'I just caught her trying to steal from my shop.'

'Oh, did you now?' Mother said, again looking from the shopkeeper to Emily.

'You need to punish her, teach her right from wrong,' he said, pushing Emily towards her mother.

'Oh, don't worry about that, she'll be punished all right.'

'Good. If she does it again, I'll call the police.' At that, the shopkeeper turned on his heel and marched away.

Mother pulled Emily into the house and closed the door. For a while, she stood staring at her daughter.

'I'm sorry, Mother.'

'You will be,' Mother said, walking away. That smile, that moment between them was gone, and, even though she didn't want to, she found herself wondering what today would have been like between her and her mother if Freya had never come.

Mother didn't look back at Emily as she walked into the kitchen. She was choosing not to punish her there and then. But she would soon enough, and it would be right when she least expected it.

Emily quietly walked upstairs and into her room. Freya was lying in her bed, crying, and Emily turned on the Christmas lights, bathing them both in red and green.

'But you said we can't have them on in the day,' Freya said, looking up, her little tears catching in the lights, making them glisten like magic itself.

'We can't, not often, but right now it's OK.' Emily closed the door and sat on the edge of her sister's bed, and Freya began to cry once more. 'What's wrong?'

'Are you in trouble?'

'It'll be OK,' Emily said, not for a second believing it.

'Mother won't like that we stole.'

'We didn't steal, *I* stole. You didn't do anything wrong.'

'I ran away with the food.'

'Because I told you to. Freya, you were only doing as I asked.'

'But Mother—'

'Will never know. Now, where is it?'

Freya lifted her covers, and Emily saw that in the space around her curled-up body was the food. She was hugging it as if it was a teddy bear. Keeping it warm, keeping it safe.

'Well done, Fry. Hide it again.'

'Emily, do you still love me?'

Emily hesitated. 'Just make sure you hide it all.'

Freya did as she was told, and Emily got up and went to the bedroom door. She opened it and looked out into the hallway, only to find Mother standing at the bottom of the stairs, looking up.

'Mother,' Emily said, hoping to hide her alarm at seeing her there. She closed the bedroom door fully, so Mother wasn't tempted to come into their room.

'I'm going out for a while. If you so much as leave your bedroom, I swear to God . . .'

'I won't, I promise. Freya won't either.'

Mother didn't reply. She simply stood there, staring up at her, and Emily couldn't help but wonder if she was dreaming up her punishment. After a few seconds, she turned and grabbed her coat from the coatrack, then left the house without saying goodbye. Emily sighed with relief, but it didn't last long because, although Mother was going out now, she would be back, and Emily would be punished.

She was on borrowed time.

Going back into the bedroom, she ran to the window and watched as Mother tried to light a cigarette. The flash of her lighter momentarily illuminated her hard features, the spark of it cutting through the falling snow. Eventually, her cigarette was lit, and she disappeared into the static.

Turning to Freya, who looked concerned, Emily sighed and then painted on a smile. 'Right, shall we get set up for dinner?'

'Where's Mother?'

'Out.'

'What if she comes back?'

'She won't.'

'But—'

'Fry, it's going to be OK.'

Despite Emily trying to make Freya feel safe, her duty telling her to, she could see she was failing. So, she came up with an idea.

'Hello, miss, what is your name?' she asked in her poshest Edinburgh accent.

'You know my name,' Freya said.

'I am Ms McConnel, and I will be your host this evening. Have you dined with us before?'

'Dined? Emily, what are you talking about?'

'Please, wait one moment, and I will show you to your table at the poshest restaurant in the whole of Scotland.'

Freya giggled, getting where this was going, and, excited to play, she started to get out of bed.

'No, miss. Please, allow me to set up first.'

Freya giggled again as Emily went over to the chest of drawers and pulled out the bottom one. She emptied the contents onto the floor and turned it over. Then, grabbing the sheet from her bed, she laid it over the upturned drawer, making a thick and uneven tablecloth.

Jumping up, she offered Freya her hand. 'Now, miss, I didn't catch your name?'

'I am Miss Freya Jones.'

'Ahhh, Miss Jones, your table is ready.'

Emily took Freya to the table on the floor and sat her down. She then turned to the pile of stolen food and began to gather it. She wanted to get a plate, but if she did, and Mother came back, she would know. So, looking around, Emily found the only thing that would pass. In one corner, in the small gap between the wardrobe and the wall, was some Lego. She grabbed the largest base plate and, using some of the bricks, she built an edge all the way around. Then, grabbing some of the bread and crisps and an apple, she arranged the food on the board and presented it to her sister.

'Ms Jones, enjoy your meal.'

Despite the meal being not really a meal at all, Freya clapped and beamed a smile to her big sister as the makeshift dinner plate was set before her. Emily then grabbed another board for herself, and plated up a similar amount of food. She sat opposite her sister, and put her plate down on their new dining table.

The girls ate in silence, enjoying the feeling as chunks of bread filled their aching stomachs, and as Emily bit into her apple she moaned in appreciation at the sweetness, the crispness. She tried to remember the last time she had an apple, or any fruit, and recalled that the last apple she had was in the summer, when cooking apples grew in the wilds behind their home. That day, she'd eaten until she was sick, but the thought didn't spoil the flavour now. It was the best apple she had ever tasted.

It didn't take long for both girls to finish their plates, and, as much as it was tempting to have seconds, Emily knew this food might be the only food they would get over the Christmas season. She looked at the small pile on Freya's bed. It wasn't a lot, but she reckoned she could make it last four, maybe five days. That would get them to Christmas Eve. After that, it was still nine days until school reopened. She would have to find another way for them to eat.

There was enough food for one to last almost until school started though, as much as she hated thinking it. If it was just her, she would be OK.

Despite wanting more, Emily could see Freya was content, no longer afraid, and Emily smiled as she yawned. Small graces.

Helping her sister change and then get into bed, Emily turned off the Christmas lights before Mother saw, and then sat in her usual spot at the head of the bed, stroking her sister's hair for over an hour until she fell asleep. Outside, the snow had morphed from blown-in static to something calmer, softer, gentler. It reminded her of a time, long ago, when she was perhaps the same age as Freya. The memory was hazy, just out of reach, but she knew it was a nice memory, and in it she could hear Mother laughing. Back when Mother was just Mummy. Back when it was just her and Mummy.

She stopped herself remembering any more, and, as it faded, the chill in the room felt colder. She gazed at her sister sleeping under the duvet, her little face barely exposed. The tip of her tiny nose was reddening in the cold.

Getting up, Emily looked out across the street. The house opposite had its lights on, and she watched as the family put up their Christmas tree. She could see them smiling, laughing. The mother and father lifting the little one so he could hang a decoration.

She sighed, looked back at her sister, and vowed to do whatever it took. She would have a Christmas just like the one across the street.

As she lay in bed, hoping to sleep without any dreams, she heard the front door open and then slam shut. She wanted to close her eyes, pretend she was asleep, but if Mother wanted to punish her she would regardless, and, if she came into the room, Freya would be woken. Emily would know soon enough. If Mother stayed downstairs, she might have an uncle with her, or she might watch some TV and pass out. If she came up, she was coming for her.

Emily didn't have to wait long, as within a minute she heard Mother approaching, and, not wanting Freya to wake, she got up, left the bedroom, went to the top of the stairs and met Mother's eye. She was halfway up, hanging onto the banister to stop her swaying. For a moment, neither moved, both just stood, eye to eye, knowing exactly what was coming.

And then Mother exploded, the monster taking hold. She ran up the final few stairs and grabbed Emily by the hair, dragging her back down them. Emily wanted to cry out in pain, but bit her lip. Freya couldn't see this, she couldn't hear this.

As Mother reached the bottom step, she flung her daughter to the floor. She leaned over her, teeth bared.

'They were talking about you in the pub. I'll teach you to fucking embarrass me like that,' she said, grabbing Emily once more, this time by the pyjama top, pulling her to her feet. As she spoke, Emily tried not to gag. Her breath was rancid, like something dying.

'I'll teach you to make me look like a bad mother in front of people,' she seethed.

Emily wanted to defend herself, but how could she? Mother was right, she had embarrassed her, she had done wrong. Stealing is stealing, regardless of context.

Mother frogmarched Emily towards the back door, and, knowing where she was going, Emily looked for her coat. She had left it in the kitchen earlier, but it wasn't there. Mother had moved it.

The back door burst open and the frosty winter air swept in, blowing snow onto Emily's pyjama top. Mother stepped out and dragged Emily barefoot into the back garden. Outside, away from Freya, Emily spoke.

'I need something on my feet. I need my coat.'

'No.'

'Mother, I'll freeze.'

Mother didn't respond, just kept dragging, and, now fearful of the cold, Emily fought to get back to the house, but Mother was too strong.

'Mother, please,' she begged, her teeth beginning to chatter. Mother didn't reply. She held firm and kept walking until she reached the shed. Opening the door, she threw Emily in, and she landed hard on the frozen concrete.

'No one makes me look stupid. No one!' Mother said, closing the shed door and locking it behind her.

CHAPTER TWENTY-ONE

I led Michelle to the living room and asked her to sit. I did too.

'Em? What is it?' she asked.

'I promise I will answer any questions you might have, but let me speak, OK?'

'You're scaring me now,' she said, shifting uncomfortably in the chair.

'Have you heard of a girl called Emily Jones?'

'Emily Jones. It rings a bell.'

'She was a little girl who was caught up in a bad case of neglect. It was on the news.'

'Oh, yeah, I vaguely remember, it was around Christmas.'

'It was Christmas Day.'

'Yeah, that's it, the girl was found almost frozen to death, in a marsh or something?'

'Yeah, she barely made it.'

'Em, why are we talking about—' Michelle stopped mid-sentence, and I watched as her mouth dropped open. 'Em? Are you telling me that was you?'

I nodded.

'What the fuck?' she said, sitting back in her chair, her hands going behind her head. 'I don't understand. How?'

'I changed my name to Claywater, my nan's maiden name, as soon as I moved to London. I needed a fresh start, you know?'

'You're Emily Jones?'

'Yes.'

'Oh shit,' she said, getting to her feet and walking away from me. 'Wait,' she said, turning to face me. 'I remember more, the sister — I mean, your sister.'

'Yes, my sister,' I said quietly.

'Oh, Em.'

Michelle came over and hugged me tightly. 'I can't even imagine.'

She let me go, then sat beside me and held my hand.

'I'm so sorry.'

'It's OK,' I said. 'To be honest, I can't remember most of what happened that night.'

'No?'

'Nope, it's all a bit hazy,' I said, enjoying that I was at least telling some of the truth. I knew my sister died, I knew she died because of me, but my subconscious mind had blocked out the exact moment. I remembered before, I remembered after, but the moment was gone, buried somewhere I'd likely never find.

'I should have told you a long time ago, but I didn't know how,' I said, lifting myself from the memory of my sister's dead eyes staring back.

'It's OK,' she said. 'You're telling me now.'

'I didn't want it to get out with the press, and you finding out that way.'

'Freya . . .' she said. 'That's why you called your baby Freya. That was your sister's name, wasn't it?'

'Yes,' I said, as I tried to push away the images. Mother's voice pushed into my head too, asking, 'What did you do? What did you do?'

'Tell me about it, Em,' Michelle said. 'Talk to me, so I can help.'

I told Michelle just enough about that time, that Christmas when my sister died. It was reported that she died of neglect. It was national news. Mother went to court, and she was found guilty and sent to prison. But I knew the real truth, and so did my mother. We both knew that I killed her. Although I didn't tell Michelle that. Instead, I spoke of how I ran away, hid in the wildlands, and would have surely died from exposure if I hadn't been found when I was. I told her of how I spent the Christmas Day of my eleventh year in a hospital ward, with police protection so the media couldn't get to me. Of how I was alone, entirely alone, until I was discharged from hospital into temporary foster placement until my grandparents could legally take me away to London. I told her of how, with my grandparents' guidance, I changed my name to begin again, desperate to leave it all behind me. I told her just enough so she didn't have any questions.

'I should have told you all of this years ago,' I said once I'd finally finished.

'I understand why you didn't,' she said quietly. 'Is that why Myers was here?'

'Yes, he wanted to know why I hadn't told the police. He asked if there was anything that might connect then to now.'

'What did you say?' she asked me.

'That I didn't know. Everyone connected to that Christmas, everyone but me, is now dead. The only thing I can think of is that Lucas found out.'

'But why would he take her for that?'

Because I killed a girl called Freya.

'I don't know,' I said.

'Do you want me to keep this quiet, just between us?' Michelle asked, and I nodded.

'It might become public, but if it doesn't I would rather it wasn't mentioned.'

'Of course,' she said, leaning in to give me a hug. 'Now, we should join the others, before they begin to worry.'

'Yes,' I said.

Back in the kitchen, Adam had arrived with food and was clearing the dining table and setting up for us all to eat.

'Everything OK?' Jack asked upon seeing me.

'Yeah. Shit, I'm hungry,' Michelle said as she took a seat and opened a container of steaming hot rice as if nothing had happened, as if she didn't know my secrets.

I felt too sick to be hungry but, as I was told I needed to eat, I did. Michelle updated Adam on everything that was known about Middlesbrough, and I was thankful she didn't mention what I had just disclosed; in fact, she acted like she didn't know at all. Michelle, a mouth full of chow mein, spoke of the link between Lucas and the north, the old friend and the ex-girlfriend who were now going to be investigated. And I held on to hope that they would find him quickly, and that he took my daughter because he was just a bad man, not because he knew that I was a murderer.

As the evening wore on, I knew it was time to say that I needed to be alone. I couldn't say my guilt was driving the decision, that these events had dragged all of the memories I wanted to keep buried to the surface.

'Guys, I'm gonna go to bed soon,' I said.

'Good idea,' Adam said.

'I'll stay tonight,' Michelle added.

'No, no, I need some time alone.'

I could see Michelle didn't like the idea of me staying alone, but she didn't say anything, and after we had eaten my friends reluctantly began to ready themselves to leave.

I waved them goodbye and closed the front door. The silence took hold, the old bricks seeped cool air.

Leaning against the wall, I took deep, measured breaths. Myers knew who I was, Michelle did too, and I had learned that my mother was truly sick when she was alive.

I felt like I should mourn Mother somehow, despite what she did to me, what she made me do to my sister. But I couldn't, I was glad she was dead.

Making sure the front door was locked, I walked into the kitchen and flicked on the lights. And in the conservatory, in the shadows, next to the whiteboard, stood my sister, watching me. Her presence made me jump. She didn't speak, she never spoke, but I heard her anyway.

'You killed me, Emily. You killed me, and they will all know soon. You killed me, and you will never meet your daughter.'

I closed my eyes, and when I opened them again she was gone. But her final words lingered.

You will never meet your daughter.

CHAPTER TWENTY-TWO

Fourteen days missing

I dreamed I was in the wildlands, standing in the middle of miles upon miles of nothingness. The same nothingness where me and my sister played when we were young, when life made a fragile sort of sense. In my dream, she wasn't there, nor was anyone else, and all I could see were shrubs and wildflowers jostling in the wind. Ahead was the marsh that connected the land to the sea. Above, clouds moved quickly, sweeping secrets over the sky. And in the distance, a tree, our tree, its branches barren, twisted fingers reaching up to the heavens. I was wearing a red jumper, and I was holding my hands under it to try to keep them warm, my fingers poking through the holes. I was looking for her, my sister. I called out, 'Fry, where are you?'

I panicked and began to run, stumbling over the uneven ground. I fell, landing next to a small pond. The water was clear, so clear I could see all the way to the bottom. I watched small minnows dance around, and then I saw something else. It was floating along the bottom, drifting in a current. I strained my eyes to see it clearly, and then it rolled over, a swirl of limbs, and my sister's face stared up at me.

I tried to grab her, but I couldn't. The surface of the water was like thick glass that I couldn't break through. I banged, screamed, kicked, clawed. Whatever I did, I couldn't get to her. Then another shape floated into my eyeline, another bobbing thing, smaller than Fry, but still human, and when it rolled over I saw it was a baby. My daughter.

Then I woke, sweating, crying, and the dread lingered.

Even though it was a dream, I couldn't help but feel like it was a reality. I knew what it meant; my sister died and I couldn't stop it, and now my daughter was dead too. But after calming myself by getting up and going to the bathroom to splash cold water on my face, I concluded my daughter, my baby Freya, hadn't met the same fate as my sister. Lucas assaulted me, injected me with insulin and then took her. Why would he go to all that effort if he was going to do something bad to her? Why not just kill me in the street? Bludgeon me to death, if that was to be her fate. No, Freya was alive, somewhere, I just had to find her. I was convinced that somehow Lucas knew what happened all those years ago, somehow he knew my secret, and he did what he did to protect Freya. She was alive, she was well. Or why go to such effort?

Today, my daughter was two weeks old. Two weeks. In the night, when the hours were long and I was unable to sleep, I did some reading. At fourteen days old, babies still can't do much for themselves at all. But they begin to know the faces in their life, recognise their voices. At fourteen days old, life was about feeding, sleeping and bonding. I was missing it all.

Even though the effect of the dream lingered, even though I felt heavy and hollow at the same time, I showered, carefully cleaning my stitches so I didn't snag them, brushed my teeth, dressed and readied myself for the day. Today, I would talk to the press again, push myself forward, give them what they wanted and pull on a nation's heartstrings until someone gave me something. My name, my daughter's name would be all over the news, but I had to disconnect from 2008. People wouldn't know, it was from another time, but someone had to know where Lucas and my daughter were.

In 2024, you couldn't hide anywhere. Social media and the digital age made it impossible. Someone had to know. Maybe they might be afraid to speak up, maybe they might feel they would be wasting time with a hunch. I needed to find them, to get them to come forward. Lucas might know what I did, but no one else did. I was the victim, I was the one in trouble. I was the good one in this, not him. People would help.

Grabbing my phone, I went into Facebook and loaded the *#FindFreya* page. I was shocked to see just how many people were now there. The community was over six thousand strong, and as I scrolled the timeline I saw it was full of well-wishers and people committing to help find my little girl. I was so moved I could have cried, but I stopped myself. Now was the time for more of everything, everything but my tears. Scrolling back to the top, I tapped the publish button and began to type.

> *I'm sorry it's taken so long for me to post on this page about my little girl. I've been having a difficult time with this, I still am. I just wanted to say thank you to you all for your kind words and efforts. It means a lot.*
>
> *I want to ask, to beg for help. If you're sitting there reading this, and something is pulling at you, something you cannot shake but are worried about wasting time by coming forward, don't worry. Speak to us. If you have a theory as to where Lucas is, talk to me. Even if it amounts to nothing, I'll be grateful for it.*
>
> *Let's bring my baby home today. Let's Find Freya.*
>
> *Em x*

I hit send, and within a few seconds my phone began to ping with likes, hearts, hugs and comments. I read the first few, thinking naively that someone who did know something was sitting there, waiting for me to post, but the comments were just more people saying they were thinking of me, and that I was being brave. I put my phone on silent. One of the volunteers would no doubt read the comments. If anyone came forward, they would tell me. And if my past was dragged up, I had to hope someone from the volunteer group, maybe Michelle's neighbours, would assume it was a troll and block them.

Closing Facebook, I opened up the news and saw our story on the BBC homepage. I didn't read the article. Instead, foolishly, I went onto Google and typed in #FindFreya. There were dozens of articles and tweets. Some from reputable sources, some not. I scrolled, hoping to see something in a tabloid that would be news to me, something that the police hadn't told us, and then I saw it. My name, followed by a statement I had hoped I would never read.

MOTHER OF MISSING CHILD'S TRAGIC PAST

My hands began to shake as I clicked the link and read. They spoke of my sister, of her death, and I dropped my phone.

'Shit. Shit.'

I should have continued to read, to find out exactly how much they knew. But I couldn't. It wouldn't be long before everyone knew of my sister, of her death, and what then? How would that help find my daughter?

From downstairs, I heard a commotion at my front door, and then three loud bangs on it.

'Emily!' a voice called. In my state of shock, I didn't place it straight away.

'Emily, it's me,' the voice said again, and I realised it was Adam. He must have seen the news too.

Running downstairs, I opened the front door and he came in, closing it behind him, keeping the cameras and questions outside.

'Fucking hell, it's mental out there.'

I didn't reply, but walked away, into the kitchen. I could feel Adam following. I flicked on the kettle and, as it began to rumble, I spoke, unable to look at him.

'I assume you know.'

'Yes. We all do. Em, can I be brutally honest?'

I turned to him and dared myself to look him in the eye.

'I am so sorry about what happened to you when you were young. And if you ever want to talk about it, I'm here, we all are. But it changes nothing about who you are, not to me.'

I nodded.

'So if you don't wanna talk about it ever, that's OK too. Because I care about Emily Claywater, and I care about her daughter Freya Claywater. Not Emily Jones and her sister Freya Jones.'

'Thank you,' I said quietly.

'Anyway, that's not why I'm here.'

'No?' I said.

'No. After we left last night, we were talking and worried the police would drag their heels, so Michelle got in her car and went to Middlesbrough.'

'What? Michelle's in Middlesbrough?'

'She said she owed you.'

'Owed me for what?'

'She didn't say. She just said she needed to do it for you. That she wanted to make amends. I think she feels guilty for not walking you home that night, we all do.'

'No one knew he was going to attack me.'

'No, but still,' he said, lowering his head.

'Have you spoken with Michelle? Has she found anything?'

'Maybe.'

'Maybe?'

'She said that if you're up for it, we should go.'

'To Middlesbrough?'

'Yes. Get dressed, I'll tell you what I know on the way.'

I nodded. Everything was happening so quickly, and despite feeling trapped in my own home, he was right, I needed to move. I needed to get out. If I stayed here, I couldn't help Freya, and I needed to help Freya. As I made my way upstairs and into the bathroom to quickly wash and brush my teeth, I saw my sister, standing by the window, staring back at me.

'Why are you here?' I asked. 'What do you want? Say something, say something!'

CHAPTER TWENTY-THREE

Then — 20 December

'Mother, how long will I be in here? Mother, say something!' Emily begged, but Mother didn't respond. Instead she double-checked the lock and walked away. Moments later, Emily heard the back door slam. The punishment had arrived, and Emily wasn't surprised. Not really. The shed was Mother's go-to. She thought it made her children think about their actions, repent, and sometimes it did, when the weather was pleasant. But if it was too hot or, like now, too cold, survival instinct robbed them of the ability to reflect. Within two minutes, Emily felt the cold had already permeated her thin pyjamas and was beginning to touch her skin, raising goosebumps and making her body shiver. And it was only going to get colder as the night took hold.

Allowing her eyes to adapt to the darkness, she began to search the small eight-foot-square shed for anything to help her stay warm. She hoped that Mother would realise it was too cold to keep her out there for long, but there was no guarantee. Mother could already have left the house again, and Emily knew it was highly likely that when she did come home, perhaps with an uncle, she would have forgotten she was out there.

Prepare for the worst. She had heard it somewhere once, although she couldn't place where, but she took it to heart. She had to prepare to be in the shed for the whole, long, bitterly cold night.

Inside the shed, cluttered with old and rusting gardening tools, was a bike that was once her pride and joy, which Mother had bought for her on her fourth or fifth birthday. Mother had taught her to ride it, stabilisers attached, and she'd clapped and laughed and hugged Emily, congratulating her. It was before Freya, when Mother knew how to love. All of her kind memories were before her sister's arrival; nothing came after but hurt and loss. As she looked at the bike, the question came again. How could she get Mother back? What did she need to do? How could she recapture a Christmas just like the ones she used to know? The answer was there, somewhere, she just had to find it.

Drawing her attention back to the bike, still with its stabilisers attached, her focus went to the front wheel, which was buckled beyond repair. Emily's heart panged remembering how it happened. Freya had just been born, Mother had just started to talk to herself like it was a conversation, and Emily was beginning to learn that Mother had changed. Mother used to love watching her ride her bike. She used to call out that Emily was her brave little girl, a pocket rocket, Evel Knievel. But that morning, when Emily dragged her bike out of the shed and called to her mother to watch her, she didn't come. So she called repeatedly, and then Mother showed herself. She looked different, and Emily didn't understand why. She didn't know then, but it was the first time Monster Mother revealed herself. Emily couldn't speak, for she was afraid of Mother for the first time, and Mother didn't say a word. Instead she snatched the bike from her daughter and stamped on the wheel, bending it beyond repair.

'Don't you think it's time you fucking grew up?' Mother snapped that day, and, recalling it, Emily began to cry. She hadn't cried at the time though; the shock was too much.

Grabbing a large sheet of tarpaulin, Emily covered the old bike. She couldn't look at it anymore.

Turning away from the bike, she fought with a broken-down petrol lawnmower to move it to one side, so she had somewhere to sit. The struggle made a sweat break out on her forehead even in the bitter cold. Completing the task was hard but satisfying, as it made her feel, in that moment, as if she was moving forward. When she had cleared a space big enough to sit, even lie down, she had to find something to cover the concrete floor to help keep the cold off her skin. Behind the old bike she found a chest of drawers and, pulling open the top, she discovered gardening gloves, holey and covered in spider's webs. She pulled them out and put them on the floor in her new space.

She was shivering now, her teeth chattering so loudly she was sure they would crack. She felt panic begin to rise in her chest. It was a hot, clammy sensation she felt sometimes around Mother when she knew things were going to get bad. But Mother wasn't here now, it was just her, on her own, and she realised she could control this. She forced herself to breathe, deep and long, until the clammy feeling subsided.

Continuing to rummage through the chest of drawers, pulling each one out onto the floor, she found an old jacket, four more old gloves, a cloth bag she could make into a hat, and dozens of old newspapers and magazines.

With the four drawers out and on the floor, she kicked off the sides with her bare feet and pulled the drawer base clear. In doing so, she tore open the cut she'd sustained in Mother's bedroom days before, and she felt the warm blood trickle over her foot and drip onto the floor. Although it hurt like hell, she didn't cry out, she didn't yelp or moan; instead she felt something else alongside the pain, a kind of relief or release. She hadn't experienced it before, but the pain felt strangely comforting. Like pain could make things OK. The feeling didn't last long before her foot began to throb, and so she continued with her task.

With the drawers' bases free from the sides, she doubled up the MDF sheets and assembled a makeshift floor, just big enough for her to lie on. Then she grabbed the old papers and magazines, tore them up and stuffed them inside her pyjamas before putting on the coat and hat. Both were damp, but she reasoned they would warm with her body. Then, sitting on her new floor, she put two of the gardening gloves on her feet, the right foot stinging as she brushed over the cut, and then two more gloves on her hands.

The stillness of a winter's night held the world in its hard and unforgiving grasp. With her voice hoarse and her strength fading from shivering so hard, she listened to the distant roar of the sea beyond the wildlands until she drifted into a brief sleep.

CHAPTER TWENTY-FOUR

I watched through my bedroom window as Adam left the house under a barrage of questions and fought his way to his car. He told me to wait two minutes and then go to the end of my back garden, where I had a gate that led to a small woodland area behind my house. He would meet me on the other side, where, we hoped, the press wouldn't be. As he got into his car and drove through the gathered crowd, I quickly readied the things I would need — painkillers, breast pumps, toiletries, a few spare clothes — and threw them in a bag. Then I put my shoes on and prepared myself to leave.

Thankfully, his plan worked, and I made it out of my garden into the small woodland area without anyone seeing me. I hid in the shade of the trees, wondering if Freya was feeling the warm breeze on her skin too. I hoped she was somewhere where she could be stimulated by nature. And I lost myself in the image of one day holding her in my arms in the sunshine, until I heard a car approaching. Unsure if it was Adam or not, I hung back until it was close enough for me to see him in the driver's seat. Behind, a car and a motor-bike followed. Adam drove fast, braked hard and flung the passenger door open.

'Get in, quick.'

I moved as fast as my weakened core would allow and climbed in. The door was still closing when Adam sped off.

'I didn't think they would follow me,' he said, swerving around parked cars that lined the road. 'They're like vultures.'

Beside us, the motorbike drew level, and a pillion passenger holding a camera started to take photos. I kept my head down, trying not to give them anything. 'Why are they being like this?'

'It's a big story.'

'But it's not helping find Freya.'

'It will,' Adam said, taking a hard right that made me have to hold on to the door handle to stop myself falling.

'Slow down,' I said, scared that he might lose control.

'Sorry,' he replied, easing off the accelerator. 'I'm not used to this.'

I didn't reply. I wasn't used to it either, but I had experienced it once. A long time ago.

'Em? Are you OK?'

I nodded, but I didn't want to talk anymore.

Adam continued to drive quickly but with more care, and, approaching a junction, the traffic lights began to turn from green to amber, and he sped up.

'Hold on.'

Adam ran the red light, narrowly missing a cyclist, who swerved and then swore at us. Behind him, the motorcycle and the car stopped. Just to be sure, Adam took several turns, leading us first away from the road we were on and then back onto it. I kept checking behind but didn't see anyone coming after us.

'I think you lost them,' I said.

'Shit, that was tense,' he replied.

'Thank you, Adam.'

'What for?' he said, his eyes firmly on the road ahead, his body still tense from the chase.

'For helping me avoid them. Now they know who I am, I can't face the questions about my childhood.'

133

Adam turned to me, gave me a look that I couldn't quite work out and then smiled. 'I'm happy to help.'

'Adam, tell me, has Michelle found anything? Why is she up there? What's going on?'

'She found Lucas's ex.'

'An ex up north?'

'Yep. And she said that Lucas had messaged her, saying he wanted to visit. But he never showed.'

'He sent her a message? When?'

'Two days after you were attacked.'

'Does she know where he is?'

'No, but the police are digging, and Michelle is too. There's a rumour they spotted his car this morning in a town just outside Middlesbrough. Michelle's there trying to find him.'

Taking out my phone, I tried to ring Michelle, but the line was busy. I then tried Detective Myers. He picked up on the fourth ring.

'Detective Myers,' he said.

'It's Emily. Emily Claywater.'

'Ms Claywater.'

'I've heard you've found his car. Where is he?'

'Word gets round.'

'Where is he?'

'We're investigating now.'

'Fucking tell me where he is!' I shouted.

'Calm down. I can't. We aren't sure if—'

'Please, this is my baby. I need my baby. Just tell me!'

Myers sighed on the other end of the line. 'His car was spotted in the Stokesley area.'

'When?'

'Three days ago.'

'Three days? He could be anywhere.'

'He could, but ANPR hasn't picked him up since. So we believe he might still be around the area. Ms Claywater, I have to go.'

'No, wait, please.'

'Ms Claywater . . . Emily, as soon as we have anything concrete, I will call you, I promise.'

He hung up and I dropped the phone on my lap, and then, reaching over, I searched on the satnav for Stokesley. It was a little under four hours away.

'What did he say?'

'They think they know where he is.'

Adam looked at the Satnav, saw the new destination, and put his foot down. 'Try Michelle again.'

I nodded and called back, but she didn't pick up, so I typed a message: *Police think he's in Stokesley. Are you nearby? We're coming now, ring me when you get this . . .*

Hitting send, I wracked my brain for anything in our past that was a link to Stokesley, but nothing came. The drive was agonisingly long, and still, nothing from Michelle.

En route, much to my dismay, we had to stop at a motorway services. Adam's car was low on petrol, and I needed to wee and express. As we climbed back into the car and rejoined the motorway, Michelle finally rang back.

'Michelle? Where are you? Why didn't you call back?'

'I got your message,' she said, ignoring my question. 'I'm in Stokesley now.'

'Have you found her? Where is she?'

'I don't know. But the police are everywhere. They won't tell me if they know where he is, but I'm staying close.'

'What if this is a wild goose chase? What if he's already gone?'

'There are so many officers around, they're frantic, he must be here. How far away are you?'

I glanced at the satnav. 'Just over an hour.'

'Get here as fast as you can.'

'Michelle, do you think my daughter is there?'

She didn't respond.

'Michelle?'

'Hang on,' she said.

'Michelle?'

'Something's going on.'

She fell quiet and I listened. There were voices shouting in the distance. 'They're moving, fast. They know something,' she said.

'What? Why? What's going on?'

I listened as Michelle began to run, her feet hitting the tarmac. The muffled phone sounds made it impossible to hear anything else. I heard a car door slam, and then a car engine started.

'Michelle!'

'They have something. They were talking with a man and he nodded. Someone's seen him. Stay on the line.'

'What's going on?' Adam asked.

'Michelle says they have something.'

'Let me listen,' he said, watching the road ahead. I put it on speaker and the sound of sirens blared through the phone.

'They're leaving the town. Sit tight, I'm behind them,' Michelle shouted over the sound of her car revving, and I sat with my phone in my hand, not daring to blink. For several agonising minutes, Michelle didn't speak, and we listened to police sirens and the screeching of her car tyres.

'They're slowing, they've turned down a narrow lane.'

'Where?'

'South of the town. It looks like a farmhouse.'

'Is my daughter there?'

'Hang on,' Michelle said again, and before I could ask any more I heard another voice.

'Hang up the phone, please,' a voice boomed over the line.

'I'm just talking with a friend.'

'I said hang up the phone.'

The line went dead.

'Michelle? Michelle? Shit. Adam, put your foot down.'

He did as I asked without hesitation, and I watched the speedometer climb to one hundred.

'How will we know where to go when we get there?' he asked.

'I don't know,' I said.

As if Michelle had heard us, a few moments later my phone pinged. I had a notification telling me Michelle wanted to share her location with me.

I put our new destination into the satnav — we were just under sixty minutes away. Sitting back in my seat, I silently prepared for the longest hour of my life.

CHAPTER TWENTY-FIVE

By the time we arrived at Stokesley, my skin itched and a red rash had spread up my neck through stress. I had rung Michelle twice in the time it had taken Adam, driving frantically, to get there, and both times she'd declined the call. I desperately needed to know something, so I messaged her.

Michelle, please tell me what you can see. I need to know something.

> *Lots of police. Road to the house closed. They're moving, but slowly. They're being careful, just in case. Just get here.*

And Lucas, can you see Lucas? Can you see my baby?

> *They won't let me close enough. I've been seen messaging. I gotta go . . .*

I told Adam what Michelle had said, and he reassured me that, if the police were moving slowly, there was no reason to believe Freya had been hurt. I wanted them to run in, to get my daughter and bring her to me. But he was right.

And I reminded myself Lucas hadn't harmed Freya; there would be no point in doing so. If he was going to kill her, he would have just killed me when he had the chance. This wasn't about him wanting to harm her, this was about him feeling he needed to do this to keep her safe. This was about my past, my mistakes, my crime. My guilt. He knew what I did to my sister, he knew the truth of what really happened that Christmas, and he was doing what he felt was right to protect his daughter from that. From me. But Lucas might panic — knowing him, he probably would — and then, in the chaos, my defenceless, innocent daughter might get hurt. It was better to prepare properly, I knew that from my own past mistakes. If they rushed it, my baby might get hurt, just like my sister had.

We had managed to shave some time off the satnav's estimated time of arrival, and, arriving at the edge of the town, we slowed and searched. Somewhere nearby was the farmhouse and my baby. The town centre was quiet. Everything but a pub and the local shop was closed. I scanned the few people who were out, paying close attention to those with a buggy. None of them were him.

'Em,' Adam said, pointing ahead. I looked and saw a single police car parked horizontally across a narrow lane. A police officer stood nearby. Adam pulled up slowly as the officer beside the car approached. I looked for Michelle but couldn't see her anywhere.

Adam opened the window as the officer drew near.

'The road is closed. Where are you heading today?' he said, and then he saw me. 'Ms Claywater?'

I was startled that he knew me and almost questioned it. I'd forgotten for a moment that this wasn't just me trying to find my daughter, the whole country knew. My face was everywhere.

'Ms Claywater, you cannot be here.'

'I want my daughter.'

'Ma'am, I can't let you down this road, not until we—'

'I've driven all this way, I want my fucking daughter.'

'Please, calm down,' he said, and I could see he understood my pain, he was just doing his job.

'Officer, who's in charge? Is Detective Myers here?' Adam asked.

'He is.'

'Could you inform him Emily is here?'

'Sir, Detective Myers is busy—'

'Have you got kids?' I asked.

'Sorry?'

'Kids, have you got any?'

'Two,' he said, after a long and contemplative pause.

'Boys or girls?'

'Both boys.'

'You'd do anything for them, right?'

He nodded. 'Yes.'

'What's your name?'

'James.'

'James, I haven't even met my baby yet. I still have stitches from where they had to take her out of me while I lay in a coma, and that man, in there, he took her from me. He took her before I could even look at her.' I had to stop. I didn't want to appear weak, and I knew if I tried to say any more I would burst into tears.

'She just wants to see her baby. She's two weeks old, Em hasn't even met her yet,' Adam said quietly, placing a hand on my knee.

The officer sighed, and, grabbing his shoulder radio, he stepped away and began to talk. A minute later, he came back.

'You can go down, Detective Myers will meet you. But you stop at him, no closer. Understand?'

'Yes,' Adam said. 'Thank you.'

Going back to his car, the police officer reversed, allowing a wide enough gap for Adam to squeeze through, before blocking the road off again. He nodded at me as we passed.

We drove for about half a mile along a road that was so bumpy my stitches pulled, the lone farmhouse at the end of it growing larger as we drew closer. On the road blocking the final approach, with his hands in his pockets, stood Detective Myers. He raised a hand and we stopped. Despite my stitches hurting, I pulled myself out of the car quickly and walked towards him.

'Where is she?'

'We're trying to talk to him now.'

'What has he said? Has he said anything? Is she OK?'

'Emily, I can't even begin to understand how hard this is for you, but try and take a breath, OK? So far he isn't speaking. We don't want to rush in, so we're trying to get him to talk to us.'

'When will I get my baby?'

'Just sit tight. Let us do this properly.'

'I need her now. Please, hurry,' I said, turning my attention to the house. My baby was only a matter of feet from me, and the draw to her was the strongest it had been. Adam held me tight, as I felt my body wanting to move towards her, to kill anyone who got in my way.

'Keep back, let us deal with this. Once we have contact, we can assess our options. OK?'

Adam nodded, but I couldn't. An old feeling stirred within. The last time I was at a house with this many police cars, a little girl lay dead inside. Dead because of my actions. I prayed to God history wasn't repeating itself.

Myers turned back and walked towards the house, and, despite him telling us not to move, we edged closer, close enough to see a woman standing on the doorstep, quietly talking through the front door.

'He's right there. Why aren't they kicking the door down?' I asked.

'I know it's hard, but be patient, they're doing this slowly, to make sure everyone is safe,' Adam said.

I watched as the woman continued to talk but looked over at Myers. He nodded and sent an officer around the back. They returned after a few minutes and shook their head. The woman on the front doorstep then backed away from the house. She too was shaking her head towards Myers, who then looked at another officer, clothed in riot gear. He nodded and moved quickly, joined by six other officers also in riot gear. One held a battering ram to break the door down. Three ran around the back of the farmhouse as the other three made their way to the front door.

Myers looked over to us, and I couldn't tell what his expression said.

'What's going on?' I asked Adam.

'I don't know, I think they're about to go in.'

'Go in? Why? What's happened? Has something happened?' I begged, fear forcing me to the cold floor. 'Adam? What's happened?' I begged again when he lowered himself to support me. But he didn't reply.

CHAPTER TWENTY-SIX

Then — 21 December

Emily lay on the cold, hard floor for what felt like the longest hours of her life, waiting at the mercy of Mother to be let out. Begging for her to remember she was there. Her little body shook violently, like death itself was crawling through her thin clothes to drag her into the cold, hard ground. The darkness was all-consuming until eventually, through the small, dirty, east-facing window in the shed, she could see a red line break on the horizon. A new day was coming, and with it freedom from the prison she found herself in. She wondered if this was her longest ever stint in the shed. In the summer she might have come close. She was punished when Mother thought she had broken her favourite mug, an act Mother herself had done in a drunken rage the night before. But it was warm then — the night came late, the dawn early, and she wasn't shivering so hard her muscles felt like they would tear.

The sun rose, tired and low in the morning sky, before fresh, heavy clouds, purple with snow, blocked it. Emily kept her eyes on the sky and her ears on the house. Mother would come, she would wake, remember and, without apology, free Emily. As long as she looked sorry for her actions. In part, she was. She hated that she'd had to steal, but what choice did she have? Steal and eat and make her sister feel happy or starve and be miserable and let her fragile plan to get Mother back for Christmas fade away.

With the clouds coming in, thick and unforgiving, forcing daylight to retreat, Emily didn't know what time it was, but hours passed, with no sign of Mother — or, more worryingly, Freya. Just as panic began to set in, real panic, the kind of panic that squeezed on your heart, threatening to burst it, the back door opened. She made herself small. She knew Mother needed to feel like she had won, that Emily had repented. But the door didn't open. Instead, a small voice called her name in a whisper that barely lifted over the wind and the sound of the angry, faraway sea.

'Emily. Are you OK?'

'Freya? What are you doing out here?' Emily said, getting up and moving to the door, straining to hear her sister through the concrete.

'I was worried.'

'I'm OK. Did she see you?'

'No, Mother's door is closed.'

'What time is it?'

'I don't know,' she said. 'Emily, I'm sorry.'

'What for?'

'I did something wrong.'

'What?' Emily said. 'Why, Fry? What else have you done to make Mother angry? I'm trying to help you, you know? To help us.'

'Please don't be mad.'

'What did you do, Freya?'

'I ate some of the bread.'

'Is that it?'

'Uh-huh.'

'It's OK,' Emily said, putting her hand on the door, wishing it was her sister's little shoulder.

'Are you sure?'

'Yes, that's fine.'

'I want a cuddle,' Freya said, and Emily sat back a little. Freya wasn't over-affectionate; showing love and tenderness was a learned emotion, one that wasn't forthcoming from Mother. Freya only wanted a cuddle if she was sick or scared.

'Emily? Emily? Do you hate me now, am I in trouble?'

'No,' Emily eventually managed to scrape out. 'Just save some food for me, for when I get out.'

'I promise.'

'Then all is forgiven,' Emily said, as tears fell down her cheeks.

'I really, really promise.'

'I believe you, Fry.'

'Emily, I gotta go, I'm cold and if Mother wakes . . .'

'Yes, go. Get warm, eat.'

'Really?'

'Yeah, just save a little for me. I can always get more.'

'I will save you some, for when Mother wakes and lets you out, I will.'

'Thanks.'

'Bye, Emily.'

'See you, Fry.'

Emily pressed her ear to the door and listened as her sister's steps crunched through the snow into the house and the door closed. With her sister safely inside, warm and comfortable, Emily paced in the limited space, as the rage and grief took hold. Freya was warm, she wasn't hungry, and although Emily knew it wasn't Freya's fault she had got locked in the shed, that the blame should lie with Mother, she still couldn't tame her rage. She grabbed an old, half-empty paint can and threw it as hard as she could at the back wall. It exploded on impact, throwing white paint over the wall, drawers and lawnmower underneath. The effort of hurling the can hurt her shoulder, and she dropped to the floor and began to cry. Curling her knees up to her chest, Emily rested her head on them as the tears fell.

As she cried, she looked across the floor. Something small and shiny caught her eye and, reaching over, she picked up a small metal object. At first she didn't know what it was, but as she pulled it from the shadows into the dim daylight she saw it was a fold-up pocketknife. She snapped it open and looked at the blade. She knew holding it was wrong, but she didn't put it down. Instead, she folded the blade and kept it closed in her palm. She didn't know how or why, but she could tell it would somehow change everything.

CHAPTER TWENTY-SEVEN

I held my breath as I watched the officers break the door in. They charged inside, a cacophony of shouting that would no doubt scare my daughter. Despite wanting them to charge in, watching them do so, I begged for them to go carefully, calmly. Freya was innocent in this. And this would scar her if they were not careful. I ran towards the house, desperate to get inside, to find my daughter and hold her and soothe her as they arrested Lucas. I didn't want her to witness any of the aggression or violence that might erupt. But before I could get into the house, I was held back by a police officer, who firmly gripped my arm.

'Woah, woah, you can't go in there.'

'Let me go. Please, I just want my daughter.'

'I understand, but I can't let you in,' he said, tightening his grip.

'Get the fuck off me!' I snapped, but the officer held firm. Adam gently placed his hand on my arm, and I snapped a look at him.

'Hey, it's going to be OK. They'll find her.'

Inside the house, I could hear people calling out the word 'clear'. Seven times in all. And then nothing. There was no sound of struggle, no arrest, I couldn't hear my daughter crying. I looked at Adam, and he almost said something, but, before he could, Myers stepped out of the house. He didn't look at me, not at first. He looked at waiting forensic officers, who nodded and began to approach the house with their kit. As they entered the farmhouse, he finally turned my way.

'Where is she?' I begged.

'They're not here.'

'But you said—'

'I know, but he has been here. Forensics will find something.'

'You said they were here! I don't understand. You said Lucas was here, and my baby was here too.'

'Emily, I need you to calm down, OK? They were, but he must have run off with her before we arrived.'

'How?'

'I don't know, but I'll find out, OK?'

'Oh, God. Please. I just want my daughter.'

'Sit tight. Look after her,' he said to Adam before going back into the house. Adam pulled me away from the front door and I began to cry, feeling too heavy to move. The adrenaline I felt was entirely gone, replaced with a deep pain in my gut that had always been there, but now it was unbearable. Adam took me in his arms and, stroking my hair, told me everything was going to be OK. He pulled out his phone and dialled.

'Who are you calling?' I asked. My words sounded thick, exhausted. Not that it mattered. Nothing mattered. Nothing but her.

'Michelle. It's gone to voicemail,' he said, as he stepped away to leave a message. 'Michelle, where are you? Ring me when you get this.'

As he walked, I found myself moving once more. I felt a kind of sad rage, something I'd forgotten was in me. Something from long ago.

'Em?' Adam said, as I stopped crying and stood up straight.

'I need a minute,' I said.

He nodded and took a step away, and as he did, with the front door of the house unguarded, I made a run for it. Before

Adam could react, I was inside the house. An officer tried to block my path, but I shoved him to the side and pressed on. The effort caused a sharp pain in my stomach. But I didn't care. I wanted, I needed to see what evidence they had that showed my baby had been there, that she was real. I wanted something of my daughter's. I needed that connection. In the living room, forensic officers were taking photos, and, seeing me, one called out. 'Hey, you can't be in here!'

I ran along a narrow corridor, into a large open-plan kitchen and dining area where more officers worked, and I was about to continue to run when I saw, on the kitchen table, a bib. Someone was shouting at me to get out, and then I felt a hand grab me. It was probably the officer I had shoved, and I managed to wrestle my arm free again, enough to fight forward, enough to reach the table. Picking up the bib, I held it in my hands. It was stained with milk — or dribble, my daughter's dribble. I lifted it towards my face and my arm was grabbed again.

'Hey. That's evidence, put it down.'

I turned, my fist clenched, ready to punch whoever was trying to stop me having one thing that was my daughter's, when a voice called out. Loud and in charge, stopping both myself and the officer in our tracks.

'It's OK! Let her have it,' Myers said. The officer let go of my arm, and I unclenched my fist.

'Thank you,' I said as Myers approached me.

'You shouldn't be in here.'

'I just—'

'I know, take it, but you need to leave this house now. OK? Something will tell us where he is, you need to let us do our jobs and find it.'

'I need to help,' I said.

'Help by staying calm. We might find something that only you will understand.'

I nodded, the fight in me dying down, and, sensing I wouldn't try anything, he led me down the corridor and out-side to Adam. I could see Adam wanted to help, but I walked away, numbness washing over me. I turned right, away from the house, and sat on the edge of an old bench in the front garden. I looked at the bib, a light-grey neckerchief style with pink stars, and tried to imagine her wearing it while she was fed a bottle. Her little eyes looking up as she drank, knowing nothing about how she had been taken, how everyone was looking for her. Not knowing that she had a mother who was desperate to see her, to hold her and love her unconditionally.

I lifted the bib to my face and breathed in her scent.

Her smell was something brand new to me and yet something I knew deep in my bones all at once.

Lowering the bib, I held it in my hands and looked at the house, my mind drifting to a daydream of how it should have been.

'Em? Em?'

I looked up. Adam was standing beside me, looking at me with concern.

'Hmmm?' I said.

'Em, you're worrying me.'

'I'm OK.'

'Look,' he started, sitting down beside me. He glanced at the bib. 'I can't imagine what you're going through, but they'll find him, they'll find her.'

I nodded, unable to talk.

'They'll find something in the house, something that will tell them where he's gone. It won't be long, you just have to hang in there. OK?'

I didn't respond.

'Em, I need you to look at me and tell me you're going to hang o—'

Adam stopped mid-word. There was a voice bellowing from the back of the house.

'Detective Myers. I need you out here!'

They sounded panicked and, assuming the worst, I leaped up and ran towards the voice. I was stopped by a police officer, but I didn't need to get any closer. Because I saw what they were shouting about, and it squeezed the air from my lungs.

Dropping to the floor, I began to wail. Inside a garage, the door wide open, was a car, with the bonnet facing out and towards me. A hose ran into the driver's-side window from the back, and inside the car was Lucas. He was in the driver's seat, his head slumped at an impossible angle. His mouth open. Even from a distance I could see his face had dropped, gravity taking hold. I'd seen the face of death before, in my sister's, and I was looking at it again. The father of my baby, the man who took her from me, was dead. There was a note pinned to the windscreen, and the officer nearest pulled it off.

Detective Myers ran out of the house, saw Lucas in the car, saw the note in the police officer's hand, and then saw me on the floor.

'Get her out of here. Now!'

Two officers came and scooped me up and dragged me away from the back of the house. Adam helped them as gently as they could, they bundled me into the back of a police car. With the door shut, locking me inside, Adam stepped away, asking what had happened.

Lucas was dead, Lucas was gone. The man who took my daughter was no more, and I prayed to God that somehow Freya was still alive. If they came out with her little body in a bag, I knew I would surely die.

PART FOUR

CHAPTER TWENTY-EIGHT

I didn't know how much time had passed with me forced to sit in the back of the police car. It might have been a few minutes, it could have been a few hours. But none of that mattered anymore. Seeing Lucas in that car, seeing what he had obviously done to himself, I knew my daughter was also dead. She had to be; they would find her in the back of the car. Or the note he'd left would tell them where she was, and I tried as best I could to prepare myself for the news. A familiar numbness washed over me. The same numbness I'd felt after that Christmas, before my grandparents forced me to get help. Without them now, I knew I'd not find my way back from it. And I didn't deserve to. I had one job, one thing I needed to do, and I'd failed. I had cursed my daughter by giving her the same name as my sister in a stupid attempt to undo what I'd done. Their blood was on my hands.

But there were no do-overs, no going back. And now my baby had paid for my crimes.

A tap on the window startled me, and I looked to see Myers standing there. He smiled weakly as he opened the door. This was it. I was about to learn my daughter was gone.

'Emily. How are you holding up?' he said, lowering himself down so we were at the same eye level.

'Just tell me,' I replied, forcing myself to hold his eye.

'She's not in the car.'

'Then she's somewhere else.'

'We're looking for her.'

'He killed himself, didn't he?'

'Yes, it looks that way.'

'Then she's dead too.'

'Emily—'

'She is, you've just not found her, I know she's dead.' I almost added that I could feel it, like before, but stopped myself.

'Emily, listen to me,' he said firmly, and I looked up at him. 'I'm sorry about Lucas.'

'I'm not.'

'But there's nothing to say she's come to harm.'

'Then where is she? Where is my daughter?'

'We don't know.'

'It's not like she can get up and walk anywhere, is it?'

'Emily. Try to stay—'

'Don't you dare fucking tell me to stay calm.'

'Emily.'

'And stop giving me this false hope. That's all you've done. You said you'd find him, but he's now dead. You said you'd bring her to me. She's only two weeks old. A baby can't look after itself, can't support itself at just two weeks old. My daughter must be dead.'

'Emily, listen—'

'No, you listen,' I said, my voice cold and quiet. 'Find her, find my baby. I need to hold her in my arms, at least once.'

Myers reached over and took my balled fist, covering it with his hand. 'I promise you, I will do absolutely everything in my power to find out what happened, and where she is. We will find her.'

He didn't add *alive*, and he and I both recognised it.

'You need to go home. To rest.'

'*Rest*,' I scoffed.

'Emily, please. Look, I shouldn't, but when we understand exactly what happened here I promise I will tell you everything.'

'And until then?'

'Go home.'

'No, I—'

'Emily, go home. You shouldn't have even come here.'

Standing, Myers closed the car door and walked away. He stopped and spoke to Adam, who nodded and shook Myers's hand and then came towards the car. As he opened the door, I saw he looked pale, like he might be sick. He tried to smile, but it didn't work.

'I've been told to take you home.'

'I know.'

'There's nothing for you here. Freya isn't here.'

I nodded, and tears fell. 'Then where is she?'

'I don't know, but I'm praying.'

'Praying? Like God is a thing? If God was real, none of this would have happened.'

Adam nodded and looked away. 'I wish I could do something,' he said quietly.

'Me too.'

Adam took my hand and pulled me out of the car, helping me stand as my legs, my entire body felt numb. He guided me away from the house towards his car, and I looked back at where the police were bustling around. I could just about make out the white tent that had been erected over the garage entrance.

I wanted to go back, to search for her, but Adam held me firm and lowered me into his car. He fired up the engine and we quietly drove away. I was leaving the last known place where my daughter was, the only place where there was any evidence of her existing beyond one photo that Adam took and a scar that throbbed across my abdomen. And still, I didn't know where my baby was.

We drove in silence. For all of the four-hour journey, I dared not let go of my daughter's bib. Adam tried several times to ring Michelle and, each time, it went to voicemail.

By the time we arrived back in London, the sun was beginning to sit heavy in the sky. I hadn't spoken the entire journey home, and after the first hour Adam gave up trying to make things all right.

As we pulled into our road, there were media vans everywhere, journalists and photographers waiting for my arrival.

'Do you think they know?' I asked quietly, my words feeling trapped in my chest.

'I have no doubt,' he said, parking the car and turning off the engine. 'Give me your house keys.'

'OK.'

As I grabbed them from my bag, people pressed up against the car. Cameras flashed towards me, and I lowered my head. Voices shouted through the glass.

'Is it true Lucas Nowak is dead?'

'Where is your daughter? Did he say what happened to her?'

'Tell us about your sister.'

'Do you think there is a connection between the two Freyas?'

Adam got out of the car and pushed his way around to the boot. He opened it and then slammed it, making me jump. He said something back to the barrage of questions, then pushed round to my side, opened the door and pulled me out. With my head low, I felt people pushing and pulling. Voices shouting at me. Cameras flashed in my face. It was completely disorientating, and I didn't know where we were until we reached the front door. Adam fought with the lock, and eventually it gave and we fell into the house. I moved towards the kitchen, as far away as I could go, as Adam fought to shut the door. When he had managed it, he slumped to the floor, panting to catch his breath.

I knew I should have thanked him, helped him up. But I didn't. I walked towards the conservatory and sat, looking at the notes and scribbles on the whiteboards, reading the comments, the suggestion of hope. Hope. Hope wasn't a friend, hope was the enemy. It always had been.

I grabbed the first board and pulled it over, sending it crashing to the ground. I stamped on it, snapping it in two, but I wasn't satisfied, not even close. I moved on to the next, and the next, until everything that the group had worked on lay in chaos at my feet. Adam didn't try to stop me either. Instead he waited in the doorway until I had run out of steam. Then I slumped into a chair, looking out into the garden. My mind, for the most part, was empty.

Adam slowly approached. 'Can I do anything?'

'No,' I replied.

'I think I should stay.'

'No, thank you. I need to be alone.'

'Em, I don't think—'

'I need to be alone,' I said with more force, and he nodded.

'OK. Listen, I don't know where Michelle is, she's probably on her way back by now. When I get hold of her, I'll get her to call.'

I didn't reply.

'Do you want me to clean this up?' he said, gesturing to the floor.

'Leave it,' I said, my voice hollow.

'Ring me if you need anything.'

I sat motionless, and Adam headed for the door. The noise briefly escalated again as he stepped out and closed the door behind him.

Now the house was silent, completely still. The numbness complete. And I didn't know why, but I thought of my grandparents. I wished they were still here.

Getting up, I walked through the house, pacing, unable to stop fidgeting, feeling lost. I walked upstairs, stopped in the doorway to Freya's bedroom and tried to imagine her in her cot, but I couldn't see it anymore. I shuffled into my room and looked out of the window at the gaggle of press. Part of me wanted to see what they were saying about my past. To know if they knew what I did, what Lucas had worked out, but I didn't have the strength to look. It didn't matter now anyway. I didn't care if the entire world knew I'd killed my sister in the wildlands all those years ago, nothing could hurt me more than I was already hurting. Sitting on the end of the bed, I looked at myself in the wardrobe mirror, seeing the damaged woman staring back, and it sent a shiver up my spine. I looked a lot like my mother, a sad incarnation of her. Behind me, I saw my sister looking at me too, no doubt thinking the same thing.

'Please, just leave,' I said to her, and I jumped when she did something she'd never done before. She spoke to me.

'What did you do, Emily? What did you do?'

I turned quickly to see her, but she was gone. I wanted to feel the connection, if even for a moment, with the first girl I let down in my life. Standing, I opened the wardrobe and pulled out the box. Removing the lid, I took out the knife, the only link between me and my past. Between me and my sister. Opening it, I pressed on the blade until my skin threatened to split. I knew what it felt like to cut into flesh. To slice it open. To watch the crimson pour.

I pushed the memory away, put down the knife, picked up my phone.

I saw the date, and my heart tore itself from my chest cavity.

It was 16 July.

Today was my due date and my baby was surely dead, and, knowing so, a coldness crept into my bones, like that from when I was young. And I knew I wouldn't ever be able to shift it.

CHAPTER TWENTY-NINE

Then — 21 December

As the day wore on, the sun resting again after its short visit, the cold set in, creeping into Emily's bones. Heavier and harder than before, and Emily knew if she stayed out there she wouldn't survive the night.

Her muscles ached, her head hurt through dehydration and her stomach rumbled angrily, the exhaustion of her body trying to stay warm made her feel weak, so weak that she dared not stand in case she passed out.

But still, Mother never came.

From where she sat, she could see through a small gap between two concrete panels in the shed wall towards the house. Although the gap was too narrow to make out any details, she could tell when the kitchen light was on. When it was, either Mother or Freya was nearby, and each time she begged to hear the back door open and the sound of footsteps in the frozen snow, crunching towards her. But every time the light turned on, it turned off again shortly after.

At some point, she must have fallen asleep, for she didn't hear the back door open, nor the crunching of wellington boots in the snow. The banging on the door startled her awake.

'Please, wake up, Em. Please, are you OK?' Freya said.

'Hey, Fry, I'm here,' Emily replied, trying to move her aching, exhausted body. Her blood felt frozen inside her veins. It hurt, but she managed to get her limbs moving and pulled herself towards the shed door.

'I thought something was wrong. I've been banging for ages.'

'Sorry, I was asleep. Why are you here?'

'Mother's gone out. I wanted to see you.'

'She's gone out?'

'Uh-huh.'

'Well, you can't be out here long, in case she comes back.'

'I know. I just wanted to see you.'

'Fry, I'm really thirsty.'

'I can get you water. Hang on.'

'No, wait,' Emily said, but Freya was already gone. Getting water wouldn't be the issue; how Emily would be able to drink it would. She desperately looked around for a solution. The window was the obvious choice. She could smash it, and Freya could pass in the bottle or cup she had collected from the house. But Mother would see it, and then she would really be in deep trouble. Mother was worse than ever, and she didn't know what she would do next. She looked at the old lawnmower and, turning it on its side, she looked at the cutting blade. It was metal, worn, but still strong and mostly rust free. Finding a spanner, she loosened the bolt that connected it to the mower. It took all of her strength, and she felt sick for the effort, but the old bolt came free, and she removed the blade from its holder. Looking around, she tried to find a gap that she could cut into and create a hole big enough for Freya to pass her some water. She knew she had to be discreet or else Mother would see. So she opted for the side of the shed that faced away from the house. She looked up at the roof, and she was sure, if she put a hole in it, right in the corner where the roof and wall joined, Mother wouldn't be able to see from her bedroom window. Climbing onto the old chest of drawers, she quickly found that the join between the roof and the concrete wall wasn't connected. Instead, the roof overlapped. It took her three attempts to wedge the blade in that gap, and, once it was stuck fast, she began to rock it back and forth. The effort made her feel dizzy. After a minute, the blade dropped out, as the gap had widened.

'Emily? What are you doing?' Freya's voice came from outside the shed.

'Hang on.'

She wedged in the blade again, slightly further along the gap, and rocked it. A large chunk of concrete, rotten through damp, broke free and dropped to the floor, creating a small hole roughly the size of Freya's fist. A small bottle of water should fit, she reasoned. Climbing down, she moved to the shed door, so close her face almost touched it.

'OK. I've made a hole at the back of the shed. Come round, I'll show you,' Emily said. 'But be quick, I'm worried Mother might come home.'

'OK.'

Emily climbed back onto the chest of drawers and, leaning against the wall, the drawers wobbling underfoot, she looked out of the hole. The wind blew hard, and her eyes began to water instantly. But, through the haze, she saw Freya come around the corner.

'Hey,' she said.

'Hey.'

'I've missed you.'

'I'll be out soon,' Emily replied.

'When?'

'Soon. Fry, have you got some water?'

'Yes, and some food.'

'OK, pass it up.'

Emily leaned back, and pushed her fingers through the hole to collect the water when Freya passed it. Freya reached as high as she could with the bottle of water. But, even on her tiptoes, she couldn't reach Emily's hand.

'I'm too little,' Freya said. 'What do I do?'

'Find something to stand on, a box or something should do it, but be quick.'

'OK.'

Emily moved away, fearing the chest of drawers would collapse. The last thing she needed was to be injured. She waited a moment as Freya found something she could stand on. A minute passed, and she returned.

'I found a box, I should be able to reach.'

'OK, pass me the water first.'

Emily watched the small hole as a bottle of water came into view and was pushed through, dropping to the ground below. Reaching across, she took her sister's fingers, inter-twining them with her own.

'Well done, Fry.'

'I have to let go, I need to pass you food.'

'OK,' Emily said. If Mother saw what they were doing, she would probably take Emily out of the shed and put Freya in, to punish them both. Moving away, she saw Freya stuff some bread in a food bag through the gap. She tried to push an apple through, but the gap wasn't quite big enough. She stopped trying, and then pushed in a packet of crisps that popped when forced through.

Freya then stood on her tiptoes and looked into the hole.

'I can get you more.'

'No, Fry, this is perfect. Thank you. Now, get in, before Mother sees you.'

'I love you.'

'I love you too,' she replied, relieved that she could still say it to her sister.

Freya moved away from the hole, and Emily heard a thud.

'Fry?'

'Oww, oww, oww.'

'Fry, are you OK? What happened?'

'I fell. I'm OK, just hurt my arm. I'm fine,' Freya replied, forcing herself to hold back her tears.

'Are you sure?'

'I'm OK. Just a graze. I'll come back later if Mother doesn't come home.'

'OK.'

Emily listened as Freya's footsteps crunched through the snow, and, jumping down, she looked through the small gap that faced the house and listened as the back door opened then closed. The kitchen light then went out. She was safe and warm. She was warm, and Emily was cold. She was safe and Emily was in danger.

It's not her fault, it's not her fault, she told herself, but it was, both she and Mother knew it.

Scrabbling on the floor, Emily found the water and food Freya had passed through, and, sitting on her makeshift floor, she opened the bottle and drank from it. The water pouring down her throat felt like it moved the blood in her body once more. Her parched throat ached for more, but she knew to sip slowly or she would be sick. With her mouth no longer dry, she put the lid on the bottle and opened the bag of bread.

'Clever Fry.'

She ate quickly, her stomach growling as she swallowed. The simple meal of plain bread made her feel happy, so happy she began to cry.

CHAPTER THIRTY

Fifteen days missing

The wildlands came to me again in my sleep. I was there, barefoot, wearing a T-shirt that had some of it torn away. The wind buffeted my side, moaning as it rushed around me, drowning out all other sound. I was walking in the direction of my childhood home. I saw a little girl moving towards the back door. My sister. I tried to call her, but my voice was gone. I ran, knowing something was going to happen if I didn't get there, and, as I approached the house, a sheet of thick ice, like a brick wall, blocked my way. I banged on it, trying to draw her attention. But even my fists hitting the ice made no noise.

As my sister opened the back door, she turned and looked towards me. In her arms was a tiny baby, my baby. She mouthed to me:

You. Did. This.

I woke and my throat burned as if I'd been shouting, and as I sat up, knowing I was in my own bed, I thought I could still smell the heather of the wildlands. I turned my head and looked out of my bedroom window, focusing on the light, slow-moving clouds to try to get my breathing under control and return my heart rate to a steadier pace. As I settled, I thought about my daughter. I was desperate to try to think of her as alive somewhere, but, as much as I fought to grab an image of her in someone's arms feeding, sleeping, crying even, I couldn't. I'd not even met her. My heart was breaking and I wanted to cry, to wail, but I couldn't. It was there, buried deep inside my chest, where my grief lived, and it wasn't coming up and out. The door that held it in was strong, fortified over sixteen years of continual work to keep my demons locked away in a vault of my own making.

Standing up, I dared to look out of the window to the street below. Journalists and reporters were still camped outside, their vans parked on the kerb. People stood around chatting. It was calm; it told me they hadn't found her yet.

Backing away before anyone looked up and caused a commotion, I grabbed my phone and saw I had several missed calls from Michelle. The first coming at just after six. I tapped her name and called her back.

She picked up on the first ring. 'Em.'

'Are you OK? Where have you been?'

'They arrested me.'

'What? Why?'

'After I called you, I wouldn't leave, so they arrested me. I got out of the cell this morning. Em, I've heard on the radio about Lucas. Is it true?'

'Yes.'

'Shit. Shit.' She paused, and I thought the line had gone dead.

'Michelle?'

'Sorry, I'm here,' she said, her voice sounding broken, small. She cleared her throat. 'What about—'

She stopped herself, unable to say my daughter's name.

'They've not found her yet.'

'Then there's hope.'

'No, no, she's dead. I just know it.'

'Hey, listen, no, if they've not found her, there is hope.'

'Michelle, don't.'

'Where are you?'

'Home.'

'OK, I'm on the A1 now. I'll be at yours in the next hour or so. Don't go anywhere.'

She tried to say something else, something about hanging on, but I moved the phone from my ear and hung up. I understood what she was trying to do, it was probably what I would do. Hope was a powerful thing. But most didn't know what I knew about hope. It wasn't benevolent, as it made itself out to be. It was cruel. Twisted. It fucking knew things didn't work out, seldom did wishes come true. It knew it was blindsiding us all, just so it could watch us fall to pieces when it all went wrong.

Hope was the enemy.

I grabbed my dressing gown and quickly threw it on, catching one of my stitches and cursing as I did, before leaving my bedroom and walking downstairs.

Making my coffee, I opened the back doors, letting the cool early morning summer air sweep through on a breeze. I could feel my sister somewhere inside the house, watching me, and I couldn't face her, so I walked outside. The morning dew soaked my feet, grounded me again, and I sat on a patio chair, staring out into the garden, focusing on nothing. I heard voices floating on the breeze from the front of the house. They started small, but quickly roused into a climax. Something had happened. Something was going on.

Then I understood: news was breaking.

They had found Freya.

I stood too quickly, the stitches pulled and white pain shot through me, but I ignored it and ran through the house and upstairs to grab my phone. As I picked it up, my stomach lurched and I threw up on the floor. I knew what I was going to discover, and I fought with myself to not retch again. I didn't want to look, but I needed to know, and I didn't want to go outside and speak to anyone, so I unlocked my phone and googled my daughter's name. Dozens of articles leaped onto my screen, and I scrolled to see what the reporters had learned. There were stories about Lucas, about his death, one headline stating he was a coward, calling it a murder–suicide. I held my breath and clicked on it. The article spoke of how he was found in the car, a hose feeding him carbon monoxide, slowly killing him. My daughter was mentioned, but it didn't say if she had been found. The article was also twelve hours old. Whatever was causing the commotion, it was immediate. Closing that page, I scrolled on. I read headlines about my daughter being missing, as well as articles about my past. I saw one about Mother but ignored it. Finding nothing to suggest they had found my daughter, I looked out of my bedroom window and several cameras raised to take a picture of me. I stood there, scanning the crowd below for something that would tell me what had happened.

Then, there was a knock at my front door. Three loud bangs.

I ran down the stairs as fast as I could, and, as I opened the door, Detective Myers stood there. His face said it all.

I stumbled back into my home, and without being invited he came inside and closed the door.

'Emily, will you sit?' he asked, and I shook my head, my words stuck. 'Please?' he said, coming towards me. He placed a hand on my arm, and with his touch my paralysis lifted and I moved towards the stairs, half sitting, half falling. As he prepared himself to talk, I stared at a natural split in the wood flooring between two beams.

'Emily, I—'

'Just say it,' I managed to whisper, unable to take my gaze from the floor.

'She's not there.'

I snapped my head up to look at him. 'What?'

'She was, there were used nappies, evidence of her being fed. She definitely was there, with him, but everything that you would need for a baby is missing.'

'I don't . . . I don't understand,' I said, trying to make sense of what I was being told.

'We knew she was fed formula milk, there was powder in the kitchen, but the formula is gone. There are no clothes, no bottles, no clean nappies. It looks like everything was taken.'

'It's all probably buried with her, where Lucas put her.'

'No, Emily.'

'You don't know, how can you be sure?'

'We discovered something else.'

'Detective Myers, don't give me hope. Don't you fucking dare. I don't want hope. I just want my daughter, but we both know I won't get that, so don't tell me things that cannot possibly be. Put me out of my misery. Just tell me Lucas killed my baby and then killed himself.'

'That's the point. He didn't kill himself.'

'What do you mean, he didn't kill himself? I saw what I saw.'

'At first, it looked evident, but he didn't. We think it was staged to make it look like he did.'

'I . . .' My words failed.

'We're still piecing it together. However, we found a small injection site in his neck. It wasn't dissimilar to what we found on you. It's not confirmed, but it's believed he was given a dose of insulin, like you were, and then placed in the car to make it look like a suicide. He's also been dead a while. We'll know exactly how long soon.'

I tried to process what was being said, but my mind couldn't. The image I had formed in my head — partly based on what I thought was true, partly based on what I assumed would become truth — was wrong. The picture was distorted.

'What are you telling me? My daughter is still alive?' I said, my voice cracking, my body shaking.

He nodded. 'We don't know who has her, but we do know it has to be someone connected to Lucas somehow. The whole country has been looking for him, and still someone knew he was there in that house. We think that whoever killed Lucas has your baby. Someone Lucas is close to, maybe someone you've even met.'

'Someone I've met?'

'We can't rule it out. We need to find that person. I need to ask you again, is there anyone from your childhood, anyone at all who we could try and speak to?'

I shook my head. The only one I knew, the only one I saw from the wildlands, was my dead sister, and I wasn't about to confess to seeing ghosts.

'What should I do?' I asked, forcing myself to stay in control. My baby might still be out there. My daughter might still be alive.

'We need to compile a list of everyone you know who knows Lucas, we need to find that link. Will you help us?'

Wiping my eyes to stop a tear from dropping, I nodded to Myers and he got up, finding a piece of paper and a pen.

'Start by writing out everyone you know through him — friends, family, work colleagues, anyone. Someone close to him must know something. His phone was found, we're trying to access it now.'

'I've done that already.' I almost told him to look in the conservatory, but then remembered I had vented my rage at the hope on those boards.

'Do it again, in case something or someone new comes to mind.'

I nodded.

'If I hear anything, anything at all, I'll call. Stay close to the phone,' Myers said, getting up and making his way towards the door.

'Detective Myers,' I called out.

'Yes?'

I hesitated. I knew hope was evil, but I wanted it, needed it still. 'You really think she's alive?'

He paused, sighed. 'You want the truth?'

'Yes.'

'This time yesterday, I was sure she was no longer with us. Now, I don't know. But that's something. In these situations, the first forty-eight hours are the most critical.'

'From when she went missing, or from now?' I asked.

He ignored my question. 'I'm heading back up to Middlesbrough now. I'll be in touch soon.'

I understood what that meant. We were on day fifteen now. Over 360 hours. His statement was clear: hope for the best, prepare for the worst.

Myers turned and headed out the front door to a roar of questions. The door closed, leaving me stunned. Getting up, I stumbled into the kitchen and grabbed a piece of paper and a pen. I looked at the blank space and started to scribble down a list of people I knew through Lucas. I didn't think it would help, but it was something. After I had exhausted my memory, I began to rebuild the boards I had destroyed. Maybe, just maybe, something would leap out at me. I picked up the first, and read the statement written in red pen. *In most cases of a child going missing, those involved are those closest.*

Those closest.

I looked at my list again, and saw I'd not written down those who were closest to me. I didn't have anyone closer than Michelle, Jack and Adam. I wanted to dismiss it, but if it was true I needed to be sure. Despite my better judgement, and with a crushing guilt, I added their names to my list.

CHAPTER THIRTY-ONE

As soon as I wrote down their names, I crossed them out again. There was no way any of them could be involved in this. But still, it niggled. Those closest. Closest to Freya was Lucas, but he was gone — no, he had been murdered by someone, murdered in the same way I was put into a coma, and that said something. Whoever had my girl, they were originally in on it with Lucas. Perhaps they had planned it together, to take her and run away and begin a new life together, a new life safe from me and my past. But then, what if that other person didn't want to share with Lucas, or they only used him to get to her? Or what if they'd planned to run away, and Lucas had got cold feet and wanted to bring her home to me? Maybe the brooch he got me as a gift was telling me he knew about my past, and wanted to be there, to understand? What if Lucas was going to do the right thing? What if that was all he ever wanted to do? Was his blood now on my hands also?

I thought about my friends, about my 'closest'. Didn't Adam say that he and Jack were thinking of having children one day? They could adopt or enter into a surrogacy pro-gramme, they didn't need my girl. And besides, they didn't know my secrets. They didn't know who I really was. I was right to cross them off. Michelle was slightly different. I knew she wanted children of her own, and I knew the struggles she faced. But she was my best friend. The closest I had to family. She wouldn't. She couldn't. But then, what if she had found out too? What if, when Lucas discovered my past, he confided in her for help, and she knew I was in fact a killer? What if they'd planned it together?

Michelle went to Middlesbrough.

Michelle disappeared off the radar for the entire night.

Michelle was my 'those closest'.

But it was Michelle, she was like family, I was being paranoid. It wasn't her, it was someone else on that list. Someone else connected to Lucas. His ex who was mentioned, or a friend.

Even with me forcing my paranoia down, I couldn't quite shake it, so to bury it entirely I grabbed a quick shower, the water as hot as I could bear, and got myself dressed. As I pulled up my underwear, I looked at myself in the mirror. Some of the post-baby swell was beginning to subside, and my caesarean wound looked like it was beginning to heal, despite the torture I was putting it through. Some of the dissolvable stitches had fallen out. My body was moving on, slowly returning to what it was before I fell pregnant, though I knew it wouldn't be exactly the same. And knowing that hurt. My body was beginning its journey into forgetting it had had a baby inside it. My body was forgetting Freya. I ran my fingers over my remaining stitches and pulled on one. It hurt like hell and centred me, making me more aware of my surroundings, and I heard noise coming from the kitchen. Someone was in my house.

Wrestling my maternity shorts on, I moved to the doorway and listened, hoping I was imagining it. Then I heard it again, and my heart stopped.

Grabbing a top, I chucked it on and moved towards the stairs as quietly as I could. Looking over the banister, I could see the shadow of whoever it was moving in my kitchen. I thought about going back for the knife but stopped myself. I had enough blood on my hands.

'Who's there?' I shouted, hoping that my fear didn't resonate.

'It's me, I'm just making a cuppa,' Michelle called back.

I sighed and began to make my way down. 'Michelle, you scared the shit out of me.'

As I reached the kitchen, Michelle came and hugged me. She smelled like old furniture. 'Are you OK?' she asked.

I nodded. 'Are you?'

'Rough night,' she said. Her voice was tired, sad, like she was grieving as much as I was, and I knew she wouldn't be aware of what I had just learned. It also told me that my best friend wasn't involved. And I felt guilty for thinking she could be. Michelle had been my rock, she had organised the search group, she was arrested for trying to find my daughter. I felt shitty for even thinking it could be her.

'I'll live,' she continued. 'Listen, I was thinking, maybe—'

'Lucas didn't kill himself,' I said quietly.

'What?' Michelle replied. 'How do you know?'

'Detective Myers just told me. It was staged as a suicide, but he thinks someone gave him an injection, probably insulin.'

'Oh shit,' she said, backing away even more, until she slumped into a chair. 'Shit, but Freya?'

'Detective Myers thinks there's a chance she's still alive.'

'Oh God. God! Shit, what do we do?' she said, getting back to her feet and pacing.

'Michelle, it's only a chance, a slim one at that,' I said. Her reaction was genuine, real. Michelle didn't know where my baby was, she didn't have anything to do with her being taken from me.

'Slim is better than nothing,' she said.

'I need to get these boards back up, will you help me?'

'Of course,' she said.

As we set to work, quietly rebuilding the whiteboards as best we could after my rage, there was a knock at the front door and we both froze.

'Stay here,' Michelle said, walking towards the front of my house.

I did as she said, but listened as Jack and Adam fought their way into the house. As soon as they saw me, they rushed over to give me a hug.

Jack and Adam still believed my daughter to be dead.

'We're so, so sorry Em,' Adam said quietly.

I opened my mouth to tell them what I had learned, that Lucas didn't commit suicide, that my daughter hadn't been found, and there was evidence that she had been moved somewhere else, but the words didn't come. It was fragile, my hope, like thinly blown glass — one tap and it would crack. Thankfully, Michelle spoke for me, as she had done several times.

I didn't listen though. Instead, I watched my three best friends talk. All animated, all passionate, but were any of them faking it, lying about everything? I looked at the board, *those closest*, and then back at my friends.

I shook away my questions. They didn't have anything to do with her disappearance, they didn't know my past. They couldn't.

To stop myself doubting it, I walked towards my daughter's name displayed on the board in red pen. Her name shouting at me. She was telling me to find her, and I would. Somewhere on these boards was the link I needed to find. A link between me and Lucas. I began to read everything that had been gathered over the past few days. I'd read it all before, but now I was looking at it from a unique perspective. I needed a name, a place, something that made sense, something that would help. Michelle, Adam and Jack helped me put up the final boards, returning the room back to a damaged version of its hopeful self from the day before. I studied the words, places, names. But the more I looked, the more the words became just words — scribbles, meaningless. Then I saw the statement again, the one I couldn't shake.

In most cases of a child going missing, those involved are those closest.

175

The statement was right, I knew it was. I was the closest person to my sister, and I killed her. Lucas was dead, I had no family, who else was there who was close to my daughter besides the three people I was with right now? I was yo-yoing back and forth, convincing myself that they couldn't possibly be involved. But my judgement had been wrong before, and I knew the consequences all too well.

I looked at my friends again, doubting everything I knew about them — and me.

CHAPTER THIRTY-TWO

Then — 22 December

When she woke, she was sure, for a moment, someone was in the room with her, but as her eyes adjusted she realised it was the remnants of a dream, one of her and Mother, laughing and hugging as they played in the wildlands. In her life before. Emily wanted to hold on to it for as long as she could, but it faded as the cold gripped her little body once more. She didn't know what day it was. The night was long, too long, and Emily was sure that more than three days had rolled into one, and, despite the hunger having been quelled, she was weak and exhausted from shivering all night. At least, it felt like all night to her. However, to her confusion, the night still held firm, the day still not even a sliver on the horizon. So it must have been only a few hours at most. Mother hadn't come for her. Instead, it was Freya's voice she heard outside the shed door.

'Are you awake?'

'Fry. Why are you out here?' she said, getting up and limping towards the door.

'Mother didn't come home.'

'But she might at any moment. You need to go inside, get into bed, be invisible like I taught you.'

'I need you, Em.'

'Fry, you can't let me out of here.'

'Why not?'

'Mother will know.'

'But, Em, it's so cold.'

'I'm OK,' Emily said unconvincingly. She knew Freya wouldn't believe her.

'If you won't let me let you out, I'm staying out here with you.'

'No, Fry, you'll freeze.'

'So will you.'

'Fry.'

'I'm not leaving.'

Emily thought for a moment. If Freya let her out, she would be in trouble, but if she stayed in the cold she might end up sick or dead. Freya had forced her hand.

'Fine, let me out.' Once again, Freya was going to make things more difficult than they already were.

Freya didn't hesitate, and shoving the shed key into the lock she snapped it open. Emily, realising what Freya would see, tried to hide the bucket she'd had to use as a toilet, but Freya noticed, and seeing what her big sister had had to endure aged her somehow.

'Hey, Fry,' she said, painting on a wide smile, and her little sister ran into her arms and hugged her tight.

'You smell funny,' Freya said, and Emily laughed. Freya joined in, until both girls were crying. They were not tears of laughter.

'Come on,' Emily said, wiping her eyes, smearing dirt across her face. 'We better get in before Mother sees us.'

Grabbing the small pocketknife from the floor before her sister could see, Emily took her little sister's hand, stumbled out of the shed and closed the door, locking it tight, before moving towards the house. At the door, she paused, listening for any sign of Mother, but it was silent, the house still. Stepping into the kitchen, the threadbare carpet under her feet felt like deep, soft quilt in comparison to the hard concrete of the shed. And despite the heating not being on, she felt her skin prickle with warmth.

Closing the back door, Emily grabbed a cup of water and drank greedily, forcing a burp after she finished to make Freya laugh. She then led her sister up to their room and closed the door. For a moment, Emily didn't move. She stood, looking at her room. She realised, although it was cold and dirty, it was hers. Hers and Freya's. It was their space, their small piece of world where they could feel safe, and she loved it.

'Em, are you OK?' Freya asked, and Emily smiled at her.

'Fine.'

Emily changed out of her damp, dirty clothes into a pair of pyjamas that were too small but dry, and flopped onto her bed. She knew there would be trouble for her being out of the shed, but in that moment she didn't care. She would make sure the blame wasn't placed on Freya. She would tell Mother she forced her to let her out, if it came to it.

Again, duty.

'What will we tell Mother?'

'I'll tell her she let me out. She might believe it, like she did when I got you out of there.'

'You think so?'

'I'm sure of it,' she replied, feeling anything but.

Freya got onto Emily's bed, and Emily wrapped her arms around her, pulling her close, hugging her tight, and Freya winced.

'Hey, what's wrong?'

'It's nothing,' Freya replied.

'Are you hurt?'

'Just a little scratch, I'm OK.'

'Let me see.'

'No, Em, I'm—'

'Fry, let me see.'

Freya sat up and rolled up the sleeve on her pyjama top. On the back of her arm, just above her elbow, was a cut, about an inch long, with an angry bruise wrapped around it. It didn't look deep, but it looked sore.

'How did you get this?' Emily asked, wondering if Mother had caused it.

'When I fell.'

'What? When you gave me food?'

'Yeah.'

'Oh, Fry,' Emily said, tears filling her eyes. 'I'm so sorry.'

'It's not your fault. I was the one that fell.'

'But you hurt yourself getting me food.'

'Em, it's OK. It's fine.'

Emily hugged her sister, and Freya continued to reassure her it was OK. But the cut looked dirty, and Emily knew she needed to clean it. Getting up, her limbs aching and heavy, she went to the bedroom door. Checking the coast was clear, she ran to the bathroom, grabbed a face cloth, soaked it in warm water and then came back into their room. As gently as she could, Emily cleaned her sister's cut before using the pocketknife to cut and tear through one of her T-shirts to make a bandage.

'Is that too tight?' Emily asked, once she had tied it on.

'No, it's fine.'

'Are you sure?'

'It's OK. Can we go to sleep now, before Mother gets home?'

'Yes. Of course.'

Climbing back into bed, Emily once again pulled her little sister in, careful not to touch her right arm. She pushed down the guilt for her sister being hurt because of her, reasoning it was only a small cut, she would be fine. It worked partly because it was just a small cut, partly because Emily was so exhausted. Freya fell asleep quickly, warm and safe and with her big sister's heart beating close to her own, and, stroking her little sister's hair, Emily closed her eyes. She felt ashamed of herself, for when she was in the shed she'd prayed — no, begged — for life to go back to how it was before Freya came. She'd realised that although she loved her sister, she hated her too.

None of it was her fault, but she had caused it all.

In the shed, Emily wanted Freya to run away, to go away, but, as Freya started to gently snore, Emily hated herself for thinking it, for still thinking it. Even with the closeness she felt, Emily couldn't deny herself. The thought lingered, demanded to be heard. Her little sister had ruined her life, and Mother's too.

As she began to sink into the bed, the physical exhaustion a stronger pull than the battle in her own head towards her feelings for Freya, she heard the sound of glass smashing outside in the street. She tried to ignore it, to continue to drift off to sleep, but her senses were heightened for it. She knew it had to be Mother.

Her suspicions were confirmed only a few seconds later, when she heard her mother's voice, punctuating the quiet of the sleeping street.

'Hurry up, I'm fucking freezing.'

Her voice was followed up by a man's.

'I'm coming, hold your tongue.'

Emily sat up and looked at Freya. Her little sister was awake; she'd heard it too and she looked scared. Emily showed another weak smile, trying to reassure her.

Getting out of bed, she moved to the window. Freya joined her.

'Keep low,' she whispered. Freya nodded as Emily dared to pull back the curtain enough to look out onto the street. Mother stood on the edge of the road, outside the front door, looking to her right. Emily followed her direction of sight to see a man stumbling up the road towards her.

'Is that Uncle Paul?' Freya whispered.

'No, it's a different uncle.'

'Really? What's his name?'

'I can't remember. Come on, back to bed.'

Emily walked back to the bed and lay in it, but Freya stayed at the window, looking down into the street. 'How many uncles do we have?' she asked.

'Fry, come away from the wi—'

Freya shot away from the curtains before Emily could finish her sentence, and she looked spooked.

'What?' Emily asked, sitting up again, her body complaining at the effort.

'He saw me, Mother too.'

'How did she look?'

'Angry.'

'Fry!' Emily said. 'I told you to come away from the—'

She was cut off again, as downstairs the front door opened and then slammed behind them. She joined Freya and looked out of the window once more. The uncle in question hadn't come inside, he was walking away, alone.

Footsteps crashed up the stairs, and from Mother's gait Emily knew it was Monster Mother.

'Get into bed. Now!' Emily whispered. 'Why can't you just listen to me?'

'I'm sorry.'

'You're always sorry.'

'Don't be angry with me.'

'How can I not be? Things were so much easier before you.'

'Don't say that,' Freya said, beginning to cry.

'Stop crying, get into the fucking bed. Don't make me ask you again.'

'You swore at me,' Freya said, afraid of her big sister.

Freya dashed to the bed, burying her sobs under the covers just before Mother opened the bedroom door. With the landing light behind her, she was mostly shadow, but her shoulders were hunched, her breathing heavy. For a moment Emily was sure she had actually turned into a monster.

'Was it you at the window?' she asked, her voice barely audible. She looked unblinking at Emily, telling her she would deal with the fact she wasn't in the shed, where she should be, when she was good and ready.

'Yes, Mother.'

'He told me he didn't want to get mixed up with someone with kids. Do you realise what you've just done?'

'Mother, I—'

Before Emily could finish, Mother shot across the room, faster than Emily thought was possible, and hit her around the face, sending her crashing to the ground.

'You always fucking ruin things,' she hissed before turning and leaving the room, slamming the door behind her.

Mother stomped downstairs, and, once Emily heard music playing from the kitchen, she dared to move. As she sat upright, she turned and saw Freya looking at her from under the covers.

'Are you OK?' Freya asked, but Emily didn't respond. She was too angry, and she knew if she said anything to her sister right now she would show as much rage as Mother had just done. Because it wasn't Emily who ruined everything, it was Freya, it was always Freya.

'Em?' Freya asked, her voice a whimper.

'Go to sleep, Freya,' Emily said back, her words hard and cold, and just like Mother's.

Freya turned over without saying another word, and Emily, finding the knife in her pyjama pocket, gave it a squeeze.

CHAPTER THIRTY-THREE

I looked back at those closest to me as Adam and Jack fired questions at Michelle. They were frantic, charged, excited even. And watching them, I doubted myself. These were not the actions of someone involved. Unless they were better at keeping secrets than me.

As they bustled around resetting the tables with the maps and notes, I watched them in turn. Adam was a man who'd gifted nappies and wipes. He was considerate, and during this ordeal he and I had drawn close. But then, you keep your enemies close, don't you? Logically, it couldn't be him, he drove me to the north, drove me home. It was impossible for him to be in two places at once. I had to rule Jack out too; he didn't have it in him. He was too chaotic, too heart-on-his-sleeve. That left Michelle. My best friend, the closest thing to family I had. She couldn't have children of her own, but she was going to be a second mum to my baby. I wondered again, a niggling thread that I couldn't help but pull on, was that enough?

No sooner had I thought it than she turned, a map in her hand.

'We'll get everyone back to help us find her, Em.'

I nodded. She was also the one who drove to Middlesbrough, she was the one chasing leads, she set up the group and spent a night in the cells, all for me. It wasn't her. It wasn't any of them. I felt terrible for thinking it even for a moment.

But someone did kill Lucas, someone did then take my daughter, and their name was somewhere in this room, somewhere on the list Myers made me rewrite. It had to be. Pulling it from my pocket, I approached the whiteboards and began to write.

'What are you doing?' Adam asked.

'Detective Myers asked me to write a list of anyone and everyone who was a link between me and Lucas. I'm just putting it up so we can all see.'

Setting to my task, I began to scribble down the names, and I was so caught up in feeling like I was doing something to help, I didn't notice Jack come and stand behind me.

'Is that my name scribbled out?' he said.

I crumpled the piece of paper in my hand. 'No.'

'I saw it, Em, and Adam's and Michelle's. Why did you write our names down?'

'I-I just . . .' I began, but I couldn't find the right words.

'You think we could have anything to do with this?' he asked. The hurt in his voice, on his face, told me I had made a huge mistake in thinking they could possibly be involved.

'No, of course I don't.'

'But our names are on it?' he said.

'I just, I'm a mess, I don't know what I'm thinking.'

'We've done nothing but try and be there for you, Emily. We've done everything we possibly can to support you through this. We're grieving too. We love that little girl as well, and we love you. How could you think—'

'I'm not thinking! I'm just afraid. I read the words "those involved are those closest", and I got confused. I'm sorry.'

'You're sorry?' Jack said.

'Hey, love, calm down.' Adam placed a hand on Jack's arm to reassure him. 'It's OK, Em's been under a lot of pressure,' he said, but I could tell he was hurt too. 'Let's forget it and focus on finding out who really has her. We all want the same thing here.'

Jack nodded but didn't look at me before going back to the table and the maps. Adam flashed me a half-smile, masking his own hurt, before joining his husband.

I turned my attention to Michelle, who looked away when our eyes met.

'Michelle, I—'

'I'm going to get some air,' she said.

I continued to write. Then, with the silence pressing, I stepped back and looked from the new list to the other names written over the past few days, trying to find a link. Each name had a small memory attached, and I wrestled to see if they could be involved somehow. Lucas had an old college friend by the name of Gary, a slight, red-headed man with the boundless energy of a puppy. I knew he lived somewhere in the Midlands. Birmingham, I thought. It wasn't listed as a place of interest. And I highly suspected someone like him had a gaggle of children, more than enough. Then there was Kate, Lucas's cousin. I dismissed her too. I'd only met her once, but she was an active member of the church. I couldn't see her being involved. Lucas's ex was next on my list. She lived in the Middlesbrough area, but if she was involved Myers would know. So, I had to assume it couldn't be her. Then, for a brief moment, Lucas came into my mind. A memory of us happy, laughing. I had to push down the fact that someone had killed him.

Round and round I went, looking at names, places, trying to find someone who pulled it together for me. That link between Lucas and me. I couldn't find it, and, screwing up the piece of paper, I threw it at the whiteboard.

'Em?' Adam said, coming over to me and gently placing a hand on my shoulder.

'Sorry.'

'Don't be. I wish we could do more.'

'You're doing so much,' I said. 'I'm so sorry I doubted you, and you,' I said, looking at Jack, who gave me a weak smile.

'We won't give up,' Jack said. 'We love you, Em. I'm sorry I reacted so badly.'

'You had every right.'

Jack walked towards me and gave me a hug, Adam did too, and for a moment we just stood hugging one another. With my head turned to the window, I looked outside and saw Michelle smoking a cigarette. She didn't know I was looking, and I saw her wipe a tear. I wanted to hug her too, tell her I was sorry, and I would, when she was ready.

'Thank you,' I said as our embrace ended. 'Boys, is it OK if I have a moment?'

'Of course, we'll make us all a coffee,' Adam said, leaving the conservatory, taking Jack with him.

I didn't know why I asked them to leave, but I needed the quiet. A moment to myself to try to process everything. Since the day I woke, I had seldom had a moment to try to let my overworked and battered mind catch up.

Taking a few deep breaths, I calmed myself and looked at the board once more. If not names, then places. I might not be able to work out who took her from Lucas, I thought, but I might be able to work out where they are.

As I looked, the words once again jumbled into nonsense in my head. My phone began to vibrate in my back pocket. I pulled it out and saw that it was Myers calling. I knew I needed to answer, but I was paralysed — until that voice in my head that kept me alive when I was young kicked in. Telling me to act.

'Hello?' I said, my voice tight and afraid.

'We haven't found her, not yet,' he said, knowing that it was the only thing I had on my mind.

'Oh,' I said, finding a chair and sitting, and I wasn't sure if I was disappointed or relieved. 'What is it, then? Have you found something?'

'No, did you write your list?'

'Yes, I can send it over.'

'That would be great, thank you. Emily, is Michelle with you yet? I heard she was arrested.'

'She was, and yes, she's with me now.'

'Great. Great . . .' He trailed off, and, like with Michelle when she was in Middlesbrough, I thought the line had gone dead.

'Hello? Detective Myers? Are you there?'

'Sorry. Yes, I'm still here.'

'Why are you asking about Michelle, Detective Myers?'

'I just wanted to make sure she got back OK,' he said, but there was a hesitation in his voice. 'I've spoken to Middlesbrough police about arresting her, it was out of order.'

'Yes, it was.'

'Can you send me the list?' he asked.

'I'll message it over now.'

'OK. Speak soon,' he said, hanging up the phone. Doing as he asked, I typed all the names into a message to send to him. I didn't add my friends' names to that list, but his questions around the whereabouts of Michelle niggled. Was he being caring, or was it something more?

Looking outside, I watched as my best friend lit and then smoked a second cigarette. She had one arm across her body, the other holding the lit cigarette up in the air. She was a million miles away. And now I wondered why. Tired perhaps, stressed certainly, but could it be something more? Could my fear, the one I pushed away as paranoia, have something to it? It had to, otherwise why would Myers want to know if Michelle was with me?

CHAPTER THIRTY-FOUR

Jack had to go back to work, and, even though I knew Michelle could stay with me, she opted to leave too. She could barely look me in the eye. They hugged me goodbye, telling me they would come back later, but I wasn't sure if I believed them. The phone call with Myers had left me feeling guarded.

After they were gone, Adam insisted several times that it was all right and that all was forgiven. But after another hour of scanning the board, exhausting my efforts to find something new, I told him I wanted to be alone with my thoughts.

'I understand. What you're going through, I can't imagine me or Jack or Michelle coping as well as you are.'

'I don't feel like I'm coping.'

'You are.'

'I just can't make it make sense, Adam. Lucas took her. But now he's dead.'

'I can't make it make sense either. You need to hang on to hope.'

'Hope isn't a friend.'

'In this case, it is. Think about it, she was there at that house with him, they have proof of that, right?'

I nodded.

'But the police said that things are now missing?'

'Yes, food, bottles. There was evidence that she was there, but nothing was left.'

'Exactly, everything was taken, which meant they needed it — for her.'

'But who? Who has my girl?'

'They'll find that link to Lucas, the person who probably planned this with him. And they'll find the reason all this has happened to you, and her.'

I nodded, and I almost blurted out that I knew the reason. This happened because I killed my sister in 2008, my mother went to jail for it and Lucas found out my secret. He must have told someone, confided in them, and together they planned to take my daughter away, fearing I would kill her too. But why Lucas had to die, I didn't know. I was missing something.

And then, Michelle came back to mind.

Adam left, kissing me on the cheek before stepping outside to fend off the reporters. He didn't look back as he closed the door, taking the noise and chaos with him. Not knowing what to do, I stood in the conservatory, looking at the photo Adam had sent me of my baby. If I'd gone to term, I thought, my baby would be a day old now. We should be in hospital, her skin on mine. She should be feeding from my body and bonding with the sound of my voice. I should be surrounded by those who loved me. I should have a hundred photographs of my little girl already. It should be the best twenty-four hours of my life. Not this. Not this.

I suddenly felt exhausted, and slumped onto a nearby chair. I had fought so hard to keep it together, to keep moving, to try to be proactive, but I was hollowed out, too tired to do anything but weep, and, burying my head in my hands, I did exactly that. I cried until my head ached, I cried until my eyes burned, until I had nothing left to cry. And in the silence after, I felt something in the room. Looking up, I came eye to eye with my sister. She was standing closer to me than ever before. So close I could reach out and grab her. She didn't blink, just like after she died. Her glassy, lifeless eyes bored into mine. I could see the betrayal, the rage in them. I could see the pain.

'Why are you here?' I asked. 'What do you want, Fry? I can't go back, I can't fix it.'

She didn't speak, but looked at me in that way she did when she was hiding from Mother, her eyes unblinking, full of fear. I couldn't bear to look, so I picked myself up and escaped to the kitchen. With shaky hands, I grabbed a glass of water and took a drink. I'd expected her to be gone when I turned back to the conservatory, but she'd followed me. She'd never followed me before.

'What do you want!?' I shouted, and still she didn't move. 'Just leave me alone!'

I threw my glass at her, and as soon as it left my hands she was gone. The glass hit the floor, shattering into a thousand pieces, and the sound of it snapped me out of my rage.

CHAPTER THIRTY-FIVE

Then — 23 December

The pain she felt after Mother hit her hurt a lot more than she let on, and all night it raged painfully, robbing her of sleep. Freya slept on, deep and peaceful, even though she'd caused Mother's outburst, even though she'd caused most of them. It seemed to Emily that maybe Freya didn't care as much as she thought. Maybe she was selfish, just like Mother. As the night took hold, Mother started mumbling. Emily couldn't make out what was being said, but it was her, speaking to no one, speaking to herself. Mother hadn't spoken to herself for a long time, and Emily had to wonder why she had started again. When Mother started talking to herself, she became more absent, more unpredictable, more frightening. But Freya had been a baby the last time, and deep down Mother had known that, so she managed it. Now Freya was bigger. Emily was bigger too, and she was afraid for what that might mean. Even when Mother stopped talking, every groan in the old house snapped her into a state of readiness.

The night dragged on, and Emily fought to stay awake. After what felt like an eternity, a new day came in, barely any warmer than the night, but now cloudless. Although she had lost sense of time, the night breaking into indistinct chunks in her memory, she was sure that at no point did she fall asleep. She hadn't heard the front door open or close, so Mother was still in the house somewhere. She had to keep Freya quiet, and she felt bad for snapping at her the night before.

As the weak winter sun rose and bled through the thin curtains, it lit Freya and she began to stir. Before she fully woke, Emily got up, turned on the Christmas lights and jumped back into bed, pretending to be asleep. She watched through one partly open eye as Freya stretched and then sat up, taking in the lights, her little face illuminated by them. Freya looked over to Emily, and Emily fake stirred awake also.

'The lights are on. You said we couldn't have them on very often.'

'I know.'

'Then why?'

'I didn't turn them on.'

'What? Then who did? Mother?'

'No, Mother wouldn't do that. It must have been him.'

'Who?' Freya said.

'Him, Santa, or at least one of his helpers.'

'Santa? Santa was here?' Freya said, her face widening into a beaming smile.

'It must have been. It is Christmas Eve tomorrow, after all.'

'Christmas Eve!'

It broke Emily's heart that her sister had forgotten how close they were to Christmas Day. She needed to do something about it. Freya needed a gift. Something to unwrap, something to show she was loved and noticed and cared for. Deep down, Emily hoped that she too would get a gift, but she couldn't say aloud what it was she wanted.

'How did you sleep, Fry?'

'OK. My arm stings, and I've got a headache.'

'You probably need a big drink,' Emily said, still feeling guilty that Freya had cut her arm giving her food. Jumping out of bed and shuffling over to her younger sister, Emily peeled back the makeshift bandage. The fabric was stuck to her wound and Freya yelped as Emily pulled it free. The cut was small, not too deep, but it looked angry, a little swollen. It looked infected. At school, before they broke up for the end of term, Emily had learned about first aid, and she knew that cuts needed to be cleaned properly. Once Freya's was clean it would heal better and hurt less.

'Come on.'

'What are we doing?'

'I need to clean your cut, put a fresh bandage or something on it. But we have to be really, really quiet, quieter than we usually would. Follow me.'

Emily turned off the Christmas lights before slowly opening the bedroom door and peeking out into the dim hall. The door to Mother's room was shut. Gesturing for Freya to follow, Emily stepped out and they began to slowly, carefully make their way towards the stairs, both instinctively stepping over a spot in the floorboards that squeaked angrily. As they descended into the gloom of the lower part of the house, which the sun had yet to find, Emily shivered, and, taking her sister's hand, she pulled her close as she moved towards the kitchen.

Opening the door, Emily was temporarily blinded by the cresting sun that was dragging itself over the roof of the shed. Without waiting for her eyes to adjust, she pulled Freya into the kitchen, and quietly closed the door behind them.

'We still need to keep quiet, OK?' she whispered. Freya nodded. 'Get yourself a cup of water from the sink, I'm going to find something to clean your cut with.'

'Will it hurt?' Freya asked, suddenly unsure.

'A little, maybe, but it's for the best. Now, drink, it will help with your headache.'

As Freya found a cup and poured herself some water, Emily searched in the cupboards for something she could use to dress her sister's arm, a box of plasters maybe, or a small first aid kit, but it was hopeless. The cupboards were bare. Knowing it was better than nothing, she told Freya to come over to the sink, and she rinsed her wound with cold water. She was close enough to Freya now to feel her body heat. She looked at her sister. Her eyes were heavy, with dark rings around them. Drying her hands, Emily felt her sister's forehead. She was hot to the touch, despite being in a room barely warm enough to stand in.

'Freya, do you feel OK?'

'Just a headache, and I'm a little tired.'

'OK. We still have some food, yes?'

'I'm not hungry.'

'Well, how about we get you back to bed? I'm sure with a little more sleep you'll feel right as rain.' Emily hoped Freya didn't sense the tightness in her voice, the worry. If Freya got poorly, Mother would be angry. Emily needed to find something to make her sister better.

In their bedroom, as Emily tucked Freya into bed, the bedroom door opened and Mother stood looking in. Emily turned to face her, frightened by her presence but holding her eye.

'Come downstairs,' Mother said before turning and leaving.

'Stay here,' Emily said to her sister.

Grabbing the knife, she made her way down, each step more terrifying than the last. Reaching the bottom step, she squeezed the knife in her pocket for comfort and then walked into the kitchen. Mother was sitting by the back door, smoking.

'I hit you,' she said. Not a question, more of a statement. 'You left the shed, ruined my evening and I hit you.'

'Yes,' Emily managed to say, and Mother turned to face her. She wasn't angry, as Emily thought she would be, but sad.

'Does it hurt?' Mother asked, looking at the bruise on Emily's cheek.

'No,' she lied.

Mother nodded. 'Do you remember that Christmas, when you were maybe four, before Freya. When it snowed, and we made a sledge out of a bin lid and played in the street?'

Emily thought, but she couldn't remember. She must have been too young.

'No, I can't remember it,' she said.

'Shame. I liked life back then. Before Freya was born, you and me, it was enough,' Mother said, stubbing out her cigarette. 'Emily, ever wish you could turn back the clock, do things different?'

'Mother?' Emily said, unsure of how else to answer. 'Mother? Have we got any medicine?'

'What?' Mother said, and Emily regretted asking, for Sad Mother faded and Angry Mother returned. 'I'm trying to open up to you, and you're asking me for things. You're a selfish little shit.'

'I'm sorry, Mother, it's just Freya—'

'Will you shut up about your fucking sister?'

'I'm sorry.'

'Get out of my sight, before I put you back in the shed.'

'Mother, we can have a Christmas like that again, we can play on bin lids.'

Mother looked at Emily, half smiled, then grabbed and lit another cigarette. Turning her attention to the window, she whispered, 'I wish that was possible.'

'It is, I promise. Me and Freya, we'll be good, and you can be happy again.'

'I don't know how to do that anymore.'

'I'll help you.'

'No, Bebe, you can't.'

Mother lowered her head and mumbled something under her breath, something Emily couldn't hear.

'Mother?'

'You used to be so small. Now look at you, where is the time going?'

'Mother, are you OK?'

'I know she let you out of the shed.'

'Pardon?'

'She let you out, she disobeyed me.'

'No, I told her to—'

'Your duty to her is admirable. But I know that she causes all of our issues. I bet it was her at the window last night. Am I right?'

Emily didn't answer, and Mother nodded.

'Bebe, is it wrong that I sometimes wish she wasn't born? That it was just you and me? I know you won't remember most of it, but do you remember any at all?'

'Yes,' Emily said.

'There were some good times, weren't there?'

'The best. I miss them,' Emily answered honestly.

'Me too. Do *you* wish she wasn't born?'

'Sometimes,' Emily said, a tear escaping.

'Good,' Mother said, and looked at Emily in a way she couldn't quite understand, as if they'd agreed on something, and, before she could ask her what it meant, Mother got up and left the room.

CHAPTER THIRTY-SIX

As day turned into night, I waited for my sister to come back to me. I wanted to say sorry for throwing the glass. For shouting at her, for being afraid of her. I wanted to say sorry for her death, but she didn't come. And, feeling powerless, I rang Myers for an update. As I dialled his number, I felt sick. What if he had news, and was trying to find a way to break it to me? What if he said he was coming to my house, as there had been a development. Fear rattled through me, but I rang anyway. The phone rang and rang, and I counted each one. He picked up on the seventh.

'Emily.'

'Hello, Detective Myers.'

'Are you OK?'

'Yes, I just . . . I wanted an update.'

'I see.'

'Have you found anything?'

'We're looking into everyone on your list, cross-referencing it with what we have. So far, nothing has come up. But rest assured, we have an entire team looking for your daughter, and as soon as I have anything you'll be the first to know.'

'Sorry, of course, I shouldn't have called.'

'It's OK, I understand.'

'OK,' I said, my voice tightening as I tried not to cry.

'Emily, I know this is hard. No, that's not the right word. I know this is unbearable. I understand — at least, empathise. I have a girl myself.'

'You do?'

'Yes.'

'How old?'

'I'm not sure—'

'Please?' I begged.

He hesitated, no doubt weighing up whether it was right or wrong to talk about his own daughter. 'She's seven.'

'What's her name?'

'Molly.'

'That's a nice name.'

'If Molly was missing, I would lose my mind. I won't stop until we find Freya. And I know what you're thinking, but there's no evidence to say she's come to any harm. Someone has her, someone close to Lucas. We'll find them.'

'Thank you,' I said, my words strangled as I fought not to cry.

'Emily, is anyone with you? I'm not sure you should be alone.'

'No, but I'm OK.'

'You should get a friend over, maybe Michelle. I suspect the nights are harder to cope with.'

'They are. I will, thank you.'

'I'll be in touch.'

Myers hung up, and somehow knowing he was a father made me trust him more, like he understood the pain I was in. And I was thankful he had told me. But something else stuck in my mind: why did he mention Michelle again? That niggle I'd felt resurfaced and I wondered, where was she right now? Remembering that Michelle had shared her location with me, I opened the app and looked to see if her notifications were still on. It told me she was at home. I could ring her, ask her to come over, as Myers suggested; but instead

I got up, put on my shoes and a light jacket, and left my house via the garden to avoid the press. Once I was through the wooded area behind my house, I put my head down and walked in the direction of Michelle's. The sweltering summer night air felt cloying and the stars were covered in thick clouds. It was a fifteen-minute walk to her house, fifteen minutes to work out what I would do next.

Less than three minutes into my journey, I had made up my mind. I wouldn't knock on her door, seek comfort, because my gut told me Michelle knew something. Myers's interest in her told me as much. I would find somewhere to watch her, to see what she was up to.

Myers was suspicious, and so was I. After all, as it said on the board, most of the time it's those closest to us that we should look out for.

CHAPTER THIRTY-SEVEN

By the time I'd arrived on Michelle's road, the thick clouds had begun to rumble and then shoot angry lightning across the night sky. Soon the rain would come, and, as I drew closer to her front door, the first spits of a downpour began.

Staying on the other side of the road, partially obscured by a van, I looked at my friend's house. The lights were out. It looked empty. I quickly checked my phone and she hadn't moved. But that didn't mean she was with her phone. Maybe she knew I would look, maybe she left it behind and was now with my little girl somewhere. Even thinking it felt weird. This was Michelle, my best friend. But she couldn't even look at me earlier. She left the room, didn't she? Said she needed air. Maybe she was worried I would be able to tell. Maybe she wondered if I already knew. And then it hit me: if that was true, she might have fled already. Taken my baby girl and gone somewhere else.

Sickness began to swell within me at the thought of her holding my daughter, pretending to be her mother. Freya would never know the truth. She would never know me. I had a choice: I could ring Myers and tell him my worries, which were probably in line with his. But if Michelle had fled, time wasn't on our side, and, as far as I was aware, Myers was still up north.

I needed to do something.

I chose badly once before. I wouldn't make that mistake again.

Keeping my eyes fixed on Michelle's lifeless house, I stalked towards it, crossing the road and passing by her front door. Three houses down there was a cut between the homes that led to the back gardens. The rain was beginning to beat down, the static drowning out all other sound. It reminded me of that Christmas. I pushed the memory down, all the way down.

At the end of the passage, I turned right and was now behind the three houses I had walked past. The narrow walkway and high fences blocked me from view on all sides. The only way someone would know I was here would be if they walked along the path. And with the rain as it was, and the time of night, I felt safe.

I stopped outside the back of Michelle's house and, finding a gap between the wooden panels of her back fence, I looked through to her house. As with the front, the back was completely dark. Part of me hoped I would see her with my daughter. If she was there, I would smash my way into that house, and I would take her from Michelle, even if I had to hurt her to do so. Then, I would hold my daughter in my arms for the first time.

I stopped myself seeing that version of things. I reminded myself, hope was not a friend.

I tried to open the back gate but it was locked. So, reaching over the top, I fumbled until I felt a bolt. I fought to wiggle it out, the effort stretching my abdomen until I was sure a stitch would pop. Thankfully, the bolt soon came free and the gate opened.

Pausing to catch my breath, I listened for any suggestion that my breaking and entering had aroused attention. Nothing but the thrumming rain.

Opening the gate wider, I stepped inside, and, as I closed it behind me, a flash of lightning streaked across the sky and lit up the garden. Fearing I had been seen from one of the other houses, I stepped towards Michelle's shed and tucked myself behind it, my eyes trained on the house. I needed to get in somehow, to find out if there was anything that would tell me where she had gone. I knew I would get into trouble for it, but if I rang the police and waited for Myers it would be too late. Michelle could be anywhere.

Feeling sure no one saw me, I moved again, edging ever closer to her back door. I picked a large stone out of her rockery, and, confident it would do the job, I raised it, ready to smash the glass. I would use the thunderstorm in my favour, and I waited, poised, for the next rumble of thunder. It felt like an eternity, the rain pummelling me, making it hard to see, but then the rumble began. As it built I raised my arm higher, and, just as I was about to let the stone explode from my hand, a light came on inside Michelle's house. Panicking, I turned away from the door and pressed myself into the wall, hoping to God she didn't decide to step into the garden. If she did, she would find me, and I didn't know what would happen.

Another light came on, this one closer, and the garden was flooded with the spill from it. She was in the kitchen. I knew it was risky, I knew she might see me, but I needed to look. I needed to see if my little girl was in her arms. Leaning away from the wall, I saw her standing in the kitchen, both of her hands at her sides, her head low. I watched as she began to cry, her shoulders bobbing up and down. I could even hear her sobs over the rain. Daring to get closer still, I looked through the back door and directly into her living room. There were no baby things, no toys, no nappies or bottles or anything that would be associated with my daughter. Michelle's house was exactly the same as it had always been. Nothing had changed.

I stepped back and watched as my friend continued to sob. She looked heartbroken, devastated, and I didn't know why. Above me, lightning danced across the night once more, but Michelle didn't look up. She stayed there, head in her hands, crying.

'Hey!' a voice shouted from my right. 'Hey, what are you doing?'

I looked up and saw an older lady hanging half out of a bedroom window, staring down at me.

'I'm calling the police,' she said, dipping back inside, and I began to run, not stopping until I was close to my house once more, my wound screaming at me for the effort. The darkness was my friend, and I was sure no one had seen me and I hadn't been followed.

CHAPTER THIRTY-EIGHT

Then — 23 December

Outside, the world was black, pitch black, the kind of darkness that Emily found both freeing and terrifying in equal measure. She knew that she and Freya were usually left alone at night. Once it was dark, Mother seldom came to them for anything. But, despite knowing they had that freedom, Emily couldn't enjoy it. Freya was still shivering, still drifting in and out of sleep. Her skin was hot to the touch, but when she was awake she complained that she was freezing. And more than that, the look Mother gave Emily lingered. Emily didn't know what to do, so as the hours ticked by, long and cold and lonely, she stayed with her sister, stroking her hair, trying to comfort her. And still the thought pulled like a hangnail, small and harmless at first, but as it tugged it tore into the skin, making it hurt, drawing blood. And the unthinkable idea that was in her mind kept wanting to climb out of the new wound.

As the lights from the houses across the road began to go out, she heard Mother moving about in her room. Emily watched her bedroom door, waiting to see the handle turn. But Mother didn't come in. She left her room, thudded across the hallway, down the stairs and out the front door, slamming it behind her. Emily stood and went to the window. She watched Mother tramp down the road, her steps unsteady, until she turned a corner and was gone, almost as if the night had swallowed her whole. She knew it was a good thing Mother didn't come in. She knew she could take better care of her sister than Mother would, she had done so for years. But, in that moment, Emily needed her to tell her everything was going to be OK. She needed her mummy.

Returning to her sister's side, she resumed the job of stroking her hair as she slept, and in the silence, in the stillness, Emily closed her eyes and daydreamed of how life could be. She pictured herself and Mother downstairs watching Christmas movies, eating popcorn, drinking hot chocolate, and cuddling under a blanket. She almost heard a laugh as Mother told a joke. She almost felt Mother's warmth as she pulled her in for a cuddle.

In the daydream there was no Freya in sight.

Opening her eyes, Emily felt the cold wash over her once more, and, leaving her sister's side, she switched on the Christmas lights. As they began to gently flash green, red, orange, white, Freya reacted, a small squeezing of her eyes, before drifting off again. Emily knew that when Mother came home she would see the lights from the street, but she didn't care, she needed to have a Christmas. She needed something that reminded her of when she was little, when Mother was happy. With Christmas Eve only hours away, Emily reasoned that surely, surely, Mother would understand. Surely she would want the same thing.

'Em?' Freya said, turning to her sister, and even in the flickering Christmas tree lights Emily could see her complexion was paler than usual.

'Hey, Fry. How are you feeling?'

'I'm OK. Tired.'

'You should rest.'

'Is it Christmas yet? Has Santa come back?'

'One more sleep. Rest now, so you're well again for Christmas Day.'

'Em?'

'Yes?'

'Will Mother be with us for Christmas? I mean, will we spend it together, the three of us?'

'I hope so,' Emily said, and she did hope, but she didn't believe it would happen. It couldn't happen, not unless . . .

The knife felt hot in her pocket.

'Now sleep, and when you wake you'll feel better.'

'And I'll be closer to Santa's visit.'

'Yes, you will,' Emily said.

'Em?'

'Yes?'

'Thank you for taking care of me.'

'Go to sleep,' she replied, feeling guilt for her thoughts.

Within minutes, Freya was asleep once more, and Em returned to duty, stroking her hair. At some point, she too fell asleep, because when she woke she was lying on the floor beside Freya's bed. At first, she couldn't place what startled her awake, but then she heard Mother inside the house, moving around downstairs. And then silence.

Getting out of bed, Emily moved towards the door and listened. She could hear crying coming from Mother's room and felt the urge to see if she was OK. She opened her door a crack, just enough to see into the hallway. The streetlight outside the front of the house cast just enough of its orange glow for her to see that Mother's door was ajar. All was quiet, besides Mother's muffled sobs.

She tiptoed to Mother's room and looked inside. It was dark, but she could see the shape of Mother on the edge of the bed, head low, hands clasped in her lap. She opened the door wider, and light from the streetlights flooded in.

'Mother?'

Mother jumped and turned quickly to Emily, startling her too.

'What do you want?'

'I heard crying.'

Mother opened her mouth to say something, then lowered her head.

'Has something happened?' Emily asked, daring to take a step inside Mother's sanctuary.

'I'm OK,' Mother said.

'I just . . . I heard crying,' she said again.

'Don't worry, Bebe. Go back to bed.'

Courage stirred in her stomach, and she took another step towards her fragile mother. 'Mother, I'm eleven now, I can help, if there's something I can do to make it go back to how it was.'

Mother looked up at Emily and, for the first time in as long as she could remember, Mother smiled at her. It was a kind, loving smile, one that felt alien and yet somehow familiar.

'You're growing up so fast. Becoming a little lady.'

Emily nodded, unsure of what to say or do.

'Come here.'

Emily hesitated.

'It's OK, come here.'

Tentatively, Emily walked to her mother's bed and stood beside it, her body rigid, worried that if she did or said anything to provoke her Mother's tenderness would slip away.

'Sit.' Emily did, and Mother took her hand in hers. 'I'm sorry you hear me cry sometimes. This time of year, it's hard.'

'Why?'

'Even at eleven, you're too young to understand.'

'I want to,' Emily said.

'I know. But no, not this.'

'I want you to be happy again. I want me to be happy too.'

'I know, so do I, but I don't know how we can go back.'

'Mother?'

'Bebe?'

'Can I tell you a secret?' Emily asked, wondering if when she spoke it she would be punished for it.

'You can tell me anything,' Mother said, and Emily wanted to label her as Fake Mother, but this time she didn't think Mother was being fake.

'Is it OK that sometimes I wish that Freya was somewhere else, someone else's problem?'

'Do you hate her?' Mother asked, and Emily didn't know how to answer at first.

'Yes and no,' she said.

'Me too,' Mother replied.

Emily nodded and lowered her head, and that thought, that hangnail, pulled harder.

Mother moved, and Emily panicked for a split second, expecting to be hit. Instead, Mother wrapped her arms around her and hugged her tight. Emily felt her mother begin to bob, then she heard her crying. And she began to cry too. She knew what this was, this moment between her and her mother. It wasn't a turning of a corner, it wasn't the start of a new life, it was just a moment, but it gave her hope anyway. And she held on to it as tight as she held on to Mother.

'Mummy,' Emily said, her words muffled in Mother's nightdress. 'Please be around for Christmas, please.'

'The three of us?' she asked.

'Yes, I mean, it has to be, doesn't it?' Emily said, wanting Mother to tell her that it did, that the three of them had to work. But she didn't say either way. Instead, she got to her feet and began to leave the room. 'Mummy, it has to be?'

'I guess,' she said.

'I wish I could do something.'

'So, do something,' Mother said, giving Emily that look again, as if to tell her they both knew what that 'something' should be.

'Mummy?'

'Do something,' she said again.

Emily froze. Had Mother just asked her to do what she thought she had?

'I need a cigarette,' Mother said.

As Mother walked down the hallway, towards the stairs, Emily didn't move, didn't blink. She had learned over the past few years that Mother had many sides: kind, sad, quiet, fake, monster. And as the silent thought they both shared resurfaced, it was the first time she understood that maybe, just maybe, she was more like Mother than she had realised.

CHAPTER THIRTY-NINE

Sixteen days missing

I didn't know what to make of seeing Michelle so distraught, and, with sleep not coming, I spent the time going over it in my mind, wondering why she was so sad. So devastatingly sad. I reasoned that it was guilt for her part in all of this. If I hadn't been left to walk home alone, then none of this would have happened. But the niggle of doubt remained and, as night became a new day, the sixteenth day of my daughter's life, I wondered if the tears were about something else entirely. Maybe the weight of hiding a secret was too much for Michelle. Maybe, just maybe, she was crying because she knew something I didn't about my daughter's fate.

I sat in the conservatory, staring out into the garden, watching the trees sway in the gentle breeze, nursing my third cup of coffee and looking at my phone every few seconds, hoping and not hoping in equal measure for it to ring. But no one called and nothing had been posted online. The few remaining press outside my house were sleepy and ready to go home.

Despite Myers's promise to call me, I was unable to bear the wait anymore. His phone went to voicemail. I didn't leave a message — he would see I called and get back to me — but I questioned why he didn't pick up. Questions, questions, and no answers in sight.

I went to dial again, feeling a compulsion to do so until he answered, thinking that maybe he was asleep or hadn't heard my call, but, as my thumb hovered over the phone, there was a knock at the door. My heart leaped into my throat and, despite knowing I needed to answer it, my legs felt hollow, unable to move. Whoever it was knocked again. This time my legs responded, and I staggered from the conservatory, through the hall and to the front door. From beyond, I could hear people talking, questions being thrown in the direction of whoever had come to see me, and as I opened the door I was shocked to see it was Michelle. I stood there stunned in full view of the press, and a fresh wave of noise erupted. Before I could speak, she bustled in and closed the door behind her.

'When will they just fuck off already!' she said.

'What are you doing here?' I blurted out before I could regain my composure.

'I needed to talk to you, about how I reacted last night.'

'Really?'

'Yes, but first let's make a cuppa.'

'Sure.'

Michelle didn't wait for me and made her way into the kitchen. I hung back, taking my time, watching her. If I'd not seen her crying in the night, I'd never have suspected a thing. She seemed like the Michelle I had always known, moving around my kitchen with ease. She was still troubled, I could tell as much by the furrow of her brow, but I wondered if she moved like a woman who had killed a man, a woman who had stolen a baby. I didn't know, I didn't trust my own judgement.

'Em? What's wrong?' she said when she saw me looking at her.

'Nothing, just a bad night's sleep.'

I joined her in the kitchen, and as she finished making the drinks she told me to sit down. I did as she asked and waited. She placed the cup of coffee on the table beside me and sat opposite.

'How are you holding up?'

'How do you think?' I said.

'Listen, Em, about my reaction. I shouldn't have left here last night like I did.'

I didn't respond.

'I just freaked out when you thought I could be involved, you know?'

I still didn't respond, trying to work out if she was being genuine in her apology or trying to throw me off the scent. What was that old saying, keep your friends close, but your enemies closer? I glanced past her, into the conservatory, the message loud and clear: *those closest*.

She saw me look.

And I wondered. If her neighbour had seen me in her garden in the night, maybe she'd seen me too. Maybe she was trying to mess with my head.

'Em, say something, please?'

'I don't know what to say,' I replied. 'Sorry, the storm last night, I could barely sleep,' I added, hoping to elicit a response. 'Did you hear it? The storm?'

'No,' she replied, unable to look me in the eye. 'I was asleep by then. Slept through it, thankfully.'

'Lucky you,' I said. It was all the proof I needed. She was hiding something.

She smiled at me, but it didn't reach her eyes, and I stared back at her. There was a flicker in her expression, as brief as one of those lightning flashes, but I saw it. And she fucking knew it too. Before I could say any more, she stood up, grabbed her cigarettes and went to stand in the garden to smoke.

I watched her walk away, blowing smoke into the air, not daring to look back at me, and I saw that in her haste she'd left her bag in the room. Keeping an eye on the garden, I slunk over, picked it up and moved further towards the kitchen side. When I was sure she wouldn't see me, I opened it and looked in. Part of me felt terrible for doing so, but I asked myself, why would Myers want to know where she was? Why would he ask twice? Why was she crying in the night, and why had she lied about being asleep? Rummaging, I felt her phone and grabbed it. It was locked.

'Shit.'

I tried her date of birth and a few obvious numbers, 4321, 9999 and the like, and nothing worked. Checking to make sure she wasn't looking, I went back into her bag to look for something else, something that could confirm my fears. Right at the bottom, my hand grabbed a piece of thick paper, and, pulling it out, I saw it was a cinema ticket.

It made me think of Lucas, of that night when he went to see a film with a friend. The night I was going to tell him I was pregnant. I looked at the date on the ticket — it was that same day.

Picking up Michelle's phone, I typed in the date on the ticket — nothing. And then I typed in Lucas's date of birth.

And the phone unlocked.

'What the fuck?'

Michelle was still smoking, her back to me. I opened her messages and scrolled through various names. Nothing jumped out. I looked through her WhatsApp, and again nothing. I tapped the archive button and saw several more conversations stored in there. Scrolling down, I saw a name I now knew I would find.

Lucas.

Opening the thread, I read their conversations in reverse order, scrolling backwards in time. They had messaged each other a lot. They were familiar with one another, really familiar. Slowing down my scrolling, I read a few messages.

We cannot do that again.

You said that the last time.

It would break her heart if she ever found out.

Emily and I are over. I want to be with you . . .

I scrolled back further and saw it wasn't the first time Michelle had said that they couldn't do it again. Some of the messages dated back to when Lucas and I were together.

Now I had a link between me and Lucas. That link was Michelle.

I thought back. Michelle not being able to have her own children. Michelle saying she'd tried to keep Freya when I was in hospital. Michelle being in Middlesbrough, knowing where Lucas was, disappearing before his body was found. And at the barbecue, before all this happened, she'd spoken of calling off a relationship, and, when Adam and I looked over, and she noticed us listening, she'd walked away, just as she'd done now, when she saw I knew she was lying.

She was his lover, she would know how to administer insulin, what doses to use; I'd learned from him too. And she was different. I thought it was because of her spending the night in a police cell, but, thinking about it, she had the look of someone who had killed. After all, I remembered looking the same way once. That was why she was crying in the night too; she was mourning her loss.

I wondered about that night at the barbecue. Michelle seemed drunk, but was she? Was she pretending, playing it up? I never asked what time everyone went home that night. I didn't know what she did after I left. Maybe she followed me, and either she or Lucas hit me, the other sticking me with a needle. Then, maybe Lucas had doubts about hiding, wanted to bring my daughter back to me, and Michelle made sure he couldn't. The whiteboard said *those closest*. No one was closer to me, no one.

Shoving the phone back in the bag, I put it back on the kitchen table and, taking out my phone, I dialled 999. I looked outside to where Michelle stood. She was staring back at me, tears streaming down her face. She knew.

I didn't move, didn't reply, but waited for her to come into the house. She knew, and yet she still tried to play innocent. As she stepped into the house, she saw the phone in my hand.

'Emily?'

I ignored her and spoke to the operator. 'Police please.'

'Emily, why are you calling the police? It isn't what—'

I lifted the phone to my ear and told them who I was, and that I needed them at my house. The operator continued to speak, but I didn't say any more; instead I placed the phone down on the table.

'Where is my daughter?' I said, my words barely a whisper.

'What?'

'Where is she?'

'Em, I don't know where she is.'

'Where is my fucking daughter!' I screamed, and Michelle stumbled backwards.

'Emily, I—'

'How long had you and Lucas planned this?'

'Planned what? Emily, it's not what you—'

'Where is my daughter!' I said, lunging at her, grabbing her by her shoulders and shoving her hard into the conservatory glass, so hard it cracked.

'I know what this looks like,' she said, trying to fight herself free. 'And I know I've done wrong. I shouldn't have slept with Lucas and I'm sorry, OK? I am. I fucked up.'

'Give her to me.'

Michelle managed to break free from my grip and stumbled outside, raising her hands in defence.

'Em, I don't know where she is, I promise you.'

'You said you wanted to keep her,' I said, bearing down on her.

'What?'

'When I woke, you said you wanted to keep—'

'Only until you woke up, Em. I wanted to keep her until you woke up, so you could have her back . . .'

'Stop fucking lying to me.'

'Em, I'm not.'

'Give her back to me!' I shouted again, lunging for her once more, but this time she was quicker than me. She managed to sidestep me, and I fell to the floor, white-hot pain flashing through my stomach.

'I know I did wrong, Emily. I know, but I didn't take her. I didn't. Shit!' she said, running back into the house and grabbing her bag. Before I could pull myself to my feet, she'd gone.

CHAPTER FORTY

Falling to the floor had torn two of my stitches and I was going to have to go to hospital, but I didn't want to, not until I had spoken to Myers.

'He's on his way, he's going to meet you at hospital,' a police officer told me as the paramedic loaded me onto a gurney and wheeled me through the house towards the front door. I didn't want to go outside and face the press again but I had no choice, and, as soon as the front door opened, they were true to form.

But I couldn't hear their questions, couldn't feel them pressing into me. All I could think about was how Michelle and Lucas had had an affair, how she had likely ruined my relationship with him and how they had planned to take my baby as their own. She knew where my daughter was, but seeing her in the night, crying and childless, I couldn't help but fear the worst.

An hour after Michelle had fled my house, I was unloaded from the ambulance and into the hospital, where a kind young doctor began to fix the mess I had caused — no, Michelle had caused. As she worked, Myers came into the room.

'How are you holding up?' he asked, sitting on a chair beside the gurney.

'You knew about the affair, didn't you?'

He nodded. 'Yes. We managed to get into Lucas's phone and found their correspondence. Did she tell you?'

'No, I looked on her phone,' I said, wincing as the doctor stitched me up again. 'She took my baby.'

'We don't know that.'

'Is that why she was arrested in Middlesbrough?'

Myers looked at the doctor, not wanting to talk in front of her, and she understood. 'I'll be a few more minutes.'

We sat in silence as the doctor finished patching me up. She told me that she had given me a top-up of my pain relief to help me relax, and I thanked her, despite not wanting to relax at all. I wanted to be out there, finding Michelle, finding my daughter. The doctor smiled and left the room. Once she was gone, Myers continued.

'Michelle was arrested in Middlesbrough because she wouldn't stay back and interfered with the investigation. With hindsight, she was afraid for Lucas, we think.'

'She knows,' I said, my voice granite hard. 'She knows,' I said again, my head feeling floaty, the pain gone. Whatever the doctor had given me, it was strong.

'We'll find her,' he said, and I didn't know which 'her' he was referring to — Michelle or my little girl? 'Now, rest. I'll keep you in the loop. We have everyone looking for both of them, Michelle and your little girl,' he added as I closed my eyes. It felt like when I first woke up after the attack. I was in hospital, and my daughter wasn't with me.

* * *

When I woke, Myers was gone. The sun was still high in the sky, so I assumed I'd only slept for a few hours. I was still in a liminal place, a mother who was not a mother, and my baby still wasn't with me. My first instinct when I woke was to move, run towards something, anything. As I jumped onto my feet, my stitches pulled and I winced. Then I heard it, the noise that must have woken me up. My phone vibrating.

At first I thought it was a message, or perhaps an incoming call, something about my baby, so I grabbed it quickly, only to discover when I picked it up that it was a stream of notifications from my various news apps. I opened the BBC one, and a title said, *Arrest made in the 'Finding Freya' case*. I opened the article and read, my eyes struggling to focus as they stirred into wakefulness. The article spoke of an arrest in connection with Freya, but it didn't mention Michelle by name. There were several highlighted links within the text, and I clicked on one that mentioned Lucas. It loaded a new page. It spoke of his death, but not of how he died. They didn't know he had been murdered. Going back, I scrolled to the related articles and saw one about me and my past. They didn't speculate that I was involved, but then the BBC wouldn't. I dared not look at what the tabloids were saying.

I pulled myself out of bed. My wound hurt, a lot, but I needed coffee, I needed my brain to work properly.

Then, in the corner of the room, I saw my sister watching me, and I didn't know what that meant.

Ignoring her, I walked towards the hospital window and looked outside into the car park below. I watched as a van approached, shortly followed by another, and a third. Men and women jumped out of the vehicles, set up cameras and began to talk into them. The press had come to the hospital to find me. I reasoned it was because of the arrest made in the case, but my gut told me something else had happened, and I needed to know what. I thought about leaving the hospital, making my way to the journalists to ask them, but as I fought with my fear I heard my phone vibrating, and turned back to where it sat on the small table in time to see the screen go dark. Grabbing it, I saw I'd had a missed call from Myers, and a few seconds later my phone told me he had left a voice message. My hands started to shake. I tapped to listen to the message and lifted the phone to my ear.

'Emily, it's Detective Myers. The press will be with you soon. Don't speak to them, and don't go anywhere. I'm coming back.'

I rang him back, but it went straight to voicemail. Something had happened, I could feel it. I opened the news articles; if something had happened outside of Michelle being arrested, it would be posted somewhere. If Michelle had told them something of interest, it wouldn't. I searched and searched, but nothing new was posted about my daughter. It had to mean Michelle had opened up.

Maybe Myers had my daughter.

Maybe he was bringing her to me.

I felt a fresh surge of hope. I moved back to the window, so I'd be able to see Myers approach. As I waited, looking out into the bright hot day, my phone vibrated again and, thinking it was Myers, I snatched it up. But it wasn't him, it was a news headline. I read it and tumbled onto the floor.

I wanted to scream, to cry, but my voice was gone. All I could do was stare at the few words that made up the headline. Six words that, now I had seen them, meant all hope, all chance, all purpose was gone.

Six small words.

BABY FOUND IN THE RIVER SKERNE

PART FIVE

CHAPTER FORTY-ONE

Baby found in the River Skerne.

A baby has been found in the River Skerne.

My baby has been found in the River Skerne.

As it replayed, over and over, I could hear my own internal monologue enjoying it. It mocked me, taunted me. She was gone, my baby was gone, and I didn't even get to meet her. She and I had never made eye contact. I'd never felt her skin on mine, her tiny hand wrapping around my finger. I'd never heard her voice. And I fucking hated myself for everything I was. I was the reason for it all. I'd asked Adam once if I was being punished, and he'd said I wasn't. But that wasn't true, I was being punished in the worst way possible. Hope was cruel, and cruelty had won again. And again, like when my sister died, I knew I couldn't stay here. So, before anyone could stop me, I grabbed my things and put on my clothes. I had to leave. I couldn't be in this world anymore.

Outside the hospital, a police car pulled up and Myers got out. He was coming to be with me, to try to reassure me, but I couldn't hear it, I couldn't hear anything ever again. So, before he entered the building, I left the room.

I made my way through the corridor and down the emergency stairs. The effort hurt like hell, but I didn't care.

I wanted to hide somewhere, like I did when I was eleven, only this time I didn't want to be found and saved, I wanted to die. Like I should have died then. If I had, a little girl, an innocent little girl, wouldn't have been made to suffer. As I slowly made my way down through the arteries of the hospital, my phone began to ring. It was Myers, no doubt trying to find out where I had gone. I looked at the display, but my thoughts were so jumbled I was unable to think of how to answer.

I kept moving until I found an exit. Alarms sounded as I pushed it open, but I kept moving, staggering into the heat, and I didn't look back until I'd found somewhere to hide, like I did after my sister died. Back then, the solitude, being connected with nature, saved me. It provided comfort in a life without any. I was ready to die that night, and I was ready now. So I kept moving.

Eventually, I came to a large wooded area and went deep into it. It was dark, cooler than the tarmacked streets, and quietly I moved through thick trees and brambles that snagged on my skin, scratching crimson lines into my bare legs, until I found a small dip in the ground, a hole in the earth, like when I was young. I sat in it and curled my legs up to my knees, just like I was eleven all over again. Back then, I shook because of the cold in the wildlands on that harsh winter night; now I shook with grief, with rage, with self-loathing. And, knowing I was too far into the woods for anyone to hear, I began to cry.

I wanted the earth to open up and swallow me whole and hide me for ever. I wanted it more than I wanted it when I was eleven. But back then, I was found, dragged back into the world and connected with my grandparents, who did a decent job of raising me. This time, there was no one to save me. My best friend was involved in my daughter's death, my grandparents were dead, and, even if there was someone, even if Adam or Jack rushed in to help me, I didn't want to be saved. I had failed to protect my own daughter. I deserved to die, and I needed to make sure I wouldn't be found. This time, I needed to ensure I truly connected with the earth. And I thought of the knife in the box in my wardrobe.

That knife that was a part of all this, of my sister's death, of my life after. It was a part of Lucas's death, of my daughter's. There were many ways I could do away with myself, but I felt it needed to be with that knife. Only that knife. It brought me into this life, it needed to end it too.

In my pocket, my phone rang and rang, but I ignored it. All I could think about was how I would get back into my home and end my suffering once and for all. Because once I was gone, I wouldn't see my sister anymore, wouldn't have to hear her questions. Once I was gone, I would be with my daughter for ever. Myers tried to call me again, and I hung up on him. Then I went online. I knew that I would learn more about how my daughter died, but I hoped that somewhere, somehow there was a new photograph of her. I wanted to see what my baby looked like before she left this earth, so that when I joined her I could find her in the afterlife. Assuming I wasn't going to hell for what I had done.

I needed that knife, assuming the pain I felt didn't kill me first.

CHAPTER FORTY-TWO

Then — 23 December

Emily sat on Mother's bed, alone, for the longest time, the knife resting in her hand, before she finally got up and returned to her own bedroom. Freya was asleep in her bed, her small body rising and falling with each breath.

Emily had worked hard to be invisible to the world, to go unseen, and out of duty she had taught her sister to do the same. Being invisible was going to serve her again. If she did it, if she changed their lives so she and Mother could be close again, just like before, no one would ever know. For those outside of the house, Emily and Freya barely existed. If she did it, she and Mother could leave, start again and live happy lives. Mother said for her to do something, Mother told her to fix it, so they could be happy once more.

She knew it was wrong, but if she did it, she also knew, Freya would no longer be afraid, no longer be so tired. No longer be hungry or cold. She would escape, and Emily would no longer be in trouble or at the mercy of Mother's wrath. Mother would be kind again, would know how to love again.

Trying not to disturb her, Emily moved quietly closer and looked down at her sister. She was still hot, still sweating.

If Mother saw that Freya was unwell, she would blame Emily for it, and the cycle would never end. And she would never get Mother back for Christmas.

Looking at the knife in her hand, she opened the blade, the snap of it locking into place somehow comforting. She held it up so the blade drew level with her sister, and Emily fought with herself not to cry. It wasn't Freya's fault, but she was to blame for it all. Emily thought about all the times she had got into trouble because of Freya. Stealing food because she was hungry. Breaking her out of the shed after she went into Mother's room. Taking the blame for her looking out of the window. Without Freya, none of it would have happened.

Mother told her to do something. She had to do something.

As she stood there, she thought about the future, and how she would actually be helping her sister. She asked herself, what kind of life would Freya have? They were destined to be miserable, unloved, until they were old enough to leave. Freya would soon be subjected to the cruellest of Mother's actions. She would experience pain and grief and fear. So much fear. If she did it, Freya wouldn't feel anything ever again. She too would be free from it.

Taking another step closer to the bed, Emily tightened her grip on the knife. Freya was fast asleep, deep and oblivious, and Emily knew that she would never know what happened.

Tears began to stream down her face. It was the only way they would ever be happy, but she still struggled with the idea of never seeing Freya again. It was more than duty, it was love. And that was why she had to do it, because she loved her sister, she loved her mother too, and this was the only way to set love free.

Freya moaned in her sleep, her fever having taken full hold, and Emily held her breath. If Freya woke, she didn't know if she could do it. The terror Freya would experience, the brief but blinding pain before she died, it was too cruel. But Freya didn't wake, she didn't open her eyes, she didn't see Emily or the knife. As she settled again, Emily pulled down the bedcovers.

Her sister's head lay at an awkward angle, exposing her slim neck. If she went in there, it would be quick, and Freya wouldn't feel any pain. One sharp movement and then, for her, there would be nothing. Freya would never feel hungry again, or afraid, or unloved. Raising the knife above her head, her hands shook, and she fought to control her breathing.

Mother's words echoed — *do something, do something, do something.*

One moment, one swift action, and everything would be OK.

One sharp moment, and everyone would win.

CHAPTER FORTY-THREE

As I waited for the sun to fade, hoping not to be found, I began to understand how my life was destined to be this way, to be full of grief, full of trauma, full of loss. I understood that I was always going to end up hiding in a ditch, waiting for night to come and a quiet moment to die. Waiting to join two girls I loved more than anything else.

When I fell pregnant, even though it was unplanned, I saw it as a way to start again, to reinvent myself as someone new. I would stop being the complicated woman, living in a big empty house that she didn't deserve, haunted by the ghost of a sister who she killed, because I would have a daughter to care for. A daughter who would be more important to me than life itself. I thought that I could raise my girl in a way that righted the wrongs of my past, I hoped for vindication. But, again, that was hope talking, cruel and twisted and malevolent hope. Now I could see I was always going to be punished. And I hated that my daughter was the focus of that punishment. She was innocent, she had done nothing wrong. I was the killer, I was the one who should have been found in a river. I wished, begged to swap places with her. But I knew that wasn't how it worked.

And yet, even though I knew it was true, that my baby was gone, a part of me still wanted to believe it wasn't. People die all the time in this world, the old and the young. That poor baby could be anyone's. I knew that hope wasn't good, hope didn't help or save anyone, but still it lingered, sticking to the darkest recesses of my mind, refusing to budge. I wanted to bang it out of my head, smash it out with a rock, but I knew, even if I did, it would still be there. Revelling in its cruelty. Hope provided a sense of warmth when the world was ice. It provided comfort on a bed of nails. Hope was there, back in the wildlands, when I was lost in the freezing-cold wilderness, alone. It was there, even after I had seen with my own two eyes that she was dead. Even at eleven I knew she wasn't coming back, and yet, as I wandered in the wilds, stumbling over brambles and heath, hope told me she was only unconscious. It told me to go back and hug her because she would be worried about me. It told me everything was going to be OK.

Hope lied.

And yet, I unlocked my phone anyway and searched for more details about the baby they'd found, because hope was telling me the same things it did before. As I typed *baby* and *River Skerne*, several posts leaped up. Details of who the baby was were not known, but every article I read gave my name. I googled where the Skerne was, and when I learned it was just outside Middlesbrough I knew it had to be her. But still, hope told me to keep looking. For what, I didn't know, but I did it anyway. I searched for something I could hang my hope on. I knew I wouldn't find it, but I carried on regardless. It was another form of punishment.

I read more articles, learned more details. She was found at just after one in the morning by a group of teenagers who were pissed and wandering the riverside. Nothing else was said about the baby, other than speculation that it was Freya, and that I had been notified. Myers had tried to contact me, at least, but I had run. There was no denying that it was my daughter they had found. And this evidence gripped that hope I had felt and butchered it with a knife. The hope in me began to fade, and it hurt like hell. I deserved as much. I continued to read, to search for things, but not to bring back hope. Instead, I wanted it to hurt so much that I didn't lose my conviction to end my life. Attached to the article about my daughter was another, which posed a question as to who took her away from me, and I opened it. I was mentioned first, and under my name was Michelle's, with a photo of the pair of us taken from Facebook. They knew of her arrest and reasoned we might have done it together. Lucas was next, with a picture of him smiling that was hard to look at. Further down I found a new article about the town where I grew up, the title a click-baiting 'Death on the Edge of the Wilds'. I began to read, wondering what link they had found, if any. They spoke of that Christmas, of how my sister had been found dead, of how I'd nearly died too, and of Mother, drunk and violent on her arrest. There was a video embedded in the article, and I tapped on the play button.

In it, a reporter stood on a familiar high street, the one from my youth. The shops were the same as back then, weather-beaten and tired. It was as if the wildlands were frozen in time.

In the video, people walked past, curious as to what was being filmed, but none interrupted. Then, someone in the background came towards the camera, a person wearing a long black top, sleeves rolled up in the heat, and a baseball hat. They were carrying two shopping bags in thin and sinewy arms. Seeing the camera, they hesitated, lowered their head and bustled out of shot.

I paused the video and, scrolling the timeline, I watched them again. I could barely make out their features, but something about them made the hairs on the back of my neck stand on end. An old feeling resurfaced, one I remembered from my childhood.

I watched it a third time, pausing it on several occasions to look at them. Finally it came to me, why I had reacted the way I did.

I pinched the screen and zoomed in on their arm. Running across it, close to the elbow, was a faded but clearly visible scar. Thick and messy, non-surgical. And I knew exactly how they got it. It was a scar I had given them sixteen years ago at Christmastime, and I knew because the knife that sat in my house was what caused it. I had carved that scar into that arm.

I'd assumed she was dead. But I could see her as clear as day. In the image, the person trying to not draw attention to herself was my mother.

I didn't know how Mother had discovered I was pregnant, or how she'd found me. I didn't know how it was connected to Lucas's death, but it must have been somehow. Mother did this. Vengeful Mother. Monster Mother. She'd taken my daughter, killed her because I'd done the same to her Freya.

I knew this Mother. I knew her well.

But apples don't fall far from trees, do they?

I could be a monster too.

Something primal flooded my veins, and I started the long walk back home, to collect my car and drive back to where this story all began, to the town that video was taken, where Mother had been captured on film. Back to the wildlands. My phone rang. Myers again. I hung up on him. I didn't want to talk to him, I didn't want to talk to anyone now, or ever again. But I did owe something to my friends, my new family. Opening my messages, I created a new message to Michelle. If it was Mother, then Michelle wasn't involved. I typed just two words and hit send, before turning my phone off.

Forgive me.

I needed that knife, but I wasn't going to hurt myself, not yet. Before that, before I left this earth to be with my little girl, to beg forgiveness of my sister, I was going to find my mother. The visit would be brief and bloody. She was presumed dead; I was going to make sure of it. And then after, I would hide in the wildlands and I would die too, and both of us would have paid our debts.

CHAPTER FORTY-FOUR

I wanted nothing more than to run home, get my car and drive to the only place I knew Mother would be. The video was from my hometown; she would be there, in that house, I just knew it. I was overcome with rage, and I wanted to capitalise on it before grief swept back over me once more. Mother would pay for my daughter's death, she would pay for what she made me do to my sister. She would pay, and then maybe I would feel some peace before I too had to pay.

It took me several hours to get home, and as I drew near, exhausted and in so much pain I could barely think, I could hear the bustle of people outside the front. The circus, no doubt enjoying the latest twist to their sordid tale. Careful to not be seen, I made my way through the small woodland to the rear of the house, to the back gate that led into the garden.

Lifting myself up to look over, I saw that the lights were on in the kitchen. Detective Myers was there with a uniformed officer. No doubt, after discovering I had fled the hospital, they had come looking for signs of my presence or a hint as to where I had gone. I would have to wait. Stepping back into the small woodland, I sat on the ground and rested against the trunk of a thick, ancient tree. As my heart rate returned to a slower pace, I thought of my girl. I wondered how she had died, if it had been quick, if she had any awareness of what was happening to her. I hoped she was too young to grasp the infiniteness of it. I hoped she simply drifted away. She was found in the river, but I hoped she'd died because of the cold, rather than drowning. I'd heard that dying of the cold was like falling asleep. I'd almost felt it once, that sense of drifting, it was peaceful. Everything just slowed down and eventually stopped. Thinking of her, in the water, floating to her end, pricked my eyes and tears began to fall. Silently they rolled down my cheek and dripped onto the hard, dry ground. Inside, I was wailing uncontrollably, screaming, begging, but outside I didn't make a sound. I would only speak to my daughter if I was lucky enough to find her in whatever came next.

I thought of Mother, of how she'd found me, of how she'd known I was about to have a baby, and I thought of Lucas. When we first found out, he'd offered to find her, to reintroduce her to our lives. I'd said no. Maybe he'd tried to anyway, and he'd found her, and she'd told him about my past, and my crime. Or maybe he never knew of what happened in the wildlands, maybe he was only trying to be a decent man, reconnecting me with my mother. Maybe it was out of guilt because he and Michelle were going to run away together. Again, questions, questions, and not an answer in sight.

But I would get my answers, I would pry them out of Mother before I let her die.

Whatever his reason, if he had spoken to her he had paid for it with his life. Somehow she'd known where to find me. I tried to remember her being there, in the underpass, when I was attacked. Would I have even recognised her if she'd walked straight past me? I had no doubt she'd assumed I wouldn't wake up from the insulin overdose, that I would stay in my coma and die. Then, with me gone, she could wait until after my funeral, and once life had moved on she'd have all the time in the world to target and kill Lucas. Poor Lucas, he was innocent in it all. I hoped he could forgive me also.

But I didn't stay in my coma, I woke, and it messed with her plans. I wondered, did she know about Michelle and Lucas? It was highly likely. After killing him, she would have wanted something to make sure no one ever looked at her. Michelle had lied, and that made her look guilty. And what about Myers finding out about my true identity? The press? Had Mother done it all?

I got up, my legs heavy and tired, and moved towards the gate once more. Looking over, I saw the house was quiet. Myers had gone. But still, I waited a moment, to be sure. Peering over, looking for movement, reminded me of the countless times I'd had to do something similar as a child, checking for Mother in the hallway of our small house. But I wasn't trying to avoid Mother anymore, I wanted the opposite. I wanted to look her in the eye, show her I was not afraid, and then end her life.

Opening the gate, I walked into the garden and made my way to the back door. It was locked. No doubt Myers or his colleague had made sure the house was secure. So, grabbing a ceramic plant pot containing a small shrub, I threw it at the glass in the door. As the glass exploded, I was sure one of the reporters would hear and would come round to investigate. Crawling through the hole in the pane, I moved quickly. Upstairs, I opened the wardrobe doors and pulled out the box, upending it on the bed. I took the knife in my hand and, just before leaving, I grabbed my daughter's bib, the only link I had to her. I wanted it with me when I had my vengeance, and when I died.

I ran back down and picked up my car keys. Moving to the front door, I looked out into the street. My car was a few houses down, on the other side of the road. Several vans were parked up directly outside. People were still milling around, but not as many as before. Myers leaving empty-handed had no doubt deterred a few from wanting to stay. Of those still there, most looked exhausted, and I reasoned that, if I left via the back and moved fast, I would be able to get to the car without anyone seeing.

Moving through the back gate, I circled back on myself and approached the car. Pulling out my phone to make it look like I was just a random person engrossed in social media, I put my head down and carried on towards it. Someone in my peripheral vision looked up but, as I was moving nonchalantly, they quickly dismissed me. I was shocked at how clearly I was able to think, how easy it was to stick to the plan. But then, I only had one thing to do now, one objective. My life had now been stripped down to basic, primal things, a black-and-white existence. It was freeing. Absolute.

Arriving at my car, I unlocked it and climbed in and, before anyone noticed, I'd fired it up and pulled out into the road. Slowly, I drove towards the journalists, keeping my pace steady, and passed without event. At the end of the road, I turned left and put my foot down. It was a long drive to the wildlands, to my old life, my old home, and my mother. And I wanted to get there as soon as I could, so I could kill her. But I knew I couldn't rush, I didn't want to draw attention, so I eased off the accelerator, focused on controlling my breathing and told myself I needed to stay calm, in control.

CHAPTER FORTY-FIVE

The hours passed by painfully, mile after mile of motorway, endlessly long and straight, and as I drove I struggled not to think of my daughter floating lifelessly in the river; but it had completely replaced any other image I had of my girl. It wasn't hard to do, I had so few. I had only seen one picture of her, shown to me first by Adam, before that same image went all over the news. The rest were just of me and my bump at the various stages of growth, from the first time I noticed a swell, to her first heartbeat galloping on a sonogram, to her first kick, to my insides feeling like they were in a washing machine as she rolled over. I fought to hold on to an image of one night when her foot pressed against the inside of me, just below my ribcage, and I held her little heel. I felt, back then, that life was coming together for me at last. I believed, I hoped, that I stood a chance, but the things in my past had caught up, and the image I fought to hold on to was replaced once more with that of her floating lifelessly.

I tried to distract myself with the radio, but even that didn't work. The news was talking about my girl, about Lucas, and then me. A news conference was playing, and I listened as Detective Myers spoke. He said he was concerned for my well-being and, when asked if I was a potential suspect, he didn't answer, only stating that if anyone saw me they should call the police. I couldn't tell what Myers was thinking. Did he know, somehow, I wanted to die? Or did he believe my flight from the hospital was enough to turn speculation into suspicion? Either way, I needed to be careful. And to be sure, midway along the six-hour journey I threw my mobile out of the window.

The further north I drove, the thicker the cloud cover was, until a few minutes from the Scottish border the heavens split, pouring rain so hard I could see it bouncing off the road in front of me. The visibility was terrible, with the falling rain and spray of the cars ahead, and everything slowed down. It frustrated me, delaying my fate, but I didn't try to pass. I needed to get there in one piece, without drawing attention. So, I tucked in, kept pace and cursed as I plodded into the country of my birth.

With each mile closer to my childhood home, the house where my sister died, where my murdering mother was hopefully living, I felt myself regress. Memories of my sister, of our short time together, came flooding back with a clarity, a vitality that I had learned to suppress. The images flashed hard and fast in my mind. The summers behind the house feeling free, the winters feeling trapped. The six hours of school time giving us an escape from Mother and her ways. I could see my sister's face, hear her laugh, I could remember all of Mother's faces as clear as if she were sitting beside me now. I wanted to scream, to swear, but my voice didn't shift from its place at the bottom of my throat. It was stuck, unbudging, exactly the same as when I was a kid.

Only now, I wasn't afraid to speak, I wasn't afraid to open my mouth in case I told someone what I had done to my sister. Of how she was dead because of me. Now, fear didn't grip my vocal cords, it was vengeance squeezing its iron-like fist around me, and I was no longer afraid of it. I was no longer afraid of anything. My worst fear had come true, nothing could hurt me now. I would stay silent until I drew my last breath, and then, only then, if I saw my daughter, would I speak. I would say how much I loved her. I would beg for forgiveness.

I had driven for over six hours, driving while fighting to contain my rage, fighting to keep my head level so I could do what I needed to do. And finally, I spotted the sign welcoming me to the town of Dumfries, the Queen of the South. My satnav told me I had reached my destination, but I hadn't; my destination was a small house a mile from the coast. I didn't need the satnav to tell me where I was going.

Slowing down, I passed the shops I had seen on the news video, shops that largely remained unchanged from when I was younger. A few had new names, a few were boarded up. But the high street was the same high street. I drove alongside the shop that I had robbed that Christmastime, and I looked in to see if I could see the same owners.

I continued through the town centre, leaving it behind. Then, a view of the wildlands revealed itself between gaps in the rows of council houses. Then, finally, I could see my road. Home. My mind wanted to go back, to think of the times I'd had there, the few highs and many lows. It wanted me to relive that Christmas Eve when my sister died. But I didn't let myself. Most of it was blocked, hidden somewhere in my mind that I couldn't recall, and I didn't ever try to find it. Maybe once I had met with Mother and killed her for taking my daughter's life, maybe then I would let myself go there, to that moment when I had the knife over my sister, Mother's words echoing in my head. I'd not let myself remember that moment since, but maybe I would tonight. A final punishment for everything I had done. Punishment for failing my daughter.

Pulling up, I looked at the home that had brought me so much suffering. At first, it looked like the place was empty, all of the windows boarded up at the front. The house was one of many that were now derelict, waiting to be reclaimed by the wildlands. But as I drew closer I was sure I could see light bleeding through a crack in one of the boards. I was sure she was inside.

Gripping the knife in my pocket, I took a deep breath, climbed out of my car and advanced towards my childhood home. I headed down the side of the house, hoping the back door was unlocked. I hoped she was there. I hoped she was unaware I was coming for her.

I hoped, as foolish as it was.

CHAPTER FORTY-SIX

The rain fell steadily as I made my way down the side of the house. The passage that led to the rear garden was largely the same. The fence was the same wire mesh, grounded with solid concrete posts. The trees that hugged the fence were the same trees, just taller than all those years ago. The bricks and mortar of the house itself remained unchanged, weather-beaten, solid, hard and cold. The only thing in the passage that was different was me. And I had to wonder, how different was I really, when it mattered, when it counted? I had spent the last sixteen years trying to forget my past, to learn and change from my mistakes, but I was back, in the wildlands, fearful and alone. I was still eleven years old, still a child, still without a clue as to how to protect a little girl called Freya.

I should have called my daughter by another name. I had cursed her to the same fate.

As I reached the end of the side of the house, the rear garden revealed itself. Tall grass and weeds covered it all, so thick and wild the path leading to the shed had vanished, and the shed itself was largely hidden from sight. But it was there, and seeing its roof peering out above the wildness sent a shiver up my spine. I could almost feel the numbness in my fingers and toes, like it was that Christmas all over again. Behind the shed, as far as I could see, sat the sprawling land that haunted my dreams. Land that had once freed me, had once imprisoned me, had once nearly claimed me. I would reacquaint myself with it soon enough.

But first I needed to see my mother.

Rounding the corner, I looked at the back door of the house. That was unchanged too. The once-green paint had chipped away in the elements, exposing dark, moss-stained wood below. Like at the front, most of the windows were boarded up. But a panel in the back door was missing. I approached slowly and tried to see inside, but the kitchen was so dark I could only make out the shape of the sides, the table, the fridge. I looked up towards Mother's bedroom window and the bathroom. No sign of light from either. If it wasn't for the fact that I had seen her, clear as day, on the news and the sliver of light at the front, I'd have thought the house was abandoned.

I wondered what to do. If I smashed my way in, I would lose the element of surprise, and I couldn't overpower her without that. She was older now, but Mother would be just as strong, just as dangerous. I had rushed before, rushed to make a decision that proved to cost me everything I'd loved. I couldn't rush now. If I failed, Mother wouldn't pay, and I needed her to pay. I would watch and wait.

Without being aware of what I was doing, I found myself drifting to the end of the garden, and, passing the shed, I dared to look at it. The door was wide open, inviting me in, and I took a step towards it. It was smaller than I remembered, and, besides the door being open, inviting the elements inside, it too was the same. It seemed time in the wildlands had completely stood still. Nothing had moved on, and therefore nothing could be forgotten.

On the floor of the shed, battered and with its edges curled through damp, lay the plywood I had used as a make-shift bed that Christmas. Paint covered the back wall from my moment of rage. I looked up and saw the hole I had made in the wall so that Freya could pass food to me. I reached up to it, thought about how our fingers touched that day. I thought of how my sister fell and hurt herself.

I found myself sitting on the floor, like I had done for two long days that Christmas when I was eleven. And every memory of that time, every moment came back to me. Things I had long forgotten, things I'd tried to forget. Maybe it was being in the shed or being close to the wildlands once again, being close to the sounds and smells of my buried childhood, but something unlocked in me and new memories flooded out, memories of that Christmas, of my sister. Memories of what happened to her. I didn't want to remember, not yet, but being there forced open the door in my mind that I had kept locked for the longest time, and I couldn't stop it coming back.

I remembered holding the knife over my sister's head, I remembered taking a breath to calm myself. I remembered raising the knife higher, readying myself to finish the job. I remembered it like I was there again, I remembered the moment I had blocked out for sixteen years. And I didn't stop myself, I let the memory come, so real, so close, I could almost feel my sister with me.

CHAPTER FORTY-SEVEN

Then — 23 December

Emily took a deep breath and raised the knife, readying herself to finish the job, but tears began to film her eyes, clouding her vision, making it impossible to see where she needed to strike. Stepping back, she lowered the knife and wiped her eyes with the back of her hand. Mother had said to do this, hadn't she? Not in so many words, but Emily knew she was thinking it, and that she was too proud, too stubborn to ask anyone for help. Mother needed this to happen. She told Emily to do something, that she wanted life to be as it had been, with just her and her firstborn. Emily wanted it too. However, as she stepped close to her sister once more, gripping the knife tight in her right hand, she thought about life without her sister. Freya got things wrong, she got her into trouble, she was the reason Mother was so unhappy, so angry all the time.

It's not her fault.

As Emily watched her sister sleeping, a voice pushed its way in, looped and wouldn't be quiet.

It's not her fault.

None of it. And yet, Emily knew someone had to be to blame for the life they lived, and if it wasn't her sister's fault, and it wasn't her fault, the blame must lie with Mother herself.

She recalled the tough times since Freya had been born, and the good times before. But in that moment, pumped up with adrenaline, Emily also remembered the times she and Freya played, how they laughed and hugged and looked after one another. No, it wasn't just duty, it was love, and the love she had was something she now knew Mother wasn't capable of.

From downstairs, Emily heard the front door bang shut, and, wiping her eyes once more, she moved to the window to peer onto the street below. Mother was outside, fighting against the wind and rain to light a cigarette, then, with her head down, she shuffled away. Mother didn't often go out in the daytime; when she did, she was always home early evening. Emily knew she would drink, she might bring an uncle home, he would leave, or not, and then she would sleep. She would then wake the next day, on Christmas Eve, and be a sad, angry monster. The cycle was never going to end, with or without Freya.

Emily's six-year-old sister couldn't be the reason their lives were so bad. It was Mother. And in that moment, Emily understood she wasn't like Mother at all, and her duty to Freya wasn't just because of obligation or love, it was because Emily was everything Mother couldn't be.

Neither she nor Freya would ever be safe here.

As Mother disappeared into the misty rain, her attention turned to the knife, and, instead of offering comfort, it made her feel sick. Dropping it to the floor, she covered her mouth and sobbed. She knew then, though she was only eleven, that she would be haunted for the rest of her life by what she had almost done.

Emily wanted to cry until her lungs gave out, but she knew she didn't have the time. Mother would soon be home again, and Emily wondered if her mother had had the same thoughts as her. She might come up and make her go through with it. Living in the wildlands would never be safe for either of them, ever again. They needed to leave. Emily would spend the rest of her life supporting and helping her sister. She would do so because, for a moment, she was going to kill her.

Still unable to stand, Emily crawled over to her sister and touched her head. She was so hot, but she shivered in her sleep.

'Don't worry, Fry, everything's going to be OK. I'm going to get us out of this. Sleep on, little sis, and as soon as you wake we're leaving here together.'

Reaching over, Emily kissed her sister on the forehead and, feeling rejuvenated for it, pulled herself onto her feet. Turning to the window, she saw the knife lying on the floor, its tip catching the orange from the streetlight outside. She wanted nothing more than to bury it somewhere far away from her sister, but, if they were going to run, she might need some protection. Though it felt wrong, she picked it up, locked the blade away and put it in her pocket.

Leaving the bedroom, Emily padded over to the airing cupboard and pulled out an old rucksack that had sat there for years, dusty and battered. She checked the straps; it would do. Going back into her room, she quietly began to pack things for the two of them — socks, pants, jumpers and trousers. Stuffing them into the bag, she looked at her sister, who remained still and silent, and tiptoed out of the room and down the stairs.

Although Emily was sure Mother wouldn't come home imminently, that fear was still there, so, moving quickly, she tried to find some food she could pack and take with her. She still didn't know if it was the right thing to do, but what she did know was that Mother would one day act on the thoughts she had shared with Emily. It might not be today, or even tomorrow, it could be weeks, months, years even, but Freya would end up hurt. She would end up dead. And worst of all, Emily still wasn't entirely sure that Mother wouldn't somehow make her do it, as she so nearly already had.

As she suspected, there was no food in the kitchen, none except in Mother's locked cupboard. She thought for a moment about breaking into it, taking everything and leaving now, but Freya wasn't ready and neither was she. Mother would be home at some point, drunk but hopefully alone, and, when she passed out, Emily was going to take the key, steal the food; and, even if she had to carry her, she was going to leave with her sister.

Feeling exhausted with the weight of what she'd almost done, what she would never utter out loud for fear she would surely die from guilt and grief, Emily made her way back upstairs and into her bedroom. In an odd way, the kindness Mother had shown had left her feeling more fearful of her than ever, so Emily dragged her bed away from the wall and blocked the door to stop her coming in. Satisfied Mother couldn't sneak in and finish what she had started, she climbed into bed next to her sister, the knife heavy and white hot in her pocket.

CHAPTER FORTY-EIGHT

I didn't kill my sister.

I didn't do it.

I had for so long accepted that because I had the knife, because my sister had died, I had murdered her. I had convinced myself so much, I could remember doing it, I could remember plunging the knife into her, just as Mother had indirectly asked me to. But I hadn't. I stopped, I realised she mattered, that Mother was the one who was bad, that it wasn't Freya's fault.

I was trying to run. I was trying to save her. We were going to run away.

I am not a murderer. I was trying to protect her in a way only a child could, by keeping the monsters at bay. There was a time when I wished her gone, but in the end I tried to save her. I wanted my sister to survive, I wanted Mother to leave her alone. Mother poisoned my mind, convincing me that if my sister was dead I would be free, happy. And I did, for a while, want to kill her. But I couldn't. I needed my sister. I had planned to run away, find my grandparents with her. I was a child, just a fucking child.

My sister's death wasn't my fault, nor was my daughter's. I had left the wildlands, I had started again, I had tried to make amends. I was ready for my baby to come into the world. I loved her more than anything else in my life. This wasn't about me, this was all about Mother. This started with her, and it would end with her. Making my way back to the house, I pulled out the knife. I knew I would lose the element of surprise if I stormed in, but I wouldn't need it. Mother might be strong, but I was a mother too, even if I didn't ever meet my child, and I was just as strong as her because of it. With the knife ready, I made my way towards the back door.

CHAPTER FORTY-NINE

Then — 24 December

It was dark when the door rattled on its hinges, waking Emily, and at first she didn't understand what was going on, until Mother shook the door again. Emily's bed held firm, and the door wouldn't open. Sitting up, Emily lifted her arm off Freya and looked down at her. She was utterly still and silent beside her. She got out of bed and took a tentative step towards the door. Silence greeted her, then, as she drew closer, the door rattled again. Mother's voice quietly slurred through it.

'What the fuck?'

The door rattled again, this time for longer and Emily covered her ears so as not to yelp. Looking behind her, she saw Freya hadn't moved. Then the rattling stopped. Emily held her breath and listened as Mother, talking to herself, walked away from their bedroom door and downstairs. Checking to make sure Freya hadn't woken, Emily dragged the bed out of the way and opened the door. She looked out into the dark landing, straining to hear Mother's voice, fragile and distant. It sounded like it was coming from the kitchen, where Emily assumed she would be smoking and looking into the wildlands.

Deciding to stay out of her bedroom in case Mother tried to come up and hurt Freya, she sat on the top step, rested her head in her hands and fought not to shiver from the cold. Eventually, still mumbling to herself, Mother came out of the kitchen. Emily stood, ready to bolt and hide, but Mother didn't come to the stairs. Instead, Emily heard a sigh, followed by the squeak of old springs as she lay on the sofa, and a few minutes later deep snores travelled up the stairs.

Quietly, Emily descended, and when she reached the bottom step she paused and looked through the railings at Mother's rising and falling chest. Taking a deep breath, she stepped into the living room then dropped to her knees and crawled towards the sofa, her face resting inches from Mother's, smelling her rancid breath. It made her think of playing hide and seek with Freya the week before.

Slowly, carefully, Emily reached up and tugged at the chain around Mother's neck, pulling out the key to the food cupboard from under her top. She tried to lift the necklace free, but Mother was lying awkwardly on her hand, making it impossible. So, finding the clasp, Emily opened it and gently freed the key from the chain. Standing up and taking a step back, Emily stared unblinking at Mother, but she showed no signs of awareness.

Daring to turn, Emily moved quickly to the kitchen, climbed onto the counter and unlocked the cupboard. As she did so, a stack of tins fell out and clattered onto the hard floor, and the crash rang through the house. Emily heard noise from the living room and, panicking, she tried to stuff the food back in the cupboard and hide before Mother walked in. No sooner had she started than the kitchen light flashed on, temporarily blinding her, and when her eyes adjusted she saw Mother staring at her, fuming.

'Are you stealing from me?'

'No, Mother, I—'

'Because it fucking looks like you're stealing from me.'

'No, the cupboard broke and I was trying to—'

'Don't you lie,' she seethed, and, knowing she couldn't convince her otherwise, Emily lowered her head and waited for the blow. But it didn't come and, when she looked up, Mother hadn't moved. The monster was there, that was clear, but this one felt different, it moved differently.

'Are you stealing for her?' Mother asked.

'No.'

'*Are you stealing for her?*'

'No!'

'Don't you lie!' she shouted, and Emily flinched. 'I thought you and me, I thought we were gonna be OK, but you're just like everyone else.'

Her voice didn't sound like her own, and Emily was more afraid of her than ever before. But not for herself. This fear was for her sister.

'I'm taking Freya,' Emily said before she could stop herself. Her duty to her sister was stronger than her fear of Mother.

'You're what?'

'I'm taking her.'

Emily expected Mother to shout, but instead she laughed, loudly and violently. 'And where do you think you're going to go?'

'London,' Emily said, and Mother stopped laughing.

'What did you say?'

'I know you hate her.'

'So do you.'

'No, no, you made me think I do, but I love her, and I'm taking her away from here.'

'You'll do no such thing,' Mother hissed, before turning and leaving the kitchen. Fearing for her sister's life, Emily ran to catch up, grabbing Mother's leg as she began to climb the stairs. Mother kicked back, connecting with Emily's stomach, knocking the wind out of her, but she didn't fall, she wouldn't fall, not down the stairs, nor for Mother's words.

Emily ran up the stairs, chasing after Mother, begging for her to leave Freya alone. But Mother didn't listen, and, as she opened the door to their bedroom, something in Emily changed, something primal, and she knew what she needed to do. Pulling the knife from her pocket, she unlocked the blade and charged at Mother, driving the knife into her, cutting deep into her forearm. The momentum carried Emily to the floor just inside her bedroom. Mother let out a scream and stumbled backwards, holding onto her arm, a line of crimson between her fingers.

'You cut me!' Mother growled, regaining her composure, her fury. She took a step towards Emily, but the knife was up, trained on her.

'Get out of our room,' Emily said, her voice shaking.

Mother took another step, but Emily stood firm, placing herself between the raging woman and her sleeping sister.

'You ungrateful little cunt.'

'I said, get out of our room!'

Mother smiled, nodded and looked down at her badly lacerated arm.

'Maybe she was never the problem, maybe it was always you.'

'Get ou—'

'It was, it's always been you. We had a good thing, then she was born, and *you* changed. You ungrateful little shit. You're the reason we live like we do.'

'Just get out!' Emily cried, tears streaming down her cheeks.

'I heard you, I'll go, I'm in no rush . . .'

Mother turned and slumped out of Emily's room, and Emily slammed the door behind her. She pressed her ear to the cold wood and listened as Mother, muttering once more, descended the stairs.

Knowing she had some time, Emily grabbed the rucksack and pushed in everything she could possibly fit, before zipping it up and hooking her arms through it, so it sat firmly on her back. She then moved to her sister, who still hadn't woken, even with the commotion. A knot formed in her stomach, a new one, but she didn't pause to think what it could mean.

'Fry, wake up. Wake up, we need to go, now,' Emily said. 'Fry? Wake up. Wake up!' she screamed, shaking her sister, but Freya didn't respond.

'Please, we have to go, we have to go,' Emily said, tears streaming down her face.

Then Emily knew something terrible had happened. Freya hadn't moved at all; she lay exactly as she had when Emily was considering the worst. She was as still as she was when Emily had curled around her, trying to keep her warm, when she realised she was nothing like her mother, and that she loved her sister.

'Fry, why aren't you waking up? Fry?' Emily said, shaking her sister hard. Still she didn't move. Panic began to rise in Emily's chest, and, grabbing her, she pulled her over, so she faced the room. Her eyes stared back at Emily. But still she didn't wake. Emily checked her pulse. She couldn't find it, and her breathing was gone too. As the Christmas lights continued to flicker, she really looked at her sister's face. The way her mouth hung open, drooping towards the floor as gravity took charge. She stared. It was still Freya, still her sister, and yet the muscles in her face had somehow melted like a wax figure in the sun, making her features seem longer and thinner.

She tried to rouse her again, shaking her so violently she was sure she would hurt her. But her body was limp, heavy. She was afraid, really afraid, more afraid than she was of Mother's wrath. The brave girl was gone, and a terrified child stood in her place.

'Mum! Mum, I need help! Please, please, I need help! Something's wrong with Freya!'

She screamed it over and over again, and, despite having cut her mother, despite knowing she would make her pay, she went to the door and shouted, 'Mummy, please!'

When Mother didn't come up, Emily ran out onto the landing, down the stairs and into the living room. She found Mother in the chair, looking at the cut in her arm, wrapping it in a towel to stop the bleeding. Emily raced over and grabbed her, startling her.

'Freya isn't waking up, Mummy, something's wrong.'

'What?'

'Something's wrong. Something's happened. I need you.'

'What did you do?' Mother said, and Emily lost her ability to speak. Mother pushed past her and ran upstairs. Emily followed but stopped at the bottom step. She couldn't go up, she couldn't see her sister like that again. Seconds later, Mother was shouting Freya's name.

'Wake up, Freya, wake up! Emily? What did you do? What did you do?'

As Emily listened to Mother trying to wake Freya, the question looped in her mind. She'd thought Freya was just sick, a mild fever; she didn't think anything would happen to her.

'Emily, what did you do?' Mother screamed from the bedroom and Emily knew she was responsible. She had wished Freya was gone, she had dreamed of it being just her and Mother. She had caused this to happen to her little sister.

Emily wanted to cry out, but her voice wouldn't free itself, and in its wake she felt the compulsion to run. If she ran away, maybe Freya would get better. If she ran away, maybe none of this would have happened. But Mother began to wail, a noise unlike anything Emily had heard before, and she knew Freya wasn't going to get better; Freya was dead, and she would be next.

Still armed with her knife, Emily ran out of the back door, past the shed, and climbed over the fence, falling and landing on the knife, which bit into her thigh. She screamed in pain but pulled herself to her feet, and then she ran into the night, deep into the wildlands.

CHAPTER FIFTY

I felt my heart rate increase and the grip on my knife tighten as I lowered myself and squeezed through the missing board of the back door. As I stepped inside, out of the rain, I allowed a minute for my eyes to adjust, and then I called her name.

'Carol!'

I listened, waited and then heard footsteps approaching. She stepped into the doorway.

'Hello, daughter,' she said, smirking at me. It was the same smirk she had whenever the monster pushed its way to the surface.

I didn't reply, but advanced towards her, the knife ready to do what it needed to do. I promised myself that I wouldn't speak again until I was with my daughter once more, but I needed Mother to tell me the truth, I needed her to say that what happened wasn't my fault, I needed her to know that I knew she was responsible all along. So I could find my peace.

'You said that day, "What did you do?" Do you remember?'

'Oh, I remember,' she said.

Mother's guard dropped, and I saw the familiar monster come forward once more, unchanged in sixteen years. 'You stopped me from going to her.'

'You were trying to hurt her. You're the reason Freya died.'

'No, you stopped me going to her. I could have saved her. You killed her, Emily.'

'No, sepsis killed her, because you locked me in a shed, and she tried to help and got hurt.'

'You were shoplifting.'

'Because we were starving. I had no choice. You forced me to steal so I could feed my sister, and she had to sneak me food and cut herself in the process. You're the reason my sister is dead, I understand that now,' I said, truly meaning it. After all those years of blaming myself, I was finally free. And that meant maybe, just maybe, when I died I would join my daughter.

'No, you took her from me,' Mother spat, slowly advancing on me despite the knife between us. 'You took my Freya.'

'So you took mine?'

'You killed her, and I went to jail. You killed her and swanned off to live your nice little life with my fucking parents, and I'm labelled a child killer. You know what they do to people in jail who kill their children? You know the suffering you caused me?'

She lurched towards me and lowered her voice to a whisper so violent I recoiled, despite being the one holding the knife. 'I've spent the last sixteen years wishing for you to suffer like you made me suffer. Then Lucas finds me, says he wants to surprise you by bringing me back into your life. He told me you were pregnant. He told me you were having a little girl, and I knew that karma had finally come for you.'

'I didn't kill my sister!' I shouted. 'She died because of your neglect.'

'We got close,' she continued. 'Me and Lucas. I learned about you, your life, the privilege you earned by ruining mine. I pretended to care, to like him, and I learned all about him too. And then he told me you were calling her Freya. I knew then, I would take your Freya, like you took mine. After I attacked you, I waited, knowing Lucas would be given custody, and then

I suggested he went to Middlesbrough. I told him to go to his ex, who he trusted, but instead I was there. Foolish boy.'

'He didn't deserve to die.'

'Maybe not.'

'So, you did all this to punish me,' I said, raising the knife and stepping towards her.

'I had it all worked out. You slip into a coma, Lucas takes her, I kill Lucas and then kill her, and you would know the level of suffering I've felt,' she seethed, advancing on me, and, even though I had the knife, I felt myself back away once more. Mothers don't lose the grip they have on their children.

'So, I'll have to kill you now,' she said. 'Bury you out there, in the wildlands. They'll never find you. And I'll keep her all to myself.'

I was confused, Mother was talking about my baby as if she was still alive.

'What do you mean "keep her"?' I said.

'I was a good mother,' she said, looking through me into nothing. 'I was a great mother, and you took that. Now I can be a mother again.'

'What?'

'I was going to kill her, to finish what I started, but I have a girl again, I can be a mother again. I can have my Freya back, and you'll still suffer.'

I was confused. Mother was rambling, her insanity making her hard to comprehend, she was talking as if my daughter was still alive. But the news, the baby in the River Skerne . . .

Then I heard a sound, a tiny cry.

My eyes went from Mother to the source, and on the sideboard sat a baby monitor. I didn't notice it when I came in, I didn't notice anything besides Mother. I shot Mother a confused look, and she took a step towards me, her hands up, ready for a fight. I looked past her to the living room and saw a changing mat and a basket with nappies in it.

Then, through the baby monitor, I heard the best and most confusing, most terrifying noise I had ever heard. A cry, a baby's cry, my daughter's cry.

CHAPTER FIFTY-ONE

'Freya?' I said, stunned to hear her cry.

'You can't have her,' Mother seethed. 'She's mine, you owe me.'

'Where is she?'

'It doesn't matter. You won't ever see her,' she said, smiling in the way that once drove fear into my marrow, but not now.

Not *now*.

I charged at Mother. The sound of my daughter's cry awoke something in me that gave me a burst of energy, of desire. It churned in my stomach, flooded my muscles. I'd come here to kill my mother, but hearing my daughter's cry, learning she was alive, I knew that none of that mattered anymore. The desire for revenge that had driven me to this point had faded into nothing at the realisation that my little girl was still alive. I didn't care for vengeance, I didn't care for anything anymore, I just needed my baby. And so, I lowered the knife, and as she charged at me I pushed her as hard as I could into the wall. She slammed into it, and I ran through the living room towards the stairs. Behind me Mother was screaming, but her voice was out of focus, because the closer I got to the stairs the more I could hear my baby and nothing else.

I took the stairs two at a time, feeling the gravitational pull of my daughter, but midway I tripped as Mother grabbed at my ankle. I fell, landing heavy on the step, and I felt white-hot pain in my stomach. Blood was seeping through my clothes. My stitches had torn. The pain was so bright, so intense, for a moment I couldn't see. I pushed the pain down and, as Mother tried to grab me again, I kicked her back. My heel landed on her chest, sending her crashing down the stairs. I knew I'd hurt her, but I also knew she wouldn't stop, so I turned and staggered up the remaining stairs, following the sound of my daughter's cries. Her voice came from behind a closed door, the same door that once belonged to me and my sister. As I opened it, a thousand memories flooded in so vividly I felt like I was eleven all over again. They tried to wash me away, back to a time that still hurt so badly, still impacted me so greatly, but I swam against the tide, waded until I was back in the present.

It was dark in the room but, despite the low visibility, there she was. Lying on her back, her head tilted towards me, her voice ringing loud and true. My baby. My girl. My Freya. My beautiful little daughter who was stolen from me, who I thought was dead. She was alive, she was well. But she wasn't safe, not yet.

I wanted to grab her, pick her up and hold her tight, but I heard Mother hammering towards me. Quickly, I slammed the bedroom door shut and dragged the furniture in front of it, barricading myself in. I started with the other bed, the one I'd slept in sixteen years ago, then I pulled the chest of drawers towards it and finally the wardrobe. With the furniture in place, I turned to my girl, and, just as Mother began to bang on the door, demanding I open it, I picked up my baby and held her for the very first time.

Her weight in my arms, her smell in my nostrils, her cry ringing in my ears. My baby, my daughter.

Despite the banging and screaming coming from outside the room, the world seemed to slow down, the noise faded, and I held her to my chest, rocking back and forth, whispering to her. I didn't know what I was doing, I was acting on instinct, but she instinctively knew me, and she began to settle.

'It's OK, Mummy is here, Mummy has you. I'm here, my baby, I'm here.'

Saying that word, Mummy, made me feel complete, like it was something I was always meant to be. Tears began to fall, a torrent that wouldn't ebb, and I rocked and cried until it had run its course. And once it had, it was clear that if Mother managed to get inside I was going to die. Freya might also. And I refused to lose her to this house, as I had lost my sister.

Mother continued to bang on the door. She kicked and screamed and punched, but the barricade held firm. She was older than before, weaker, I was stronger now.

'Baby, we're going to get out of here, but Mummy needs to put you down for a moment.'

I laid Freya back in her cot, and she began to cry once more. It broke my heart having her cry when I was here to soothe her, but I needed to get me and my daughter out of this house, this hell.

Moving towards the furniture, I grabbed the wardrobe, the last piece of the barricade, and prepared to move it. Then, when Mother pushed, the door would give a little. She would think she had overpowered the barricade, and that was exactly what I needed her to think. I pulled the wardrobe free, and, with her next attempt to get in, the door opened an inch or so. I moved to the other side, where she couldn't see me, and called out, 'Please go away, please leave us alone.'

I needed to sound pathetic. I wanted her to compare me to the eleven-year-old girl who she had targeted years before. I needed her to think I was weak, powerless, afraid of her wrath.

But I was no longer that little girl; I was a mother, and I knew exactly what a mother should do for her child.

'Please, please, leave us alone,' I called out again, sounding more pathetic than before, and I saw the door begin to budge. The chest of drawers toppled, and hearing it crash to the floor, Mother pushed harder. The door opened by another few inches, enough for Mother to be able to look inside. Before she could see me waiting, I lunged, grabbing her head in both hands. I shoved with all my might, and her head made contact with the doorframe. I did it again and again, smashing her head into the wall until I felt her weight buckle. I let go, and she dropped to the floor, moaning quietly. I looked through the gap, and she was slowly getting to her feet, the side of her head a bloody mess, but she didn't wince. She simply stared at me, wanting me dead. The child in me was terrified, but I held her eye, unblinking.

'You will not have my baby.'

'She would have had a good life here with me, she would have been the daughter you took all those years ago,' Mother spat, and I understood: if she couldn't have Freya, no one would. She exploded into a fresh rage, charging at the door once more, and, as she did, I moved quickly and slammed it on her. Her hand was trapped between the door and the frame, crushing it. She let out a deep scream, more rage than pain. I opened it again and she dropped to the floor once more, her left hand disfigured and broken. This was my window to escape.

She will not have my baby.

I quickly pulled the drawers back further, and then, picking up Freya, I stepped over the bed and into the hallway. Mother lunged for me, but I was too quick. I stamped on her damaged hand and she buckled once more, wailing in pain. I took the stairs as quickly as I could, running through the living room, into the kitchen and back out into the garden. The rain was lashing down so hard it roared as it hit the ground, and I did what I could to keep the elements off my daughter's skin.

Behind me, Mother stepped into the kitchen, wavering on her feet, the left side of her head covered in blood. And the way she looked at me, I knew I was going to die, we were going to die, unless I ran.

261

Turning away, I hastily moved to the rear of the garden, and, climbing the small fence, Freya crying in my arms, I ran out into the wildlands. I fought to keep my balance as I moved. But the land had largely remained unchanged, I knew the terrain well, and my muscle memory kicked in. And so, even being careful with my precious daughter, I was still faster than Mother, who slipped and stumbled as she chased us. I knew if I could put a big enough distance between us she would stop, so I kept moving deeper and deeper into the wilderness, and, after ten or so minutes, panting and in pain, I stopped and looked back. Mother was nowhere to be seen, but that didn't mean she wasn't there, searching.

Finding the same tree I had stopped at that Christmas, the same tree I tried to bury myself in when I was eleven, I took shelter, the thick trunk acting as a rain break. Leaning over her to stop any more raindrops hitting her skin, I whispered to her, trying to sound as calm as I could. Quietly begging her to stop crying.

'Please, Freya, please, my baby, she'll find us.'

Realising she was possibly hungry, I pulled my top up further, lowered the cup of my bra and placed her on my breast. I didn't know what I was doing and, even though I had continued to express, I didn't know if she would take. But, to my relief, I felt her latch. It was followed by more pain, deep inside my breast, and I grimaced slightly, not daring to move. I listened as Freya began to swallow, and my pain was replaced with euphoria. I was giving her life, I was finally giving her my milk. We instinctively knew what to do. She knew I was her mother. She knew I was there for her. As she drank, I quietly cried, keeping one eye on my beautiful daughter's head, the other on the wildlands.

CHAPTER FIFTY-TWO

Then — 25 December

All night, Emily shivered in the ditch in the middle of the wildlands, waiting to be caught, with the wind as her only companion, the violent sea a distant friend. She wondered what punishment she would receive for what happened. She knew whatever it was, it would be worse than anything she had faced before. And she realised she didn't care. Freya was gone; whatever punishment she received, she deserved.

I killed her.

I killed my sister.

I have just killed my sister.

As the night pressed on, the sky began to show the signs of dawn, and pretty soon Emily thought she could hear the sound of children waking to discover Santa had been. Of course, she knew that she couldn't actually hear anyone, she was too deep into the wildlands. But she let herself continue to think she did. She imagined a warm room, lamplight casting shadows over piles of boxes wrapped in colourful paper. She pictured two children, two girls coming into the room. They looked a little like her and Freya, and their mother followed closely behind. Smiles and kindness and love. The two children were passed a gift each, and they opened them quickly. There were hugs, head kisses and giggles.

And then the warm room was gone, replaced with Freya's unmoving body. Her unblinking eyes.

I have just killed my sister.

More voices travelled on the wind, more figments of her imagination — only, they didn't fade when Emily forced herself to push the silly thoughts away. They persisted, grew louder. It wasn't her mind playing tricks on her, they were real voices, and they were coming her way. Daring to lift herself up, she looked out across the wildlands and saw two torch lights cutting through the night. The voices were calling her name.

'Emily? Emily?'

She hid again in the ditch and, grabbing the wet, muddy edges, she pulled it all on top of her. She smeared it into her face, submerged as much of herself as she could, hoping that Mother wouldn't see her.

'Emily Jones?'

The voices were close now and, pressing her head against the cold mud, she closed her eyes.

Lights shone towards her, and a voice called out. 'Hey, she's here. I found her.'

Opening her eyes, knowing her time was up, Emily shielded her face with her hand. Her eyes adjusted. She saw it was not Mother, but someone else.

'Emily, hey, it's OK. Emily, we're here to help. We're going to take you somewhere safe.'

Emily dared not move in case it was a trick, but then the second person approached and looked down at her. A woman with kind eyes.

'It's OK, Emily,' she said. 'Everything's going to be OK.'

As her eyes adjusted further, she could see that the man and woman in front of her were police officers, and, knowing she was safe, that Mother couldn't hurt her, she began to silently cry. They would learn of what she had done though, and she knew she would go to prison for her crime, but even knowing that she still felt safe.

The man stepped into the ditch and grabbed Emily under her arms, lifting her free from the ground and placing her in the arms of the female officer, who held her tight and whispered that everything was going to be OK. Emily held tightly too, not wanting to let go. It had been years since someone had hugged her without her feeling like at any moment she might be struck.

The two officers trudged with her out of the wildlands, and, as they drew closer to the house, Emily could see two police cars and an ambulance out front. The female officer felt her tense up and, knowing she was afraid, she held Emily tighter.

'It's OK, no one is going to hurt you. We're taking you somewhere safe until we know what happened.'

Emily knew what happened, she knew what she had done, but, as she opened her mouth to confess, no words came. Her voice was gone.

The officers arrived at an ambulance, where Emily was placed onto a gurney. She was covered in a foil blanket and two paramedics began to check her vitals.

'You're one lucky girl,' one of them said. 'A few more hours out there and you would've got hypothermia.'

She nodded, but she felt anything but lucky.

The paramedics then turned to the police officers and spoke quietly, but Emily could still hear them.

'What the hell happened to this girl? She's not been washed in weeks. She's so thin.'

'Is she OK?'

'She will be, but she was lucky. And the other girl?'

'No,' the officer said, and Emily closed her eyes as tight as she could, hoping to block everything out.

With her vitals checked, they loaded her into the back of the ambulance and closed the doors, and as they began to drive away she saw Mother in handcuffs being escorted to the back of a police car. Sad Mother was back, until she looked up and saw Emily, and then the monster returned.

As the ambulance began to pull away, Mother mouthed to Emily, 'You did this! I'll make you pay!'

CHAPTER FIFTY-THREE

Freya fed for around twenty minutes, and then, with her tummy filled, she managed to sleep, her tiny cheek resting on my skin. I stayed hunched over her, doing what I could to shield any of the rain or wind from hitting her precious skin. I knew I had to wait it out, wait for the cover of darkness before I ran. I wanted to run there and then, but with the weather so bad, and the ground so uneven underfoot, I risked slipping and falling and hurting my baby. And Mother was still out there, silently hunting. I had no choice. Wait for darkness, wait for the weather to ease, and then we would make our escape and find the help we both needed.

For hours I sat in the ditch, protecting my baby as the night began to take hold. Watching my daughter sleep, my beautiful and precious daughter, I couldn't help but compare now to back then, how I'd wanted the ground to swallow me whole, how I'd wanted to be gone. The last time I was here, my life felt like it was ending, and now it was beginning. I didn't kill my sister, I didn't owe a debt, I wasn't being punished by God. My sister wasn't haunting me, she was trying to tell me I'd done nothing wrong. For years, the memory had been jaded. I had been gaslit by my mother, I had been made to distrust my own memory.

I needed to find a way out of the wildlands. I owed it to my daughter, to my sister, to myself.

In the distance, I heard a voice on the wind. That Christmas, when I'd heard voices, it was people trying to help me. But now I knew it was Mother. Help wasn't coming this time, no one was going to save us. I had to save us. My baby wasn't going to die in this place.

Keeping low, I looked over the ridge of the ditch and saw, just like back then, a torch beam cutting through the night. She was drawing closer, and soon she would find me. The tree and the ditch had been mentioned in the news reports following that Christmas. Mother likely knew.

I knew I had no choice, I knew, unless I fought, she would find us and kill us. So, I did something I never wanted to do. I put my daughter at risk once more.

Digging into the side of the ditch, I created a small shelf in the bank, sheltered from the rain, and, even though it went against every fibre of my being, I laid my daughter in it. She began to cry, and I wanted to scoop her up again. I almost did, but I stopped myself. We would never be safe, not until I removed the threat. And, I reasoned, I was only putting her down for a minute, two at most, and then I would never put her down again.

'I'm sorry, Freya,' I said, before climbing out of the ditch and snapping a branch off a tree. I hid behind the trunk.

I watched as the torch homed in on my daughter's cries and advanced. Mother rushed towards us, but even in the low light I could see she was uneasy on her feet. As she drew closer, I raised the branch over my shoulder, then I swung it like a baseball bat. I wanted to hit her in the face, but the branch was too heavy, so instead it dropped and I hit her in the stomach. As it made contact, she cried out in pain and doubled over, but managed to hold on to the branch and snatch it from my grasp. I thought I had done enough to grab my daughter and run away, but I had underestimated her and, before I could reach my girl, she picked herself up and shoved me against the tree, the branch pressing into my throat. As I tried to push her away, she smiled at me, her teeth clenched, seething like the monster I knew from my childhood.

'You won't have my daughter,' I said, my words tight as I fought to free my neck.

'You don't deserve her,' she hissed, pressing harder into my neck. I managed to wriggle a little and relieve the pressure, but, as soon as I did, Mother sidestepped and hit me in the face with the end of the branch, just below my eye, sending me into the mud face first.

Mother didn't look back, but instead made her way to my crying baby and lowered herself into the ditch. Before I could get back onto my feet, the vision in my right eye all but gone from the instant swelling, she had Freya in her arms. I stood uneasily, my hands going up in defence.

'Let her go. If you want revenge, I'm right here.'

'Look at you, standing there all smug.'

'I just want my daughter.'

'You kill my little girl, and what do you get? A life in a fancy home in London with my fucking parents. Money, a good job. And what did I get?'

'I don't know.'

'Charged with neglect. Sectioned. Years of my life gone. In and out of hospitals. There's no justice.'

'If this is about money . . .'

'Don't you patronise me. No, it's not about money, it's about balance. It's about what's right. You took a daughter from me, now I'll take one from you.'

'Don't. Please, Mum, please.'

'And now you call me Mum,' she said. 'I wanted her dead in the beginning, but then I wanted to keep her, to be a good mother. I wanted to raise her as my Freya. Now you've left me no choice. Another Freya is going to die because of you.'

Mother covered Freya's face with her hand, suffocating her, and I lunged towards her. With Mother holding Freya in one arm and smothering her with the other, I was able to grab her and pull her hand off my baby's face. Freya began to cry and, as I tried to take her from my mother, I was hit in the stomach. The pain was immeasurable, and I doubled over onto the floor. My already torn stitches began to bleed heavily, and I knew I was in trouble. I forced myself upright and, shaking the rainwater out of my eyes, despite the blinding agony, I lunged again. I grabbed Mother by the arm that held Freya and squeezed her broken hand. She screamed and let go of my daughter, who I caught before she hit the floor. I heaved myself out of the ditch and started running. But I was bleeding heavily, and the world swam. My eyes struggled to focus, and I stumbled badly.

Behind, Mother drew closer, and, as much as I tried to outmanoeuvre her, she caught up. Grabbing my hair, she yanked it, sending my head snapping up and dragging me towards her. I fell heavily onto my back, my arms wrapped around Freya, shielding her as much as I could.

Mother then started to kick me, first in the stomach and ribs, then moving to the side of my head.

I tucked into a ball, Freya against my heart, as my body absorbed the blows.

Mother stopped kicking and, leaning over, she pulled me by my hair again, forcing me to look at her.

'You fucking ruined my life,' Mother said, and, as she was distracted, I felt around in my pocket for the knife. Pulling it out, I used my thumb to force the blade open. 'You ruined my life when you came into it, and you ruined it when you left.'

As Mother stepped back to deliver another kick, I thrust the knife towards her and buried it into her standing leg. I pulled it out again and felt Mother's blood squirt onto my face. She dropped to the floor. Howling. Rage and pain in equal measure. Getting to my feet, my daughter still in my arms, I staggered towards the house, feeling that at any moment I was going to pass out. I stumbled several times, the pain in my body like nothing I had experienced before. But still, I kept moving. If I stopped, if I gave up, my daughter would die out in the wildlands. I almost gave up once, I would never do it again.

Finally the house came into view, and, falling over the fence, using my body as a shield for my daughter, I managed to reach the back door. The light inside flooded into the garden and, looking down, I checked Freya was OK. She was shivering, her little lips blue. I moved faster and, inside the house, I stripped her wet clothes off and wrapped her in a blanket from the living room. My clothes were covered in blood. Underneath, my caesarean wound was almost fully open. Daring to put Freya down, I searched for a phone, finding a landline behind the sofa. I lifted it, dialled 999, and, as the operator spoke, I staggered back to my daughter, my baby, my reason for living, barely resting my hand on her before I passed out.

PART SIX

EPILOGUE

Three days later

I heard a giggle, one I once knew, one from long ago, and I tried to open my eyes. But I couldn't see anything. I thought I was blind, but it wasn't darkness, it was the opposite. It was light, bright light, and it blinded me. Like the flash from a camera bulb. But the flash was permanent and unmoving. It made my eyes burn. I thought I was back at the beginning, back when I woke from the coma. And fear shot through me.

I tried to move, to turn my head, but I couldn't. My body hurt all over. In the brilliant white light, I thought I could see a girl of around six. Then, as the memory materialised slowly, floating out of the black, she faded into the white.

Freya.

I tried to sit, but the pain in my stomach was too much, and beside me the effort of me trying to move set off sensors and alarms.

Freya, where is Freya?

I tried to move again, but this time two hands rested on my shoulders, stopping me from doing so.

'Hey, no, don't try to get up, you'll hurt yourself,' the voice said, and, as my eyes began to focus, their outline came into view.

'Michelle?'

'Hey, Em. Now, don't panic, OK? She's here. She's right here.'

'Where? Where is she? I need to see her,' I said, feeling an awful déjà vu. Fear flashed into my mind. I didn't remember someone coming to help; what if Mother had got to her first? What if I had failed again? 'Please, tell me she's OK? Please.'

'Hang on, don't move, OK?'

I nodded, tears in my eyes, and Michelle stepped back. Only a few seconds later she returned, and in her arms was my sleeping daughter. The tears that formed began to freely roll down my cheeks. Michelle cried too.

'Can I hold her?' I said between sobs, and Michelle nodded. 'Of course.'

Michelle lowered Freya onto my chest, and I held her in my arms. 'Is she OK? She was so cold.'

'She's fine, more than fine, you saved her life.'

For a moment, I couldn't speak. 'Michelle, I'm so, so sorry.'

'Hey, it's OK, don't be sorry. She manipulated it to be that way.'

'I should have trusted you.'

'You were under so much pressure. And I wronged you, I failed you. I'm sorry.'

'It's OK. I should have trusted you,' I said again.

'It's forgotten. I'm here now.'

'Thank you.'

I looked down at my daughter and could make out the slight outline of a bruise on her cheek.

'She was hurt?'

'Superficially. She has a couple of small bruises, no broken bones. They said, if you hadn't shielded her like you did, she would have died.'

'Are you sure she's OK?'

'Yes,' Michelle said, placing a hand on my shoulder. 'Honestly, she's fine. You, on the other hand, you gave us quite the scare. Are you OK to hold her? Do you feel strong enough?'

'Yes,' I said.

'Great. Sit tight, I'm going to get a doctor, OK?'

I nodded, and, as Michelle went to leave the room, I looked down at my daughter once more. The bruise on her face broke my heart, but she was with me, she was in my arms. She was OK.

'Wait, Michelle,' I said as Michelle reached the doorway. 'Where is Mother?'

Michelle turned back to me and hesitated.

'Michelle? She won't come back to get her, will she?'

'No, she won't.' Her look told me all I needed to know. 'You're safe, both of you are. I'll be back in a second.'

Michelle smiled and stepped out of the room. Freya wriggled in my arms and began to cry. I wanted to try to feed her like before, but I could barely move. I tried to rock her gently, to comfort her, but she continued to cry. Michelle came back into the room, followed by a doctor.

'I can't get her to stop crying,' I said.

'It's OK. She's fine,' Michelle said, taking her from me. She bobbed her up and down and Freya settled, and for a split second I thought maybe Mother was right, maybe I didn't deserve to be a parent.

'Hey,' Michelle said, as if she could read my thoughts. 'You saved her life. You and her, you'll bond. OK?'

I nodded but didn't reply.

The doctor checked me over. Told me about the injuries I had sustained, how I very nearly bled to death. I had several broken ribs and a broken wrist, but the worst was my abdomen. The blows I had taken had completely ripped open my caesarean scar and it took a lot of work to save me. I would not be able to have any more children. The damage was extensive, and they had to perform a hysterectomy. I tried to absorb what was being said, but it was too much to process.

As the doctor left, he told me that a detective was waiting to see me, and I said they could come in. Then Myers walked into the room.

'You are one tough cookie,' he said. 'How are you feeling?'

'Like shit,' I said, and he laughed.

'Yeah, well, that's probably an understatement.'

'I don't remember what happened.'

'You dialled 999 and when the operator tried to talk to you, you were unresponsive. They tracked the landline and sent help. You were found face down in the living room of your mother's house. At first, they thought you were dead, and were shocked when they found you had a pulse. You'd lost a lot of blood. Freya was on the sofa, crying, but mostly unhurt. They rushed you here.'

'How long have I been here?'

'Three days.'

'What's going to happen to me?' I asked.

'It's an ongoing investigation, but what you did, it was self-defence. You had no choice.'

'And my mother, did she . . .' I said, not daring to finish the sentence.

'Yes. We found her in the land behind your house.'

I nodded, trying to process that I had killed my own mother. But again, I couldn't.

'I didn't kill my sister,' I said.

'We know.'

'Mother said I did, but I didn't, I was trying to save her—'

'Your mother was a poorly woman, you and your sister should have been taken into care. You were failed, but you did nothing wrong,' Myers replied, and I burst into tears. Sixteen years of holding it in, sixteen years of believing I was a monster, that I was Mother, and I was finally free.

'Emily, there will be questions, of course. But right now, you need to rest, to recover. Be with your beautiful little girl.'

'Myers? What about that baby, from the news?' I asked.

'A tragedy. But because of you and your actions, there weren't two tragedies that day.'

'Thank you,' I said, remembering what I told Michelle once, that children aren't spared from trauma, they aren't spared from tragedy.

'I'll be in touch, OK? But don't worry.'

'OK, thank you, Detective Myers.'

'Steve,' he said.

'Steve,' I echoed.

He smiled, nodded to Michelle and left the room.

Freya started to complain in Michelle's arms, and she started bobbing her again. 'I think she's hungry.'

'I wish I could feed her.'

'Do you want me to help you?'

'Please.'

Michelle came over, helped me lift my top and unclip my maternity bra, then, handing me Freya, she guided my daughter to me, and I felt her latch. I didn't know if I would still produce milk, it had been days, but to my delight I felt her draw from me.

'She's feeding,' I said, fresh tears swelling in my eyes.

'See, you were meant to be her mum,' Michelle said, crying too. 'I'm going to message Jack and Adam, they wanted to know when you woke up.'

Michelle kissed me on the head and stepped out of the room, quietly closing the door behind her, leaving just me and my daughter. I looked down at her as she fed, and, for the first time I could ever remember, I felt truly at peace.

Freya fed until her little tummy was full, and then, after I'd winded her, she fell asleep against my heart. Despite the pain I was in, the trauma I had been through and would have to face, I felt the best I had ever felt in my life.

The wildlands would stay with me, they were just as much a part of me as my daughter. But I knew then that I would find a way to place it behind me, that I would find a way to move forward and give my daughter the life that I deserved, that my sister deserved.

I knew that one day my daughter would have questions about what had happened, and when they came I would tell her the truth. Maybe one day I would take my daughter up there, show her where her aunty lies at rest, show her the wildlands where we first met.

I was aware of movement in the room, and, looking up from my daughter, I saw my sister standing in the corner. She smiled at me and, when I blinked, she was gone.

'Em, what are you looking at?' Michelle asked, coming back into the room.

'Nothing,' I replied, returning my gaze to my baby once more.

THE END

ACKNOWLEDGEMENTS

About a year ago, I was scrolling aimlessly online, and stumbled upon an article which grabbed my attention, and started to turn over in my mind. The article was about a handful of pregnant women, back in the height of the pandemic, who were incredibly sick with COVID-19 and placed in medically induced comas. The article went on to discuss how some of these women had to have their babies delivered while they lay comatose. I'm not a woman, I'll never be a mother, but the idea of that moment being taken away broke my heart. It also planted an idea in my head. What if I created a character who had her baby taken? From there, Emily — her story, her past — came rushing at me, and *The Night They Stole My Baby* began to form. But, even feeling inspired, even having a good sense of the story I wanted to tell, and my reasons for it, I haven't done this alone.

Writing *The Night They Stole My Baby* was, in the truest sense of the word, a team effort. Without the countless words of encouragement, many conversations, hundreds of 'what if' moments, this book would still be a scratchy idea and the reasons I wanted to craft it would be lost. Some people who have helped me on this journey I didn't even know — their ideas came in the form of conversations I overheard, or moments I watched (not at all weird!).

So, to begin, I would like to thank those people I will never know, who serendipitously turned up to answer questions about Emily's story when I was stuck. Cheers, strangers.

To my editor, Steph Carey: from the very first conversation we ever had, I knew we were going to click. Thank you for championing me and this story, and providing insight and lifting it so that whoever reads it can have the same visceral feeling I had when I read that article. Thank you to the whole team at Joffe Books: Sam Matthews for guiding the editorial process, and to Tia, Hanna, Sasha, and Gemma for marketing this book. This is our first time working together, and it's been everything I could have hoped for. Thank you to Mathew Grundy Haigh and Jacqui Lewis for line edits and proofreads. To Nick Castle for that cover, and to Nina Taylor for all of the production work.

To my agent, Lisa Moylett. I am the luckiest author I know. In the short time we have been working together, everything feels different. Everything feels possible. And to Zoe Apostolides, thank you for all of your notes, feedback, time and kindness. I really do have a dream team at CMM.

I'm also very lucky that I get to talk to other lovely authors, but I want to especially mention Lisa Hall, John Marrs and Michelle Adams. Over this past year you have been there to talk, share ideas, lift me when it felt hard, and I am forever grateful.

To you lovely readers right from NetGalley, to Goodreads, to blogs and vlogs, to you who post on Instagram, and engage with online book clubs. To everyone out there who takes the time to read, and comment and speak about my stories. Thank you. Without you, none of this would exist. What you do for authors has by far the biggest impact on whether or not a book does well and all of my success so far is down to the tireless work you do.

And finally, to my son, Benjamin. Without you, there is no motivation, no determination, and no inspiration. And I will forever try to repay you for this.

THE JOFFE BOOKS STORY

We began in 2014 when Jasper agreed to publish his mum's much-rejected romance novel and it became a bestseller.

Since then we've grown into the largest independent publisher in the UK. We're extremely proud to publish some of the very best writers in the world, including Joy Ellis, Faith Martin, Caro Ramsay, Helen Forrester, Simon Brett and Robert Goddard. Everyone at Joffe Books loves reading and we never forget that it all begins with the magic of an author telling a story.

We are proud to publish talented first-time authors, as well as established writers whose books we love introducing to a new generation of readers.

We won Trade Publisher of the Year at the Independent Publishing Awards in 2023. We have been shortlisted for Independent Publisher of the Year at the British Book Awards for the last four years, and were shortlisted for the Diversity and Inclusivity Award at the 2022 Independent Publishing Awards.

We built this company with your help, and we love to hear from you, so please email us about absolutely anything bookish at: feedback@joffebooks.com

If you want to receive free books every Friday and hear about all our new releases, join our mailing list here: www.joffebooks.com/contact

And when you tell your friends about us, just remember: it's pronounced Joffe as in coffee or toffee!